# Changelings: An Autistic Trans Anthology

Edited by Ryan Vale & Ocean Riley

# Copyright

Dedication

For everyone who's ever felt like they don't belong.

# Contents

# Introduction

by Ocean Riley

THIS ANTHOLOGY IS for every autistic trans person who has ever felt misunderstood or underrepresented. As an avid reader, I felt a distinct lack of characters that represent us at this intersection. So, as Toni Morrison once said: "If there's a book that you want to read, but it hasn't been written yet, then you must write it."

Alas, creative writing is not my forte, but I decided that co-editing an anthology was absolutely within my capability, and thus, *Changelings* was born.

Research indicates that autistic people are far more likely to be transgender than their allistic counterparts. It's not easy to be autistic, or trans, especially in the current climate; but to be both is to face attacks on all sides simply for existing. We deserve stories that represent these integral parts of our identity together.

I hope you find a story within these pages that resonates with you; you deserve to be seen.

You are enough. You are worthy. You are loved.

# Introduction

by Ryan Vale

THE CHANGELING IS a creature found across European folklore. A human baby gets replaced by a faerie or otherwise inhuman creature. Often portrayed as a strange, quiet child with large eyes, unusual sensitivity, and poor social skills. Unsurprisingly, historians and folklorists have linked the myth of the changeling to the reality of autistic people.

The other meaning of "changeling" is, of course, a shape-changer: someone or something that alters their appearance. To be both trans and autistic is to be a changeling on all fronts. This term may have been used to harm in the past but we chose to reclaim it here when titling this anthology.

This book was created to share the authentic experiences of autistic trans masculine and non-binary people; stories told by us, in our own voices. The diversity of our community and its creativity was shown by the submissions to this anthology.

This book was written for all the autistic trans changelings in the world. Thank you for picking up this book. I hope it means as much to you as it does to all of us.

# The Door

Laurie Doyle

Content Warnings: Gender Dysphoria

# The Door

Laurie Doyle

THERE'S A DOOR in my bedroom.

I guess that doesn't sound all that strange, really. It would be weirder if there wasn't a door. I mean, how would you get in without one? The window works, but only if your room isn't too high up. Or maybe–

Wait, I'm getting off-track.

Let me start over.

There's a door in my bedroom that shouldn't be there. I don't know when it appeared, just that I noticed it one day, half-hidden behind my wardrobe. I was in the middle of clearing out a bunch of old clothes, sorting them into bags to take to the local charity shop, and I came across the outfit Mum had made me wear for my brother's wedding a few years before. Plum-coloured dress, white cardigan, slip-on shoes that made my feet ache with the memory of staggering around in them that endless day.

Anyway, I found that outfit and immediately dumped it in one of the bags. I mean, I'm not going to wear it again, not unless there's a secret third child in my family who also wants to get married.

So I tucked the dress, cardigan and shoes into the bag and, at that moment, I noticed the door. It stood there, the same magnolia as the walls, just about my height—which isn't that tall. Most doors are eighty inches high; I'm not even sixty.

Of course, I dropped what I was doing and dragged my wardrobe away from it, inch by inch, until I could get a better look.

It was just about the most bland-looking door I've ever seen. No panels, no engravings, just a flat rectangle of what felt like wood beneath a layer of off-white paint. It did have a handle, though—a brass knob, scratched and dull—and, below that, a keyhole.

"Huh," I said, which didn't convey my feelings at all. I mean, most people might be a little thrown off, finding an extra door in a room they've spent most of their life hanging around in.

For me, it was more than that. My bedroom is my sanctuary, a place where everything can be just right. I've got books slowly cascading from my shelves to the floor, notebooks full of scribbled ideas for the table-top games I want to make, mugs of pens, piles of cushions, matchboxes of pins and staples and paper clips, all in the Right Place.

So seeing something that shouldn't be there—something I *hadn't noticed*—made my chest go tight, my jaw clench, my skin prickle with unease.

I stood there for a long moment, facing off against the door. It stayed bland and ordinary, strange and unsettling. I reached for the handle. I needed to find out where it led, what it was doing there. But the door didn't budge. I yanked and shoved, gently at first, then putting my whole body weight behind it. It still didn't move.

I stepped back, breathing hard. Frustration swelled in my chest, gathering like a storm, and I forced myself to look away before it overwhelmed me. See, sometimes I get overloaded, like a computer with too many programs running. My fan will start whirring, my processor slowing, my internal temperature rising until I can't ignore it any more and either burst into flames or shut down completely.

Not the best experience. So right then I turned away from the door, letting myself calm down before I went back to it.

It helped. A bit. I tried the handle again and, of course, the door didn't budge. Which meant my next point of call was the keyhole.

Obviously, a keyhole means a key and, despite my parents calling my room 'absolute chaos' and 'a disaster zone', I know every single item in here. There are no keys.

Still, there are other keys in the house. Keys to every window and door and cupboard—and keys that don't seem to be for anything at all. My house is old. I mean, really old. It was built centuries ago and, even though the landlord tried to spruce it up for us renters, he left the wonky window frames, uneven floors and cracked slate roofing in as 'features' that my parents have to pay for the privilege of enjoying. And by enjoying I mean freezing in draughts, propping shelves up with books, and constantly alerting the landlord to the damp patches on the ceiling after heavy rain.

These keys I'm talking about were handed to us when we moved in, a massive bundle so tightly packed it barely jingled. My parents asked what they were for and the landlord pointed out labels he'd helpfully stuck to most of them. 'First floor bedroom left window', 'kitchen door', 'cupboard under the stairs', stuff like that. Still, a fair chunk had been left blank and, when my parents pointed those out, the landlord just shrugged and repeated his usual spiel about this being a beautiful old house, full of character. Which my parents seemed to like.

I figured maybe one of those keys would help me get this door open, so I rushed downstairs to the kitchen and made a beeline for the top drawer next to the washing machine where my parents keep the toolbox, loose screws, elastic bands, stray bolts—and the spare keys.

They were easy enough to find, given their immense size, and barely a minute passed before I was racing back upstairs.

I tried the keys one by one. Some didn't fit, which made them a quick 'no', but others I spent a good few seconds struggling to turn. Like I said, my house is old and some doors or windows have to be jiggled about a bit if you want to get them open.

By the time I reached for the last one, I was getting tired, and when I jammed that key—my final hope—into the lock only to find it wouldn't turn, I had to bite my lip to keep from hurling the whole bundle across the room.

Still, there was nothing I could do. Short of getting my hands on a battering ram, there was no way for me to make the door open without a key.

Tension squeezing my shoulders, I pushed my wardrobe back into place and continued sorting my old clothes. I needed to think of a plan.

Said plan is currently underway. I lean against the wall of the maths building, drumming my fingers in a steady rhythm against my arm and waiting for Alice to *finally* finish talking with Mr Owens.

Students stream past me, all heading for the main gate in a desperate rush to their parents' cars or the bus stop. My school's out in the middle of nowhere, surrounded by open fields and rolling hills. Which means it's pretty picturesque, but no one's walking home.

It also means that, thanks to Alice being set on discussing coursework with our maths teacher, I'm going to miss the first bus.

I scratch my neck, the rough polyester of my shirt a constant itchy reminder of how uncomfortable I am. This stupid uniform seems like it's designed to quietly torture the wearer by being too cold in winter and too hot in summer, coarse no matter how much fabric softener you use, and with a collar so stiff, it's liable to take your eye out if you look down too fast.

It's uncomfortable for other reasons too. Girls aren't forced to wear skirts anymore, but they're still expected to have trousers from the women's section, a shirt that's fitted, and a ribbon instead of a tie. All those components come together to make me feel like I'm wearing some fancy dress costume and, any minute, people are going to notice how ridiculous I look.

So waiting for the next bus isn't my idea of a good time.

I'm on the verge of leaving to find a bench, so I can at least take off my tight black shoes for a while, when the door bursts open and there's Alice, tucking a notebook into her bag.

"Sorry about that!" she says, shooting me a smile. "Just needed to get a couple of equations checked."

I shrug. Honestly, I don't understand why Alice is so worried about this piece of coursework. It's ten percent of our total grade—basically nothing. But then, I'm not the one aiming for straight As. "Any chance we can still make the bus?" Alice asks.

I push off from the wall and peer at the gates up ahead. Fewer students pass us now, the stragglers who were either too busy chatting with friends or talking to teachers to get out quickly.

Still, I haven't actually seen the bus go by yet, so—

"Ah." My shoulders slump at the roar of an engine. Seconds later, a double-decker bus rushes by like it's as desperate to get home as I am.

"Oh well." Alice sighs. "I guess we should head to the orchard."

The orchard, as it's generously named, is a patch of grass off to the side of the main gate with three scraggly apple trees overlooking a bench. Alice sits, but I stay standing. I've had to wait all day to tell Alice about the door, what with her lunch break taken up with an extra class for gifted students, and now the time's come to do it, it's hard to figure out where to start.

"What are you doing next week?" Alice asks, startling me from my thoughts.

I blink at her. Next week?

"Activities week," Alice says, raising an eyebrow. "You never told me what you picked."

Oh. The reminder is like stepping on a sharp rock I didn't realise was in my shoe. Activities week is my least favourite time of the year. Sure, it's nice not to have to go to classes, but it's a series of forms and deadlines and changes in routine that make my stomach clench. I'd like it more if they just gave us the whole week off.

"I don't know," I say, dropping onto the bench beside Alice. "I forgot it was that soon."

"Isn't the deadline for your choices list tomorrow?" Alice asks.

I nod. It's hard to focus on something as small as that when the door fills my mind, a mystery I can't let go of.

"What?" Alice leans forward, peering at my face with a frown. "Is something wrong?"

Yes. Of course it is. I sigh.

"I saw something weird in my room yesterday," I say.

"Weird?"

"A door."

Alice's frown deepens. "What, like a secret door or something?"

I almost smile. That's what I like about Alice: she always seems to grasp what I'm trying to say. It's not like with other people, where they look at me like I've suddenly transformed into some bizarre creature the moment I open my mouth.

"Yeah," I say. "Behind my wardrobe. But…"

"'But' what?"

"There's something weird about it." It sounds stupid when I put it like that so I quickly add, "I mean, sure the house was furnished when we moved in, but there's no way I'd miss a whole door, right?"

Alice nods thoughtfully. She knows better than most that I notice even the smallest details. A frayed thread on the curtain across the room? A thin layer of dust along a half-hidden skirting board? The faintest creases in the spine of a book? I spot them before anyone else.

So if the door has been there since I moved in, how come I've never seen it before?

"Did you open it?" Alice asks.

I shake my head. "I couldn't. It's locked."

"Huh. Weird."

"Yep."

"So what are you going to do about it?"

"Ah." I hold up a finger. "That's where you come in. I was thinking you could, you know, pick the lock?"

Alice narrows her eyes and I flash her my most winning smile. Technically, I'm not supposed to mention her lock picking skills; when she told me she'd been teaching herself using online videos, I blabbed about it to my parents and they, in their infinite wisdom, told Alice's dad what she was up to. Alice didn't get in trouble—it wasn't like she'd broken into anywhere—but she told me her dad gave her a long lecture about consequences.

"My parents are out until later," I say. "If you're still around when they get back, I'll just say we're working on that maths coursework together."

Alice's eyes narrow even further. "Have you even started it?"

"Sure." I've drawn one whole graph. "Come on, it'll be fine. Please?"

For a moment, I think she's going to refuse, but then she sighs and pushes herself to her feet.

"Fine," she says. "But you owe me."

I leap up, unable to bite back a grin. Without the key, Alice is my only shot at getting this door open.

And this is one mystery I can't let go unsolved.


"This is it," I say, waving Alice into my room. She's still struggling out of her jacket and shoots me a disapproving look that I ignore. No time for social niceties when I'm so close to getting this door open.

I drag my wardrobe aside and Alice folds her arms, staring at the door like she's sizing it up.

"Someone's painted over it," she comments.

"Yeah." I run my fingers across the smooth, magnolia surface. "Which makes me think it's been there since before my parents and I moved in."

"Except you didn't notice it."

"Right."

"Okay, then." Alice pulls a paper clip from her pocket and sets about unfolding it. "This might take a while. You keep an eye out in case your parents get back early."

I start to protest—it feels like I should be right there with her the moment the door opens—but Alice's expression makes me swallow the words. If she gets caught lock picking, she'll be in for another lecture and, when she's doing me such a huge favour, it's only fair I do my best to help her avoid that.

So while she hunkers down beside the door, I lean against the wall, straining my ears for any sound of a car pulling in or a key in the lock. The neighbourhood's quiet at this time, when kids are home from school and adults are still at work. Mostly, I use this little bubble of peace to just lie on my bed and let all the tension that's built up over the course of the day filter out of me. Each clatter of a chair, each shout, the bright lights, the overpowering smell of cooked lunches, and the hum of the crowded bus: it all drifts away from me, like invisible particles seeping from my skin until I'm finally calm again.

Now though, I'm anything but calm; my heart drums against my ribs and I bob up and down on the balls of my feet, twitching my fingers and battling the urge to ask Alice how it's going. She's got her back to me, long hair brushed over her shoulders and one ear right next to the keyhole. I don't know much about lock picking, but I do know how to recognise when she's focusing hard. The last thing she needs is me breaking that concentration.

Then suddenly, she sits back on her heels and breathes a sigh.

"All right," she says. "It's open. I think."

My stomach lurches and I hurry over, so fast I nearly trip over my bag. The door stands motionless, of course. No sign anything's changed.

"Want to do the honours?" Alice asks, stepping back.

I nod. My pulse races, excitement like sparks in my veins. I don't know why, but it feels like this door is important—something I need to open.

To see what's inside.

But as I reach for the handle, my hand's trembling, fear shivering up my spine. Once I open this door, I won't be able to unsee what's behind it. Sure, I can close it, maybe even lock it with Alice's help, but that knowledge will stay with me.

I swallow, pushing those thoughts away. It's some empty cupboard, that's all, full of dust and spiders. Nothing special.

So why does this feel so huge?

"Go on," Alice says and the sound of her voice helps me remember to breathe.

The brass is cool beneath my fingers, smooth despite the scratches. I turn it, feeling the mechanism inside click, and gently tug it open.

"Woah," I say.

There's no cupboard inside. No dust, no spiders. Instead, a wall of solid darkness faces me, unmoving despite the light streaming through my window.

Well. That's not how darkness works.

"What the…" Alice trails off and I feel her lean over my shoulder. "What is that?"

I don't reply. There's no way I can even begin to describe the feeling growing inside me. The cool certainty that this darkness isn't meant for Alice, or my parents, or anyone else.

It's for me.

"Hey!" Alice grabs my sleeve and I flinch, finally pulling my eyes away from the inky rectangle. Her brow is furrowed, fear bright in her eyes.

"What are you doing?" she asks.

It's only then I notice I've stepped forward, toward the darkness.

"I need to see where it goes," I say. "It's connected to my room, remember?"

Alice chews her lip, eyeing the door like she might a venomous snake. "You don't know what's in there."

"Exactly."

"You know what I mean. It's not…" She waves a hand. "It's not right."

She has a point. Darkness shouldn't be so solid, so unmoving. The light from my window should be enough to chase it away.

Still, something inside me knows—not thinks, *knows*—I don't need to be afraid. That I have to do this.

Alone.

"It'll be fine," I say, shooting Alice the best smile I can muster. "I'll be back before you know it. Okay?"

"No, not okay! What if there's something in there?"

"Like a monster?" I grin for real. "If there is, it's being pretty quiet."

Alice glares at me. "This isn't a joke. What if you get hurt? I could…I could come with you."

It's a tempting offer. The idea of stepping into the unknown by myself is a bit like diving into a lake without knowing how deep it is. If Alice came with me, maybe it would be easier.

But I find myself shaking my head. "No, thanks. I'll be fine, honestly. You just wait here and, if my parents get back, tell them…" What? That I've stepped through this weird door into who knows where? I shrug. "Tell them I've gone out, or something."

Alice gives me a long, hard look. "You're really doing this?"

"Yeah." I have to.

"Fine," she says. "But be careful, okay? If anything happens to you, I'll…"

I place my hand over hers and give it a squeeze. She sighs, so quiet I barely hear it, and releases me.

I step through the door.


The darkness isn't cold. I thought it would be, like the gloom of a deep cave, but the air is still and warm. Which is no more weird than anything else about this.

My feet scuff against a wooden floor, mostly smooth, but with the odd splinter here and there that makes me wish I'd left my shoes on. It feels a lot like walking around my bedroom, which makes sense seeing as this place is connected to it I guess. Whoever built this passage must've used the same materials.

I try to focus on that rather than the nagging sense that I'm at the centre of some immense space, too big to possibly fit inside my house, and the fact that the light which should be filtering in from my room is gone.

That I'm in the dark, alone.

I dig my nails into my palms. There's nothing to be scared of. Monsters aren't real and, anyway, it's not like I've heard anything moving around in here.

Except… There *is* a sound. Quiet, distant. A scratching. Not like the tiny claws of mice, but softer. Strangely familiar.

It's the only sign of anything in this world of darkness, so I head towards it, step by careful step, the sound growing steadily louder, clearer. A pen, that's what it is. Pen against paper. Someone's nearby, writing furiously.

Without a light to see by?

No, there *is* a light. It's so faint, at first I think it's my eyes playing tricks on me, but then I make out a tall rectangular shape in the blackness.

A doorway.

My heart begins to pound. I haven't gotten turned around, I'm sure of it. Which means this door is connected to my bedroom.

That's an uncomfortable thought, one I don't want to deal with right now, so I inch closer, stepping quietly, heel to toe. There's something across the doorway, blocking out most of the pale light that's trying to filter through. I place my hand against the blockage, fingers brushing a smooth wooden surface. There isn't enough room around whatever this is to squeeze past, so I roll my shoulders back and give it a hard rap with my knuckles.

"Hello?" I say. "Anyone there?"

The scratching stops. Somehow, that's worse—the knowledge that someone really is around to hear me.

"Hello?" I try again, the words trembling on my lips. "I'm, uh...I just want to..."

To what? Talk? I don't even know who this room belongs to. I might have wandered down some convoluted passage into someone else's house for all I know.

But I don't think that's what's happened.

There's a grunt and a scrape and the thing blocking the door shifts sharply to the right. I blink against the flood of light, so bright that for a moment I can't see anything at all.

Then it fades. And I can.

A room spreads out before me, bed crammed against one wall to make room for a desk and chair, a colourful rug spread across the wooden floor. Books spill from their shelves, mugs of pens strewn about on the desk and window sill. Posters hang from the walls, bright and cheerful.

Identical to my own.

This is my room. There's no mistaking the scuff marks where I've scooted my chair across the wood, the sheets of homework scattered across my desk. Everything is the same, so much so for a second I'm sure I must have accidentally wandered back the way I came.

Except there's no Alice here.

Just a figure. Vague, shadowy. They hover in the corner of my vision and, when I turn to look at them, they shy away.

"Where– Who–" I bite my lip, trying to pull my whirling thoughts back together. "This is my room."

The figure bobs their head. A confirmation. Maybe they don't want to talk to me. Maybe they can't. But whoever they are, they're in my room.

And I want to know why.

"Who are you?" I ask, watching them shift uneasily. "Why are you here?"

They shrug, a loose motion that's weirdly familiar. All of this is.

"You knew about this?" I say, gesturing to the door.

A nod.

"Have you been through it before?"

A pause, thick and heavy. "No. It wasn't made for me to use."

A shiver creeps up my spine. I know that voice. I hear it every day, at school, at home. No matter where I am or what I'm doing, it's waiting, ready the moment I open my mouth.

My voice.

"What are you?" I ask, turning. Once more, the figure flits away and I reach for them, but my fingers shift through their body like I'm grabbing at smoke. "There's no way you're– You can't be me!"

The figure rubs its arms, awkward now. "I'm not. Not exactly. You're you: a whole. I'm just a part of that."

"Which part?"

"One you've been ignoring for a long time now."

"What?"

The figure waves a hand impatiently. "Think about it. Think about the times you've felt tense, uncomfortable."

"Right," I say slowly, cautiously. I don't know what this person is driving at. I just know the unease I should've felt walking down that dark passage is hitting now. I should've listened to Alice; I shouldn't have come here alone. "Everyone feels uncomfortable sometimes."

A sigh. "You know what I'm talking about."

"I really don't think I do."

"All right. When did you first notice the door?"

That makes me pause. The day I saw it, I was in the middle of clearing out my wardrobe, stuffing all those old clothes into bags to take to the charity shop.

But what does that have to do with anything?

"The dress," the figure offers. "Remember the dress?"

I stiffen. Of course I do. "You're saying this door appeared because of a dress?"

"No. Because of the feelings you had about it. About your uniform too."

"I don't have any feelings about them." Except I do. That discomfort, the sense I'm wearing some stupid costume and, any minute, everyone's going to realise I'm not what they think I am.

Because I'm not. I'm not a girl, even though my birth certificate says I am, and I'm not a boy.

So what am I?

"You're you," the figure says, as if reading my thoughts. "Just like everyone else. Gender isn't something which has to match your sex the moment you're born and it doesn't have to be binary. Some people are men, others are women. Some are both. Some are neither."

"No," I whisper. I picture my parents, who bought me that dress, who looked so happy as they took photos of me wearing it. That's what I'm supposed to be.

But I can't deny those feelings, can't deny how much better it is to wear clothes that match who I am inside. That help people see me for who I am.

"It's hard," the figure says, softly. "And I understand why you left me here so long, even though you wanted to find me. You thought it would be easier to continue playing your part, pretending to be the person everyone expects."

They're right. Except it's not easier, not at all. It's just quieter, like I'm standing in a transparent box that's slowly filling with water. If I don't mention it, no one will notice, even when my head goes under.

Except for me.

I'll notice.

"And that matters," the figure says. "You'll know it's all wrong. You've known for a long time now. So why not try accepting it?"

I shake my head. The thought of telling my parents—of telling Alice—is too big, too heavy. If I try to deal with it now, it'll crush me.

27

"I didn't say you had to." The figure tilts its head. "Not yet, at least. Take it one step at a time."

I breathe a humourless laugh. "All right. What's the first step?"

"Accept it. Accept me."

The figure holds out a hand. I turn to them and this time they don't shy away. They stand there, identical to me except for their smile which is bright and warm and everything I ever wanted.

I glance at the darkness behind me, the passage that will lead me back to my room. I could leave right now, let this part of me stay hidden forever. No one has to know it exists.

My lips twitch. No one but me. I'll know. I always have.

And now is the time to accept that.

"Fine," I say. "I guess we're going back together."

I grasp the figure's hand and, somehow, their smile grows even brighter. Sparks burst from their body, brilliant blue and red and yellow. They dance around my fingers, up my arm, into my chest.

"Thank you," the figure says.

I open my mouth to ask what's happening, but then there's a flash and warmth rushes through my chest, filling a hole I didn't realise was there.

"What was that?" I whisper, but there's no one around to answer my question.

The room is empty.

The figure is gone.


It doesn't take long for me to work my way back up the passage. For one thing, the darkness has lifted, showing me a narrow walkway of wooden floorboards suspended between walls of light. Not the painful fluorescent kind, but soft, gentle, like the final rays of the setting sun staining the sky with colour.

Being able to see helps, but it's the rush of joy in my heart that propels me forwards, lifting me like a feather in a breeze. I race along, lighter than I've ever been, yet also more solid, more stable. I'm a painting after the final brush stroke, a story after its final word. I'm whole, complete.

I'm me.

There's the door, just ahead. There's Alice peering through, face creased with worry. I wave but she doesn't seem to see. Maybe she can't, not yet. Maybe the light that fills this space is for my eyes only.

I slow as I reach her, step out carefully so I don't startle her too badly. She still jumps a little, then sighs with relief.

"You took your time," she says.

I nod. Light flickers in my chest, a thousand brilliant, swirling colours. They dance inside my heart like fireflies, burst through my veins like fireworks.

"Hey," Alice says as I step past. "Are you okay?"

The light shimmers beneath my skin, warm and bright. I've never felt more whole. Never more like myself. Even if the path ahead is long, even if it's hard, I know who I am.

Am I okay?

I turn to her.

I smile.

"Yes," I say.

# Vanishing Names

## Mary Buffaloe

Content Warnings: Controlling Parents, Homophobia, Transphobia

Author's Note:

Mary Buffaloe is a non binary American writer. Vanishing Names is dedicated to anyone who has ever felt out of place in the world, and my brother August.

# Vanishing Names

Mary Buffaloe

BABYSITTERS ARE THE backbone of the global economy. I should know, I've been one since I was twelve. The premiere child supervisor for the central Arkansas area. Like my sister before me, I am the top name in every mom's address book when they need to go to work, go out, or they're just tired.

I won't be able to get a work permit until I turn fifteen in January, so for now I have to satisfy myself with twenty to forty bucks at a time. There's a box in my room that's hidden between my mattress and the box spring where I've kept it all. When I see it nestled under the sheets I feel like a little dragon, even if my riches are meagre. My mom asked me what I was saving for, and I shrugged my shoulders and said 'a car' though it was a lie. Every time I think about telling her it's for the rainy days when I'm out of her house and I can re-sculpt my body, the words turn to sand in my mouth.

My parents are just people. I don't think I know anything about them or that they know anything about me. They go to church, my dad works in finance while my mom stays home, and has one of those walls of crosses that is a necessity in the respectable Christian home. My eldest sister, Elsie, set the bar too high. I think they didn't really need another kid after her. She won homecoming queen, went to University of Arkansas, and she's getting married next summer to a guy that was a soldier in Afghanistan. My younger sister is only five so there isn't much of a personality there for me to work with yet, but it means my parents are so preoccupied with her they often forget about me. Now that it's August they barely remember to take me to babysitting gigs.

Today, I set off under the dying sun to the Murphy's, the humidity plastering my hair to my forehead.

My head twitches with joy, causing sweat droplets to fly out as if I'm a dog after a bath. Secretly, I like this more even if it means I have to cycle five miles in sweaty air that crowds too close to my skin. I've found other people don't really like quiet people: teachers like them enough in class but something about a fourteen year old who can be self-contained and is happier to sit in a corner staring ahead is disconcerting. I forget I'm doing it, my knees softly thump together for an hour before someone has to tap me and ask if I heard the question.

That's why even if the parents don't like me, the kids all like me just as much or even more than Elsie. All they want to do is be left alone or tell you about the book they read on dog breeds. They exist in a space before they understand all the rules, and that makes things easier for me because I don't understand the rules either. It's better I just stay quiet than make a mistake, but the kids don't notice the mistakes.

The apricot walls of the Murphys' house is a welcome sight for my legs which are now twitching with strain against the gears. I jump off the bike and lean it against the house before ringing the bell. As it rings I realise I must look crazed, but there's no way to change what the night air has done to me.

Mrs Murphy opens the door and I can see the frown which hides in the creases of her forced smile. I wipe a hand against my sweaty face to see a line of grime on my palm. No wonder she's looking at me like that, my sunburned-pink skin must be caked with dust from the road.

"Bethany-Ann! My... you look– well, why don't you come in and I'll make up some lemonade before me and Mr Murphy have to go."

God, I hate my name. My parents did the southern thing where they picked the two frilliest names in the world and smushed them together to create a monstrosity. Friends at school took to calling me Beth, but that still feels like there's water in my ears I can't dislodge when they say it. Often I find myself fantasising about my first day in college when I can just say anything when people ask what my name is. Maybe when they ask I'll know what I want it to be.

I follow her into the heartless suburban stucco walls and I am immediately greeted by Axel slamming into my legs.

"Bea, have you seen Clone Wars?"

My grin widens on my face, but before I can answer, Mrs Murphy puts her hands onto his shoulders and steers him away with an apologetic grimace.

"He's been asking everyone that, sorry. And Axel, you know her name is Bethany-Ann. Come on, show some respect."

I suck breath through my teeth in annoyance without thinking, I much prefer Bea because it makes me envision myself buzzing from flower to flower under a rising sun, and it seems easier for the kid to say.

His eyes, which are much too big for his head, leave my face and stare at his socks in shame. "Be-Bepony, Betan–" He scrunches his little face in frustration. The two missing teeth in the centre of his face aren't helping matters and I can tell he's struggling with the 'th' sound.

As his mom scurries out of earshot, I lean down so we can look eye to eye. "Hey, I like Bea better anyway, okay?" He smiles with relief and slams me with a hug again. "Plus, I have seen Clone Wars so you'll get to tell me all about it, okay?"

He begins to vibrate with joy and a laugh escapes my throat. His mother returns with the lemonade pitcher and puts it on the imitation marble countertop before looking at us with exasperation. I've found parents really don't appreciate it when their kids like me more than them.

She shrugs off her irritation as Mr Murphy strides in and gives him a kiss on the cheek before turning back to me. "Number's on the fridge, pizza should be here within fifteen minutes." Her body swings to face Axel. "And bedtime is nine. Got it?"

Axel nods and I can see by how his feet twitch on the tile that he is ready to see them off. So am I. Frankly, I'm excited to hear his Star Wars opinions.

"Okay, we should be back by ten but I'll tell you if it will be later. Have fun!" With that they slink out in the August humidity and I hear Mr Murphy mutter curses at the sun before the car disappears down the driveway.

"So," I say with a widening grin, "Clone Wars?"


"I like R2-D2 best." Axel says with a solemn tone as if we are discussing world politics.

"Why?" I say before lowering a slice of pizza into my mouth.

"Because R2 is funny. And I like the beeps." He proceeds to perform the entire audio sequence from the space battle of Phantom Menace and I can't help but think that if the people I had engaged in a 2,000 note long argument on tumblr about Obi Wan's strength of character had the same nuance of thought as this child, the world would be a better place.

I nod as if hearing the wisdom of a sage. "My favourite is Darth Maul because he looks cool."

Axel absorbs the sentence then folds his little hands into his lap with the same reverence I afforded him. "And he has a cool lightsaber."

"He does."

"He was too cool to die."

My smile widens knowing I am about to make Axel's night. "He's not dead in Clone Wars."

His eyes widen and then he's clamouring over me for the remote, smacking my pizza into me in the process, which makes me laugh harder than I have in months.

He extends the remote to me. "Show me." He frowns after the words leave his lips as if contemplating something internally. "*Please.*"

I would have done it without the politeness, but he is a southern boy after all.

My hands mechanically flip to the episode and switch it on. I feel his head fall into my arm so I ruffle his hair with my clean hand as he snuggles closer.

By eight-thirty he passes out but I decide to keep the show on for a bit anyway. Watching the jerkily animated Anakin Skywalker brings back the memory of seeing it for the first time on Cartoon Network and wishing my hair would fall like that, that my seven year old jaw would grow into that, and my collarbones would sharpen. At first my sister made fun of me because she decided it was a crush, but it was more like a burning hole in my chest which could only be satiated by theft. I wanted Natalie Portman to look at me like that. I wanted to be him—the angsty scar did something to my brain chemistry. It's with a sudden moment of irritation that I realise my current fringe resembles Anakin's far too much for comfort.

Axel's head falls from my shoulder into my lap, and I figure it's time to get him to bed. One night without brushing his teeth won't kill the kid, so I just lift him up, put on his pyjamas, and then settle him under the covers.

I return to the couch to resume the show, but my phone rings. Figuring it is Mrs Murphy I flip it over and answer before checking the ID.

"Hello?"

"Bethany-Ann?"

"Um, yeah–"

"Oh good, your momma told me you changed your number after I called the old one a couple of times."

I struggle to place the voice which is somehow both raspy and soft. "Mrs Nichols?"

She chuckles with something nervous behind her tone. "Sorry, I should have said that, yes. I was wondering if you could watch Lily this week, say, Monday through Wednesday from eight am to nine pm? I'll pay you 200 dollars per day. Mr Nichols is on a business trip, and the regular sitter is not available—you know how it is."

My heart stops in my chest, everything past '200 dollars' becomes white noise in my ears. That would be the most money I've ever seen in a week. I measure my voice before I instinctively blurt out that I will do anything for that.

"Yeah, um yeah. Of course!"

"You're a lifesaver! Normally Lily would come with me or Mr Nichols but– well, um she's been a bit difficult. Can't sit still and all that. Just to warn you." Her voice sways as if that would change my decision to help, but the dragon hoard in my bedroom is already pulsating with the promise of having 600 dollars added to it in one week.

"No problem, I'll see you on Monday."

She breathes out something relieved I can't properly hear. "Thank you, Bethany-Ann. Thank you so much."

The phone is already dark when I move to end the call, so I throw it back down and resume the show. I haven't babysat Lily since she was nine, and even then she was a bit too old for it. Our moms had met through PTA, when Mrs Nichols' birth daughter Josie was in the same class as Elise. It had been my momma who had suggested Lily be my babysitting trial run for just a few hours while they were at Bible study.

One day Mrs Nichols just stopped calling and it would have been rude to just cycle over uninvited when Lily had never asked to see me. Now she's twelve and I can't imagine why she isn't allowed to stay home alone, but I consider gleefully that with the sudden influx of funds, I may be able to draw from the hoard to order a binder from one of those discreet sites and tell my parents I bought a pottery making kit or something.

Lily's a weird kid, and it wasn't just the homeschooling. That's why we had always gotten along. Normally, I consider kids I babysit to be my fun little clients, but Lily was the first kid I was trusted with and we were only two years apart so she felt more like a friend I was being paid to be around. Mrs Nichols told me she had once bitten Elise, which had forced me to hide a shrieking giggle. She didn't like to be told what to do and seemed much happier to sit at the bank of the pond, which was nestled behind her house, and catch pygmy frogs. When I had watched her for the better part of a summer, we had gotten sunburnt catching dragonflies one afternoon. Lily had interrupted her mother when she scolded me for letting it happen, telling her that it would have been rude to just leave the dragonflies. I'm curious to see her again, and even more curious what 'difficult' means.


The Nichols house lies hidden down a gravel path which is obscured by a whispering army of weeping willow trees. Writhing air rises off the gravel as it crunches under my feet and the hums of cicadas echo in my skull which feels screwed on too tight under the beating sun. I'd forgotten this was one of my favourite places in town. It's a proper house, unlike ours, which is one of the units that got carved in half so some landlord could make twice the rent. For a moment the money seems unimportant compared to spending three days surrounded by the green, which seems to breathe heavily into the still air.

Lily sits on the porch staring ahead, her hair twisted into a long braid which she pulls at over her shoulder. She is much taller than I remembered, her gangly arms hang to her mid thighs and her dark brown skin seems taut over her bones as if they grew before the rest of her had a chance. I can hear she is babbling to herself, some of it incoherent, but I pick up bits about some kind of bird creature living in her attic.

My foot breaks a fallen twig and she snaps her neck to appraise me with her gaze. I feel an involuntary shiver run over me, and I swear her pupils are wider than those of any other person I've seen.

She rises mechanically, walks into the house and returns with her mom, who cannot yet see me nestled amongst the green. When I enter her view she slumps with relief and moves toward me. Mrs Nichols is wearing her work clothes, a white satin shirt and navy slacks, with her brown, thinning hair curled to give the illusion of thickness.

"Bethany-Ann! Oh, it's so nice to see you. You've cut your hair; it was always so beautiful long."

My breakfast sours in my stomach and I force a smile. Lily cocks her head as if she can read my mind.

"Well, I'm off, I'll be back at nine." She turns to Lily, nervous. "Be good."

Before I can ask about numbers on the fridge or food she has leapt into the truck which rumbles down the driveway. I watch the dust settle before turning back to Lily, and I jump because she has moved from the porch and now stands right in front of me. Up close, I can see she is only a head shorter than me.

"Uhhhhhhh, hey."

She blinks. "It is you."

"Ummmmmm, yeah. What's up?"

"My mom does not like to be alone with me."

I open my mouth and close it again, every response feels stupid. Finally I let out a shaky breath, I can feel the back of my t-shirt beginning to dampen. "So, do you wanna go inside?"

Finally her face contorts into a definite expression: disgust. "No, anywhere but in there. Would you like to see a snakeskin I found?"

That I understand and a grin spreads across my face. Who doesn't love a snakeskin?

Lily sets off before I can respond and I struggle to keep up with her. The grass is pulling at my ankles, but she appears to glide over it. We arrive at the base of a cypress tree and she points to a particularly long milky white shell of a snakeskin.

Before thinking, I kneel and take the treasure in my hands. It's rare to see one fully formed like this, I can even see where the head had once filled this husk. My breath catches as I thumb over each scale and when I turn to Lily she almost seems happy.

"You found this here?"

She nods and moves next to me to lightly thumb over the rough scales as well.

"It's a cottonmouth," I say without asking if she wants to know, but I'm already on a roll. "You can tell because of the markings." My fingers trace over the spots and her nails scratch over the markings as I point them out. "They're very venomous, if we got bit by one of these guys it would suck because I only have a bike and the hospital is about ten miles away."

"How would you die?"

"Well, you could have internal bleeding, muscle atrophy, if it's bad enough you could even lose an extremity." I freeze realising this is not something I should be telling a kid. "Sorry, I–"

"Why are you sorry?"

"I–" My tongue feels heavy in my mouth under her curious expression. It's a completely earnest question, but there is something in it which alarms me; maybe it's that her eyes seem darker than I remember or that all of her features are sharper. Or it could be that this is the longest anyone has paid attention to me in a while.

It must be hotter than I thought. "Um, yeah, I guess. No one really wants to know how a snake's gonna kill them."

"I do."

"Why?"

"Because there's one in the tree."

My head whips up to see the cream mouth of the snake and I scramble backward, falling over a rotting log which erupts with millipedes, but I don't care. My eyes are on the snake which is now at Lily's eye level.

"Uhhh, okay."

*Don't swear, don't swear, keep it cool*, I tell myself.

"Um, Lily, just walk backward, um slowly, no sudden movements–"

"Linus won't hurt me."

"Linus?!"

She smiles and I watch in horror as she extends her arm and the cottonmouth slithers onto her and wraps itself around her arm, its head nestling on her shoulder. It's almost like it's kissing her cheek.

"Would you like to meet him?"

"WHAT?!"

Lily frowns. "No loud noises. Linus doesn't like them. I thought you would sympathise."

I ignore the intimate knowledge this child has of me and instead turn to look at the snake. Should I hit it with a stick? Take the risk it would bite me instead?

"I wouldn't hit him. Linus only wants to meet you." She moves forward before I can object and suddenly the deadly snake is wrapped around my neck like a poisonous chain.

"Hi, uh hi, Linus." I hope my voice isn't too squeaky but Lily grins, and I swear her teeth seem...sharper.

"That's his skin you found. He thought it was very sweet how much you liked it."

"Uhh, oh, um yeah. Very good work, sir. In one go? Impressive." I'm talking to a snake. Why am I talking to a snake?

For a second I think the snake smiles but that's impossible because they don't have those muscles in their faces. Then it nudges me with its forehead and I feel I may pass out from the oddity, the heat, or both.

Lily reaches her hand back out and Linus happily glides onto her extended forearm. She walks to the water's edge and lowers him so he can dive into the water. A few thumps of his clubbed tail and he's gone.

I collapse onto the floor and hold my knees to my chest. Lily watches me.

"That didn't happen."

"Didn't it?"

My eyes search her face for some kind of gotcha moment, but it is completely earnest again, it's almost irritating. The worst part is I think I'm shaking from pure joy rather than fear.

"I'm– um, I'm going to get some water. Do you– do you want something from inside?"

"A peach, please."

"Yeah, okay, um, I'll– I'll go get a bunch of peaches and we'll have a little lunch, okay?"

Before she can respond, I'm running to the house and when I throw open the door I almost run right back out. It's in complete disarray; there are what look like claw marks on the wall as well as spots of mildew where it seems water has corroded the floorboards. I gag on the smell of mould and hurry to the fridge so I can get out. No wonder the kid hates the house.

My brain plays over the feeling of the snake on my arm and I hate the delighted pit in my stomach which hopes it will happen again. Something is wrong and I can't figure out what, but the lengthened points of Lily's teeth remind me of something from a folktale.

The rest of the day passes without incident as we gorge ourselves on peaches and catch pygmy frogs like when she was smaller. I can't shake the feeling the snake was some sort of trial run, but we don't see it for the rest of the afternoon so I hope it really had been a heat-induced delusion.

Mercifully, the sun begins to dip below the horizon around eight as the sky bursts into a ripple of indigo and the burning air finally had rest. Next to me, Lily seems to be buzzing as new ribbons of colour burst from the dying sun, and I realise it is the happiest I have seen her.

The orange glow of the sky grazes her cheek and I swear her skin has an undertone of deep emerald. It's as if her whole being is one large gem which can only be seen in the transitions of the day. She catches me staring so I direct myself to my ruddy hands and focus on pressing pink thumbprints into the side of my arm which fade as the pressure recedes.

Lightning bugs begin to illuminate the rapidly approaching twilight. One lands on Lily's hand and she giggles. I smile and hold out my hands which soon accrue upwards of ten scuttling bugs along my arms. Other people are bothered by the brush of little legs but, for whatever reason, and all my sensitivity, the feeling has never bothered me.

I don't even realise it's nine-thirty until Mrs Nichols walks up behind us saying something about traffic and needing to stop for gas. The lightning bug spell is broken as Lily suddenly rises and dashes into the house before I can say goodbye for the day.

Mrs Nichols sighs and waits for me to shake off the bugs before helping me to my feet.

"Sorry about that."

"No, no, it's fine. I'll see her tomorrow anyway."

She blinks. "You'll come back?"

I frown and then chuckle. "Yeah? We had a good day."

"No...problems?"

Consciously, I omit the snake. "No, none at all. We just walked around the pond all day. It was really nice."

That still doesn't seem to calm her but she hands over the 200 dollars and pats me on the shoulder anyway. I fight the urge to run my hands over it methodically to revel in each individual fibre.

"Well, I'll see you tomorrow, Bethany-Ann."

As I leave, I can see out of the corner of my eye that she shakes before entering the house.


The next morning, I get a text from Mrs Nichols letting me know she had to leave early and that she left Lily outside. I roll my bike up the gravel driveway and part of me thinks the willows turn to stare as I make my way to the house. If there was even a slight breeze, I could excuse the feeling they're watching me, but the air only hangs like stagnant breath on my cheek.

This time Lily isn't waiting for me, but I can see her dark hair bobbing in the pond. I frown, I thought it wasn't safe to swim in because of the snapping turtles and water snakes, but the memories of the day before flood in and I know she's not in any danger.

Suddenly, her head shoots up, droplets of water clinging to her loose coiled hair which twinkles iridescently in the sun. I can see there is a flopping catfish hanging out of her mouth. Those too sharp teeth bite down and the fish goes still. I don't realise I'm staring with a mix of shock and fascination until she begins to glance about, her eyes settling on my face. There's a grin of satisfaction in her eyes.

After propping my bike against the house I go to grab water. It seems I must have lost some of my sanity on the ride over. When I close the fridge, she is standing before me on the corroded wooden floor, her feet surrounded by a puddle. There are traces of mud and pond scum around her lips and when she smiles, I can see bits of pink flesh in her teeth. So I'm not insane.

"Hello," she says.

I swallow the lump which has been building in my throat. "Hey."

"Would you please come outside, I hate being in here. I can't feel things right."

My mind ignores the creepiness of the statement in an effort of self-preservation and I nod slowly. "Uh, yeah, I can tell." Unconsciously, my eyes dart around the dilapidated house. She smiles smugly.

"Your work?" I ask.

She shrugs. "Would you mind if it is?"

In my pockets, my hands ball into fists and release repeatedly. "Uh, not really. If it was earned."

Her expression darkens with something I cannot read as she pulls her arms up to her chest. "It was earned."

"Well then, um, I guess I don't mind."

Lily's expression softens slightly and I feel like I've passed another small trial. "Come on."

"It's not Linus again, is it?"

Her self-assured attitude fails as she cracks a grin and suddenly she seems too much like the little girl I used to know. Just like how it was with the lightning bugs.

"No. I want to climb."


We run out of the house and, again, I trail behind her. Her limbs extend when she runs and her body suddenly becomes more elegant than the gangly mess of limbs which I had first seen thrown together on the porch.

She's a blur of motion as she scrambles up an oak before settling on the highest branch she can get to. I follow along at a much slower pace and, by the time I get to the branch below her, I'm gasping for breath. My heart thunders from wondering if we're safe up here and with exertion from the hot sun. Though now the clouds are gathering, a storm is coming, and that ought to cool things down.

Lily watches me as I situate myself as comfortably as I can on the branch, her hair like one of those saint halos in a Renaissance painting. "Are you okay?"

I don't respond and instead shield my eyes from the sun so I am able to look at her. "You don't use my name."

"You don't want me to," she says matter of factly.

"How do you know that?"

"I just do."

"Can you read minds all of a sudden?"

Lily smiles, but it's sweet rather than her usual uncanny one. "You made a face when my mom called you it. You're a very expressive person."

"Oh."

"I'm not sure how everyone doesn't just read your mind."

I shrug. "I don't think anyone looks at me all too much." Part of me knows this is not a conversation to be having with a kid, but I cannot stop myself.

She frowns sadly. "I would have looked at you. I always missed you. You were nicer than all the other babysitters."

"Why did your mom stop asking me?"

"Thought you were weird. Called you a word I don't know."

My chest tightens. "Oh."

"She talks to your mom. Your mom said the word too. They didn't think I was listening. They didn't want you to be a bad influence on me."

I shove down what feels like tears prickling at the back of my throat. "Then why am I back, Lily?"

"Because I asked and said I wanted no one else. You saw the house. I am very persuasive."

A smirk rises at the corners of my lips and she echoes it with a little smile. "How did you do that by the way? It looks like a swamp monster went through the place."

Her smile falters. "You think I'm a monster?"

I sit up too fast to clarify and I shake a bit on the branch. "No, oh god, no. Sorry. It's just the water, the greenery, the house looks like it has just… like a… well, something natural, I guess, living in it." I laugh nervously. "Really Lily, if you were a monster, what would that make me? You're the most normal person to me, the most sensible that I've ever met, I remember thinking that every day I cycled home two summers ago. That's not really a compliment by general standards but I think I understand you. If monsters are like us, maybe it isn't so bad to be one."

She watches me for a moment and I can see her pupils widening and shrinking rapidly. "Ask your question." Lily whispers, eyes still locked on my face.

"Are you human?"

"Not really. Are you a girl?"

"Not really." My heart stops. "I've never told anyone that."

"No one else knows about me either."

We sit in silence with her legs dangling near my face. When she speaks I can hear the tears behind the words. "I– I think you're the best friend I have ever had. It was so lonely when I didn't see you. But I didn't know where you lived and Mamma wouldn't tell me."

"I didn't realise how lonely I've been until yesterday," I say, and once it leaves my lips, I know how true it is. "People don't really make any sense. They have all these little rules, they won't just say what they think, they– they talk behind your back: I don't understand."

She shifts on the branch and I reflexively look up. "Do– do you wanna be like–"

Before she can finish there is a rumble of thunder and I feel the twist of the air as it is charged by electricity. The rain is inevitable, but the instinct within me that scurries out of swimming pools when god claps his hands hurries my descent down the tree.

"Come on, if there's lightning—and there will be—this is the worst place we can be."

She nods and, before I can do anything, she drops from the tree. I let out a choked scream as she falls, but she lands in a crouch and, once standing, looks back up and grins.

I scale the rest of the way down and when my feet hit the mossy ground, I breathe a sigh of relief. She's still smiling at me, the pointed teeth on full display. Now it seems as if it has always been that way and I was only slow to notice.

"Race you!" she yells, but she is already tearing off through the trees. I know I am going to lose but I trod along after her anyway.


We huddle underneath the porch with a basket of plums between us that we are happily ripping apart. A graveyard of pits rests at our feet and I find each one sweeter than the last.

She looks over to me with curiosity. "What are you going to do? About not being a girl, I mean."

The original tension I held when she asked before is now replaced with a cool serenity. I haven't gotten to tell anyone about this, and there is no prejudice in Lily's expression. Kids are cool like that.

I shrug. "Wait, I think. Probably until college. Just change my name, everything. I'm saving money for when I need it. I dunno, I'm still figuring it out."

"What name do you want?"

Laughing, I bite another plum and speak through the mouthful. "No idea. Sometimes I look at baby name websites but I don't want any of them. I'm kinda hoping someone will just call me something and then I'll like it enough to keep it."

"They'll take your old one."

"Why would they want my name?"

She smiles. "No, your name is very ugly, no one wants that." I throw back my head and laugh, plum juice dripping down my face. "I meant they'll take it. Like payment for a wish. Then it won't be yours anymore. And no one will know it ever was."

"They can do that?"

"Yes. And then you would become like me."

"What– what is like you? And who are they?"

"The mushrooms. I just asked them politely and they made me into this."

I snort, but her face is neutral with truth. "Oh, um, sorry. Soooo you… just asked?"

"Pretty much. And they said they'd be happy to have me. And then I went with them, and came back… me… but not completely. Just a bit more green in my blood."

"You're not Lily anymore?"

She lays back onto the deck and takes a deep breath. "Depends what Lily is. A name? I gave them my old name, no one but them remembers it." Lily laughs, watching me scrunch up my face when I realise I hadn't even noticed Lily hadn't always been her name. "Not even you. You can't" Her chest rises and falls for a few silent beats. "I think I'm more Lily, more whole, than I've ever been. A whole person. It's why I hate the house, I can't feel all of myself in there."

Nodding, I continue cautiously. "I think I understand. I never feel like all of me."

Her head whips up and she props herself on a forearm. "Would you like to? I tried to ask earlier but the sky interrupted me."

"They– they could do that for me?"

"If you wanted. You don't have to leave everything behind, but you can if you want. You could talk to the snakes."

My face widens into a grin, and I can see her eyes brighten with the knowledge that this was the main draw for me. "Really?"

"Yeah, I could introduce you to Linus' whole extended snake family."

"You should have led with that!" Laughter rumbles with my words and my mind is immediately preoccupied with all the questions I have for the snakes.

She smiles and opens her mouth, but then the headlights of the truck are blinding us. Disappointment surges in me as I know that there is only one day left of this. I hadn't even noticed it was so late because the weeping sky had obscured the sunset.

Mrs Nichols runs out of her car and onto the porch and seems genuinely confused when she sees us there, the remnants of smiles and juice still on our faces. "Come on, Bethany-Ann, I can drive you home."

My bike is loaded into the truck before I can say anything and I only have time to turn and give Lily a small wave before I am ushered into the passenger seat.


Rain obscures the view from the window so I have to content myself with picking at the skin around my nails and following the shaking of a Batman bobblehead with my eyes.

Mrs Nichols clears her throat, but the twitching plastic has me in its grip. She coughs and says my name: "Bethany-Ann."

"Yeah?"

"Ummm, first I want to say thank you for helping these past two days." Something in my stomach begins to tighten. "But, um, I took work off tomorrow so you're off the hook."

"I don't mind, really." My voice comes out hurried and desperate which causes her to tighten her lips into a thin line.

"No, I was– I talked with your mother today. She uh, well, she had better tell you, not me, and we both agreed we were right a couple years ago."

"Why?" I can't help myself. Every cell in my body knows why but I need someone to just say it to me.

"You're just not the kind of girl I want influencing Lily, she's already so... volatile... so suggestible. When we adopted her, we wanted to make sure she grew up...right. You're a sweet girl, really, it's just it would be a shame if that...conscious upbringing went to waste now. I'm– I'm sorry about the money. I put in an extra fifty for tonight."

Words stick in my throat and I shove down the emotional onslaught. My bed seems so welcoming in my mind and I can't wait to leap out the truck and dive head first into it.

When the truck pulls up to my house, I snatch the money and slam the door open and closed before running into my house. In the periphery I can hear Mrs Nichols call out "Bless your heart" before pulling away and I want to bang my fists on the hood, but I don't. I am prepared to make a beeline to my bedroom until I see my hoard sitting on the dining room table. Next to it is a diary, my diary. Bile rises at the back of my throat.

My mother is crying. How dare she. When she speaks, it's strained. "Oh baby, oh my little girl." She tries to reach forward but I snatch my hand away, my breath thundering. My father doesn't even look at me.

"I– I was just cleaning. And I found it–"

"It was hidden. You would've had to have been looking."

She takes a breath and I can see the anger behind the tears. "Maybe I was. I'm entitled to know what's going on in our house. You don't tell me anything! We– we need to get you help, Bethie–"

"No."

"You're confused–"

"No!"

"Tomorrow we'll go to the doctor." She turns to my father. "I told you we should have taken her a long time ago—we shouldn't have let it get this far."

"Well, we didn't know the extent. Just thought you were antisocial." My father interjects without emotion.

"And now! Now we'll have to send you off to one of those camps for the rest of the summer or– I don't know, it's just so horrible–"

My dad finally looks at me. "It's for the best."

"We'll put this money in the bank for you. You have really accumulated a chunk of change. I can't imagine– Oh. *Oh!*" My mother devolves into tears and shakes against my father's shoulder. "I always knew you were… were…" I realise she can't say it. My queerness hangs in the stuffy air between us. "…one of *those* girls. But this! God doesn't want…"

Sobs overcome her before she can finish and my father wraps his arms around her as if protecting her from me. "We'll discuss this tomorrow," he says quietly.

I tear off to my room, my heart aching when I see the emptied place where my treasure had once laid. My body falls into the sheets and only then do I let myself cry. The sky wails with me, and somehow I know, in the Nichols house, Lily shrieks for me too. I rise and move to my alarm clock, determined, setting it to five am before anyone in the house will wake. At the very least, I need to see Lily one more time.


Luckily for me, the screen on my window is pretty easy to knock off. I haul myself out the window and thump onto the grass outside. When I climb the fence which separates our backyard from the road and land onto the driveway, I hum with annoyance seeing my bike has been locked in the garage overnight. The Nichols house is about seven miles away, and before I even move, my limbs whine in protest at the prospect of walking that far in the heat.

I throw off my discomfort and disappear into the trees across the street. Figuring it would be stupid to stay close to the road on the likely chance my parents come looking for me, I stick to the brush. It's stupid how you're only important when you've done something wrong. There's a path which ends at the Nichols house if I remember right; one time I had gone wandering and found it.

Unfortunately, the trail has grown over in the years that this has ceased to be a road by which kids go to school. Branches stick in my hair and I trip over tree stumps more than once. Tears make my face sticky as the humidity won't let them dry. I don't know if I just want to say goodbye to Lily or if I want to take her up on the offer.

Then I see a trail—or what looks like a trail—softened by moss. The trees are parted here which makes my passage a little easier. I plod forward through the brush, the sound of the road now fully deafened. My hand reaches into my back pocket for my phone to use it as a compass, and I let out a relieved laugh when I see I've been going in the right direction.

It seems the walk is becoming easier, the sun doesn't feel so hot under the trees and my feet don't protest when they are lifted into another step. My head twitches back and forth involuntarily, swishing my hair from side to side, and I realise I am happy in spite of myself. I don't know what awaits me at home, but under the trees I feel okay.

A crunching at my feet draws my attention and I can just make out the snake camouflaged in the brush.

"Linus?" I whisper as I kneel down. If it isn't Linus, this would be a really stupid way to die.

I almost scream with glee when the snake glides up my arm before I remember he prefers the quiet. It nuzzles my neck and I use my thumb to caress its head. This means I must be close.

My feet seem to follow the path involuntarily, and by now I know the trees are making way for me. Two days ago I would have laughed it off as a beautiful dream but now I know better.

The branches part to reveal a clearing and the sun, which is now directly overhead. My heart races with recognition. I see the tree we climbed yesterday and I let out a small sob of joy. Lily comes crashing through the brush, her eyes wild.

"You–You found it." Her eyes hone in on the snake. "Thank you for bringing him, Linus."

I let Linus onto the ground where he disappears into the roots of an oak. "I had to come say goodbye."

"No–" She begins to cry as if she knows it all, and her tear tracks are light green, like chlorophyll spilling down her cheeks.

"My mom found my diary—told your mom, they're– they're going to send me away."

"No."

"Lily–"

"No!" Her hands dig into mine and I can see her nails are sharp like her teeth. "I told you. You can be like me, with me. A new family. They– They," she gestures wildly towards her house, "They only wanted me to feel better about myself. I need to be a part of a family who wants me. I'm never going anywhere. *Please.*" Lily's voice cracks and I hug her.

"They'll worry. It's not fair–"

"You can come back. I'm still here, aren't I? You can go anywhere you want. Please, you could be whole."

My breath hitches in my chest. "You promise? All of it?"

There's a call from far off, it sounds like Mrs Nichols, maybe my mom. We have to hurry.

She nods ferociously in response, her own eyes darting anxiously to the source of the sound. I look back at the path I came from and shudder at the prospect of going home or them discovering me here. My hands find hers and I squeeze. "Okay."

When she pulls me through the trees it feels like we're going faster than it should be possible to run. My feet barely touch the ground and I can't hear the crunching of our steps. No branches hit me, and the sun feels pleasant on my skin with the aid of the breeze Lily is stirring up. It is over before I want it to be as we stumble into a small clearing.

There is a council of mushrooms, just like in a storybook. They sit in a circle and the breeze sounds like murmuring. No, they're actually speaking.

The one at the head of the circle speaks and I cannot tell if it is only in my head or carried by the wind. Its voice is tender but deep and listening to it feels like lichens are sprouting in my ears. "Lily?"

She steps forward into the circle. "Yes."

"What have you brought us?"

"A friend. He's come to ask for the gift you gave me."

There's a murmuring amongst the mushrooms and, though they have no eyes, I know I'm being appraised.

"And he knows the price?"

"Oh, I am happy to give that to you guys. I hate that thing." I scold myself internally for speaking out of turn but the chorus of mushroom voices are now blooming in my ears.

"Sit down, boy."

Lily moves from the circle and I sit where she had stood moments ago. I cross my legs, then uncross them, then cross them again. The tingling up my spine tells me the mushrooms are laughing.

"Uhhh what do I do now?"

"Ask."

"Um–" I turn to look at Lily but she is only watching me curiously. "Would you– would you all please, um, let me be– be whole? I'm tired of this feeling, I'm tired of my clothes fitting weird, I just– I just want to be whole. I want to feel how I feel when I'm lying in dewy grass or–" I look at Lily. "Or how I feel when lightning bugs crawl over me at twilight. I want to be that peaceful all the time. So please. Have my name, I never want to hear it again. And– and um, yeah." I stare forward at the head mushroom.

"Oh, sweet child, the world has lied to you. You have always been whole, it's not your fault the limited minds of others cannot fathom the enormity of you. You have always been as you wish, and we will show you. Give us your name, boy."

Shaking, I lean down onto my forearms to whisper into the mushroom. My lips form the name but the second it leaves my lips I cannot fathom what it once was. Joy seems to be rapidly expanding in my chest and when I wipe my hand across my face, I can see the chlorophyll tears.

Lily watches me, and the moment I exit the circle, she tackles me and pulls me into her chest. When she releases me, she's grinning, and I realise she's looking up at me now as if I've grown taller in the past few minutes. Maybe I have.

"How do you feel?"

"Like I've always felt. Only now–" I take a deep breath, my head shaking back and forth in spite of itself, bangs fluttering on my forehead. "Now it feels easy. But like it's always been easy and I just didn't know it yet." I don't know what will happen next, but I'm not sure it matters now. My life is mine for the first time.

"What do you want your new name to be?"

I look around and then settle back on her. "Could you give me one?"

She smiles and steps back like an artist at the foot of a sculpture. Then she moves forward again to whisper in my ear, like I did to the mushroom. Her voice is cool, like there's a washcloth being pressed against my brain.

"For the summer air that now fills your lungs, and the green in your veins, I give you August."

When she steps back it feels like something has slotted into place over my old name and my face hurts from smiling. "Yeah. August. I like that."

# Fate Turns the Light On

Rafaella Rul

Content Warnings: Panic Attack, Fascists Attacking a School, Implied
Death

Author's Note:

I sat down to write "Fate Turns the Light On" after a long discussion
with my mother about the longevity of The Sound of Music. As is the
way of ideas, when I started typing, it became something else entirely
—I had a very specific scene in mind and I think if you're familiar
with the soundtrack you'll recognise the title (from which you may
draw your own conclusions).

In 2022 in the United States, where I was living at the time, there were
fifty-one school shootings resulting in injuries or deaths. In that same
year 278 bills were introduced targeting the queer, especially trans,
community—many of them in the name of protecting children. It
reinforced something I'd always known: kids are always having to save
themselves. The law always waits outside for the danger to pass them
by, when they're not actively causing harm themselves.

All of that was on my mind—The Sound of Music included—as I
wrote this short story, featuring an autistic trans masc kid, who just
wants to try on his very first binder in peace. Alas, things do not go as
planned.

# Fate Turns the Light On

Rafaella Rul

THERE IS A fucking alarm going off *again*, and this is the worst one so far.

The Five Rings Academy of Astronautical Navigation, Discovery, & Friendship has many, *many* different alarms for all the things that can possibly go wrong in a space-station based boarding school attended by the children of five separate sentient species—so *many things* are always going wrong here.

One of the first things each new student is made to learn is what each alarm means: there are different coloured lights, different patterns of flashing, different sounds, different *patterns* of sounds, and a seemingly endless combination of all four. Each alarm signals a different disaster. Though, some can hardly be classified as disasters.

For example, an alarm had gone off eight days ago for, as of yet, unknown reasons.

And last month there had been a migraine-inducing alarm that had been set off across every Ring, entirely by accident—or so the professor is insisting—in the chemistry labs on the Fourth Ring.

Last year, again on the Fourth Ring, there had been a memorable incident where a professor had *intentionally* shut off the artificial gravity of the Ring to give his students an up close appreciation for space, because living year round on a fucking space station was not enough. He had been fired on the spot. Or, well, he had been fired as soon as the artificial gravity was reinstalled and the deathly loud alarms turned off.

All of the alarms are supposedly different. Distinct. Easy to distinguish which disaster has currently affected the school.

But to Dax Astra, fifteen and in his fifth year at the Academy, all of the alarms are the same, all of them variations on eardrum-shattering sound or panic inducing lights or *both*.

He knows if the brain melting loudness is paired with the bone crunching bright flashing lights, he should be making an attempt to find an adult and an escape pod.

Dax knows, right now, as the lights flash against his closed eyelids and the most unforgivable combination of blaring noises he has ever heard in his entire life are going off around him in his room, that he should, *right fucking now*, be leaving his room and the station.

Instead, on top of the Noises and the Lights, Dax is fighting a third constriction: his very first chest binder arrived today and, after an uncertain amount of after class time spent simply running the smooth silky stretchy soft fabric against and through his pale fingers and holding it pressed against his chest, Dax had finally fought himself most of the way into it, when the horrible, *fucking awful*, alarms went off.

He's not sure which is worse.

The SOUNDS—

The LIGHTS—

Or the way one of his arms is *stuck* at a rib cracking angle inside the binder and neither his arm nor the binder will *move*.

There is also the unfortunate burning sensation in his eyes, and the heavy tracks down his cheeks from where tears have escaped but he can't wipe them away because, well, his free hand is pressed hard to his corresponding ear in a futile attempt to block out the alarms.

He keeps his eyes squeezed shut, but it does not help; the lights are still flashing behind his eyelids and covering one ear makes the alarm dissonant, which is nearly worse except uncovering his ear makes him wonder if he could somehow heave himself to a nearby airlock instead.

If this alarm spells his death, Dax can only spare this one thought: he hopes it is quick.


A hand on his shoulder adds to his panic: too close to sending him over an irreconcilable edge, but then there is another hand on his opposite shoulder and they squeeze just tight enough to ground him.

Metaphorically speaking.

"Dax? Hey, hold on–" the hands leave but the words do not stop. "Where are those space-damn headphones you're always wearing— shit, yeah, you know we should really clean up in here– ah ha! Okay–"

The headphones slip over his ears. Proteus North, the most recent in a long line of changing roommates, has to pry his right hand away to fit them on correctly but he is unexpectedly casual about it.

As a roommate, Proteus North has been… interesting. His side of their shared room is as messy as Dax's, but where his mess is organised and methodical, Proteus' side looks like a storm has blown through. He is the first roommate who has not complained about how unsocial Dax is; something terribly looked down upon in the Friendship Track.

There is this expectation, on the Fifth Ring, that everyone be sociable at all times. That, on top of classes and group projects and sharing rooms, everyone is always available to do 'things'. Dax does not know what 'things' is supposed to mean, or who has the time to do them. He does know that after talking to people *all day long*, the very last thing he wants to do upon returning to his dorm, is go back out or invite people in.

Dax leaves the safety and quiet of his room and his noise blocking headphones, for two things: class, and flying. Proteus, who invites him out frequently, is the first person who has never pushed, wheedled, or whined when Dax says no.

Proteus had also helped Dax cut all his hair off six days ago. Which makes him the closest thing Dax has had to a friend since he chose the Friendship Track five years ago.

With the loud alarm sirens decently muffled, Dax dares to open his eyes again and meets Proteus' lightning blue stare. It is neither pitying nor annoyed. It is... different. He is not sure what the look is, and he cannot make out what he is saying anymore between the headphones and the muted sirens and the disorienting flashing lights.

Dax gets the gist, though, when Proteus tugs his binder into place, freeing his trapped arm, and throws Dax the extra soft sleep shirt from the edge of his bed. Proteus does not wait for him to tuck it all the way into the waistband of his uniform trousers before grabbing his hand and pulling him out of their shared room. Dax can tell from the way his mouth is moving that Proteus is still talking but he is hoping it's nothing he will need to remember later because he doesn't think now is the time to learn how to lip read.

He focuses on the feeling of Proteus' hand around his own to distract himself from the lights. Proteus has a strong grip but soft skin. He does not like the dampness, the sweat building up, but he is not sure if the sweat is his or not. It would be embarrassing to blame Proteus if, in fact, Dax is the one responsible. Dax's free hand is not sweating, and they are moving along the corridors too fast to tell if Proteus' other hand is sweating. Maybe it is their hands together causing the problem. Why do so many people hold hands if it is always this damp? Is it always this damp? Maybe Dax *is* the problem and Proteus is secretly regretting holding his hand–

This is the least helpful distraction Dax has ever come up with. He needs a new one, and he needs it fast.

Dax gets what he asked for as they turn into the next corridor and regrets his request immediately—the flashing lights change colour. Between one flash and the next they go from blinding white to an angry red, and Dax does know this one. It is a blessing on their retinas and a curse on literally everything else:

Life support has stopped working.

The amount of breathable air left depends on a lot of factors:

First, how many lifeforms are still inside the Academy, something neither of them are in a position to know. Then, what caused the malfunction, and whether or not air is actively being removed from the station. There's also how soon they can get to an escape pod or a classroom equipped with oxygen masks because they are too far from their room to risk turning back, or–

He thinks back to eight days ago when this same alarm had gone off—the only reason he recognises it—how no one figured out how or what had set it off. Life support had not actually failed eight days ago, but Dax does not think they are lucky enough for two false alarms in as many weeks.

They should have reached an escape pod by now, they should be off the station and waiting to be collected by the local team of United Conglomerate First Responders, *not* to be confused with the United Conglomerate Armed Forces, and ushered to the nearby moon for an emergency headcount.

It occurs to him only now—distracted as he has been—that Proteus did not find Dax to rescue him, and had possibly never intended to take him to the pods.

Perhaps his estimation of possible friendship was too hasty.

Dax stops abruptly, unintentionally yanking on Proteus' arm—he is not sorry about it—and Proteus' mouth is moving as he turns but Dax cuts him off: "Where are we going?"

Like he can hear the answer, he cannot even hear himself.

Proteus seems to know this, so he must have been talking this entire time, not to converse with Dax, but to hear himself talk. More generously, to distract himself, but Dax is not feeling particularly generous, what with everything—whatever 'everything' is—going on.

Proteus tugs his hand and points with exaggerated emphasis to the right, and with a more observant look around, as fast as he can under the circumstances, everything clicks—it has been a *long* day. He especially understands why Proteus bothered coming back for a roommate he hardly knows.

His roommate has been paying closer attention to him than he realised.

They are headed for the jet hanger. Proteus needs a pilot. And Dax–

Dax has no idea what is going on, or what the plan is beyond hacking into a ship, but he no longer cares. Anything, *anything at all*, if it means he gets to fly.

He cannot stop the smile that bares his teeth and he does not try to. And, despite the thinning oxygen, Proteus gives him a broad, wild, grin when Dax squeezes his hand; his free hand flexes, open and closed, and back and forth because *yes*.

There is one thing, and only one thing, powerful enough to pull Dax from his books and his stories, one thing in all the universe, and it is the feeling of space outside the small cocoon of a thrumming engine, his hands at the controls, thrusters on full and a sky full of stars.

Life support inside ships and shuttles run off different power systems from the station, which is good because it would have been massively unpleasant to come all this way only to suffocate at the last hurdle. As it is, Dax and Proteus stumble to their knees as the ship door glides shut behind them and the power kicks on, gulping in air as it filters in around them.

It takes them both a minute to readjust, a minute Dax has no idea if they have time for. He still does not know what the alarm was for, beyond it being real this time around, or why Proteus thinks a ship is better than an escape pod. He could make an educated guess, but he does not particularly care to.

He is too excited to *fly*.

And in all honesty Dax hates the escape pods. Hates, hates, hates them.

There is no control.

Proteus tugs him back up to his feet and taps his own, uncovered, ears with his free hand. Dax looks out the front window, the view screen not turned on yet, where the flashing red lights are still flashing. In theory, they should be totally insulated from the Academy alarms in here, but his ears are sensitive and he would rather be safe than trigger overstimulation again. He shakes his head and buckles himself into the pilot seat—finally letting go of Proteus' hand, without asking where he means for them to go. Dax will ask when they are free of the dock.

They say there is no sound in space.

Dax does not doubt that is true. He is certain that, without a ship or a suit, he could experience the true meaning of silence. He is not certain he would care for it. Even if he were alone in the ship right now, he would be aware of the humming engines; he finds the sound comforting. After living his entire life on one space station or another, he thinks total silence would be jarring. The idea that he might need to set foot on a planet, or moon someday is something he keeps putting off. He would rather not deal with it at all, but he will settle for not dealing with it now.

After removing his headphones, all he can hear is Proteus narrating their every action. Perhaps that is the trick to going planetside: bring a friend who will not shut up.

Still, he feels no guilt cutting him off: "Where am I taking us?"

"Away from the Academy a bit, then turn us around and stop. We want to see what we're really dealing with before doing anything else."

Part of Dax thinks he should ask what 'anything else' might entail. Would someone else ask? Is he supposed to? He thinks, probably, somebody else would have asked a long time ago, would have asked before letting a practical stranger who is only *possibly* a *potential* friend drag them through the screaming alarms of the Academy and into a small, and by most definitions stolen, ship. Should he?

He does not ask. Mostly he wants to know what is going on, what is happening to the Academy, and Proteus is right, it will be easier from a distance.

Dax flies them a few miles out and turns them around, where the view stops them better than he could. Time seems to stop, too—seems to, because he knows time cannot actually stop. No matter how much he would like it to right now.

Academy shuttles and ships are battling non-Academy ships, and for a full second it floods Dax with icy fear—but the Academy vessels are not being blown to stardust as he would expect, and for another full moment he does not understand why.

Students! The other Academy ships must be piloted by other students. They must have organised quickly, likely they had all run for the ships as soon as the alarms had begun to blare. While his classmates had leapt into action to save their school, Dax had had a meltdown. He would have died in his room, tangled up in his binder, but for Proteus.

Would Proteus have come back for him if he was *not* the best pilot at the Academy?

He cannot–

He cannot follow that thread, cannot unweave the tapestry here, not right now.

He has to keep breathing, he has to learn to breathe with his binder on.

Dax focuses on the controls, traces each and every shape along the console with practised precision and by the third time around he can bring his focus back to the present, he can breathe without focusing on the way his lungs expand against the smooth and pleasantly constricting fabric of the binder, just in time to hear Proteus say:

"That'll be the Humanists—Professor Quasar kept telling the headmaster they'd come after the school but he kept insisting they wouldn't. *'They wouldn't dare attack children!'* Unbelievable. This was avoidable, if only the old man wasn't completely–"

Proteus goes on but Dax has stopped listening. He knows about the Humanists, some; as much as any student—the school attempts to keep its students in the dark about all things that deviate from the Academy's values, and the Humanists deviate, but when an extremist group wants two thirds of the student body dead at worst and expelled entirely from the galaxy at best, well. News finds a way.

Everyone knows the Humanists want a human only galaxy.

Dax, ever a devourer of stories, knows that monsters like the Humanists exist in nearly every story. In stories, they are supposed to be defeated by young nobodies who become heroes on a journey that usually starts much smaller than saving a universe; usually, the hero only sets out to save a family member or friend, and saves the world in the process.

Heroes do not go out seeking glory. He knows that.

And Dax has no family at the Academy anymore, his sister graduated the year before. He doesn't even have friends anymore, not really. Some acquaintances.

Dax could be a hero. Probably.

He considers Proteus in the seat beside him, talking still. If either of them is a hero, it's Proteus North, who has friends to save. Who saved Dax, even if it was only because he needed a pilot. His hands itch over the controls.

Maybe it is more complicated than that. Maybe, because Dax wants to help without anyone in particular he *needs* to save, maybe Dax wanting to save classmates he does not know can mean he is also a hero.

He is not entirely sure how it works outside stories.

Dax is not seeking glory. Not really. But there is a fight going on in front of them and he knows they—he and Proteus—can help. They can make a difference. They can save someone who might not have survived otherwise.

"–And I know it's a big ask, but Quasar says you're the best pilot at the Academy, so I figured, together, we could–"

"Yes." Dax flexes his fingers and looks away from the battle ahead to take in Proteus' pale profile, almost glowing in the ship's violet-tinted lighting. His blond hair washes out, blends right into his skin, a stark line against the colour of the purple Academy uniform. "If you're asking if I can fly us into that, and get us out alive again: yes."

Proteus grins at him, wide enough that Dax has to turn away, face the battle again.

Sometimes in stories, total strangers bond over a shared goal and become lifelong friends. Maybe that will happen here. Maybe, when they are done, Proteus North will be his friend. That, he thinks, would be nice.

"Good." Proteus pulls up the weapons controls, overriding whatever safety measures adults had previously installed to keep kids like them from doing exactly the kind of reckless, very dangerous, thing they are about to do. "Hit it!"


If Dax had to explain why flying through a battle, with the crashing lights and ships and phaser beams, does not freeze him down to his knees, the short answer is that, despite Proteus keeping up a running commentary, battle is quiet. The longer they fly the less he notices Proteus rambling—he had stopped trying to navigate quickly, after Dax had zigged and zagged them through two colliding ships unscathed.

He is fairly certain Proteus talks for the same reasons he does not, the same reasons Dax sometimes needs to wear his noise cancelling headphones. He does not ask, but he wonders how their classmates in the other ships differentiate between the ramblings and the commands Proteus delivers nearly simultaneously over the comms.

The Humanist ships are easy to differentiate from the subtle grey and black hulls of the Academy vessels, the violet Academy insignias on the ops of their ships don't stand out in quite the same way as the bright red stripes painted across all sides of the Humanist ships.

"They've made themselves into easy fucking targets," Proteus says, laughing like this is a test simulation, not like there are real lives on the line.

Dax keeps forgetting too, if he is totally honest, and unconsciously he pushes away the thought that after this is done there will be bodies to count and some of them could belong to people he knows and sits with in class. He will think about that later.

He cannot think about it now.

Now, he flies.

There were people on the Humanist ships too, people his flying and Proteus' shooting have killed. Are killing. *Us or them*, he thinks, consciously this time because it does not hurt when the deaths are faceless and evil.

"Nobody takes a bunch of kids seriously," Dax says quietly, and barrel rolls them around and through the wreckage of a Humanist ship. Very determinedly, he does not differentiate between the rigid shapes and the softer lines of the debris.

Proteus laughs, sharp and jagged this time, like he too is ignoring that occasionally Dax flies too close to other ships to avoid bumping into any bodies. "This bunch of kids are kicking their bunch of fascist dicks collective ass."


By the time the United Conglomerate First Responders, and Armed Forces, arrive, in ten sleek blue ships that make Proteus roll his eyes—

"They're literally seconds away, you know that? Mom helped design those ships, they spent a *disgusting* amount of resources on making them capable of jumping literal fucking galaxies in an instant, and they can't be fucked to come save a school full of literal children until *after* we've done their job for them? Bet they take all the credit too, the space fuckers."

—all the Humanist ships have been destroyed. Dax does not say anything, there is hardly a need to. Proteus is ranting loudly about everything that crosses his mind, colourfully.

"Ten fucking ships. Space Jesus. They could've routed the Humanists with *one* of those ships. Typical UCAF, overcompensating for their massive fucking incompetence."

Dax decided, sometime in the last few hours of daredevil manoeuvrers, well aimed shots, and more lucky breaks than he even wanted to keep track of, that he likes the way Proteus talks. The sound of his voice, the calm narration even in the worst of tight spots, had been grounding.

Metaphorically speaking. And the way Proteus swears, like someone casually commenting on the environmental controls, has actually made him laugh more than once.

He does not know how, but Proteus talking is better than near silence.

He is fascinating.

Both of them sober when Dax docks their ship; they are the last ones back in, and three spots, out of the ten spaces in this bay, remain empty. If the same amount of ships are missing from each bay, they'll have lost fifteen ships. Optimistically thirty students. It is possible these are the only missing ships, only missing three ships, a minimum of six students. It is even more likely their bay suffered the smallest loss. It is possible only seven ships survived, at least fourteen students.

He cannot bring himself to start considering the survival probabilities of the escape pods.

Dax fights for his next inhale, his fingers flay across his console, searching for life support and—that cannot be right, it says all systems functioning, but that makes no sense, there is no more air on the ship–

Proteus spins his chair to face him and holds his face between both his hands and Dax wants to tell him to let go but he squeezes, just a little, fingers tangling in Dax's badly cut black hair and it is just enough pressure, just enough that he can breathe again.

"I know," Proteus growls. For a moment Dax thinks all that rage in his blue eyes is directed at him, until he says, "But it's *not* our fucking fault, got it? The whole space fucking *school* would've been dust if it wasn't for us. Blame the Humanists, fuck, blame the UCAF, *but not us.*"

Dax grabs at his hands when Proteus pulls away. "And the headmaster, for not listening to Professor Quasar."

Proteus barks a laugh and pulls him to his feet. "You're right, fuck him too."

They walk down the gangplank together holding hands again, and by the looks on the faces of the headmaster and the UCAF officers, Dax has no idea if he and Proteus, and their classmates already facing off with the adults, are about to be celebrated or expelled.

What makes a hero, he thinks again. There are stories where the hero is never recognised for their actions, and others still where the hero is made out to be a villain. Sometimes the history is revised after their death, a hero post mortem.

But Proteus is right, they saved the school. Whether or not the teachers and the UCAF officers choose to acknowledge their actions.

Still.

Where do their actions leave them?

Proteus squeezes his hand and whispers in his ear, "We're a team. We've got this."

Whether they have, actually, 'got this' or not, Dax is reassured, at least, that they face the consequences together.

# A Chrysalis for the Emperor

## Briar Ripley Page

Content Warnings: Ableism, Insects, Animal Death, Vomiting, Teacher Bullying/Abuse, Confinement, Body Horror

Author's Note:

This story was difficult and emotional for me to write. Unlike most of my fiction, it draws heavily and directly on my own childhood experiences. But I can't help thinking it's important for that reason. When I was a child and teenager, I very rarely encountered fiction in which the protagonist was autistic or otherwise developmentally disabled. I never found any fiction that reflected the difficulty, alienation, and occasional trauma of being a special ed student.

I think if I'd been able to read stories with disabled heroes that dealt with those topics, I would have felt less ashamed of myself, less like all my suffering was my own fault, and less like my only options in life were "become neurotypical-passing" and "become an un-person permanently". Terrible options, and even more so when passing as neurotypical feels irrevocably entwined with cisness, heterosexuality, and gender conformity.

One story I did connect with a great deal in middle school was Kafka's The Metamorphosis, to which "A Chrysalis for the Emperor" obviously owes a debt.

# A Chrysalis for the Emperor

Briar Ripley Page

BUG WATCHES THE big nightcrawler in her best friend's hands as it twists itself up and down and around. The worm's skin is slick with mucus, and Kieran's fingertips are glistening under the high noon sun.

Bug is no kin to annelids; she finds them as gross as most people do. Still, she feels sorry for the fat red-brown creature.

"Hey," Kieran says, "C'mon, Bug. You gotta choose. Should I let him live, or execute him?" His fist begins to tighten.

Bug gives the thumbs-up. If Bug gave the thumbs-down, Kieran would smoosh the worm until there was nothing left of it but sticky paste. This, Kieran says, is how the ancient Romans decided whether or not to kill prevailing gladiators: ratio of thumbs up to thumbs down from the crowd in the arena, and the emperor overrode them all. "You're the emperor, Bug," he told her, the day he invented the game. He put a hand in her long, wild hair and only winced a little when one of Bug's chitinous insect antennae, hidden in the curls, grazed his palm. "I'm the executioner."

Bug is a benevolent emperor. She always lets the prisoners go.

"Shit." Kieran drops the worm in the grass. He drops himself in the grass too, stretching out on his back. "You should let me kill one sometime, Bug. Just once."

Bug shakes her head. She's not a killer. She's not a bad kid—she hopes she isn't. She tries to affect a stern facial expression, but she's not very good at facial expressions in general. The muscles and skin of her face feel wrong to her; too tight or too loose or something, alien.

The bell rings. It's time for class. Bug pulls on Kieran's shirtsleeve when he shows no sign of moving. He rises slowly, groaning and rolling his eyes.

"Aw, c'mon, Bug. Just this once, let's skip. We could hide behind the woodshop shed. They'd never find us before the period's over."

Bug shakes her head again. She shapes some words carefully, forcing them through her throat. They come out in the creaky, hissing voice nobody wants Bug to use, not the girlvoice she's supposed to practice, but Kieran's the only other one here and he doesn't care.

"Come," hisses Bug, "More trouble tomorrow if we're gone today."

They walk down the gentle slope of the hill to the low brick school building together.


In Special Ed. Mr Corcoran is trying to teach Kieran math. Kieran is twelve like Bug, but he still can't do multiplication or division without a calculator. The most rudimentary pre-algebra fills him with rage. Bug can hear him shouting from the room next door: "Screw this!" There's the sound of paper ripping and crumpling. "I don't need to learn this shit! I don't *want* to learn this shit! Stop talking to me like I'm stupid, you big walrus!"

Bug would laugh, if laughing didn't get her in trouble. Mr Corcoran really does look like a walrus, with his tiny eyes and bristling moustache.

"Samantha?" says Mrs Metzger. "Pay attention."

Bug looks at Mrs Metzger's nose to simulate appropriate eye contact. She nods.

"Show me what you've practised since last week, Samantha," says Mrs Metzger.

Bug sits up straight in her hard plastic chair. "My name," Bug lies, "is Samantha Gregory. It's a pleazzzure to m...meet you."

Mrs Metzger winces. "Samantha. Be honest. Have you been practising at all? At home after school like I've asked you?"

"Yezz," Bug lies. Speech therapy has turned her into a liar. If Mrs Metzger has her way, Bug will eventually become so good at lying that even Bug believes herself to be telling the truth.

"*Samantha.*"

Bug closes her eyes.

"Samantha, please look at me."

Bug opens her eyes. Mrs Metzger is leaning forward with her elbows on her knees, trying to seem sympathetic.

"Samantha, I know this is difficult for you. I know it's embarrassing to have to practice things that come naturally to others—" Mrs Metzger begins. She's interrupted when the door between the two small Special Ed. rooms swings open. Mr Corcoran has Kieran by the arms. Kieran makes a big show of stomping and cussing but doesn't really try that hard to get away, doesn't do anything that would give Mr Corcoran license to throw him to the ground in a more painful kind of restraining hold.

Mr Corcoran marches Kieran to the Quiet Closet. Through the doorway, Bug can see the other three kids in Kieran's remedial math group sitting in a circle around the particle board table, pretending not to stare.

"Phil, please," says Mrs Metzger. "This is the third time this week."

"Not my fault, Janice," says Mr Corcoran through his moustache. Then, to Kieran, in a much louder voice: "All right, you. Fifteen minutes. After that, you can sit with the group until the end of the period if you're calm." He opens the door of the Quiet Closet and thrusts Kieran inside.

Bug's antennae rise involuntarily from the mass of her hair. They're chitinous, matte black, about nine inches long and as thick as Bug's pinky finger. They have a sense the rest of her body lacks; a sense that is sort of like touch and sort of like smell and sort of like dreaming. Through her antennae, Bug feel-smells Kieran in the Quiet Closet, exuding something sour and despairing and joyous all at once.

Mrs Metzger sits across from Bug in a haze of feel-smell like tobacco and dish detergent wrapped in denim. "Oh, Samantha," she says, with a disgust she thinks she's hiding. "We *talked* about this. Look at me."

Bug stares at Mrs Metzger's nose again. She wishes she were anyplace else.

"You're really a bright child," said Mrs Metzger, "despite your...difficulties. Your condition is mild; you're lucky in that. Many children with your disorder have no chance of living a normal life."

Bug nods her head up and down, conscious of its relative normalcy. Apart from the antennae and a certain glossy stickiness to the palms of her hands and the soles of her feet, she just looks like a short, ugly twelve-year-old girl. She has a cousin a few years older than her who looks like a five-foot-six cockroach. He can't talk at all, or hold a pencil, or go to a regular school. His mom, Bug's aunt, thinks her son and Bug are the way they are because of vaccines, and now every time Bug gets a shot she wonders if she's going to wake up with compound eyes and an exoskeleton. Sometimes Bug even thinks that might not be so bad.

"But Samantha," Mrs Metzger sighs, "you have to *want* a normal life. You have to want it, and you have to be willing to work for it. To cooperate with of all us here who are trying to help you. Otherwise...

well. Who knows." she looks pointedly at Bug's antennae. "Now. Do ordinary girls have antennae?"

"No," mumbles Bug in a girlvoice.

"What's the appropriate thing to do when we find ourselves growing parts that don't belong?"

"Cut them off," mumbles Bug in a girlvoice.

"Yes!" Mrs Metzger smiles in a way she probably imagines is warm and motherly. "Looking after our hygiene and personal grooming is so important, especially as we approach our teen years. I want to see you with a smooth, clean head when you come in tomorrow, Samantha."


Bug sits next to Kieran at their usual Biology table. It's at the back of the classroom, in the corner closest to the door. She hoists herself up on the tall metal stool and lets her backpack slump between the stool's three long legs. She watches her distorted reflection shimmer alongside Kieran's in the dull silver of the little sink set inside the black tabletop.

"Hey," whispers Kieran.

Bug holds up one finger: *Wait a second.* She gets her notebook and pencil out of her backpack and starts writing on a blank page. It's much easier than talking.

"Are you okay?" Bug writes, "How was the Quiet Closet?"

Kieran shrugs. "Same as ever," he says. "It's really not that bad. Beats having to sit through the whole math period."

Bug shudders. Her antennae rise into the air again and sense the slimy glint of a lie around Kieran.

"Whoa," Kieran says. "Dude. I thought they told you to cut those things."

"They did," Bug writes, "I forgot." She hesitates, then scribbles heavily over "forgot".

"Screw that, then. I like your antennae."

"Girls don't have antennae," writes Bug.

"So you're not a girl." Kieran shrugs again. "You're you. You're Bug,"

Bug smiles. Her antennae stretch higher, like plants seeking the sun somewhere above the roughly textured paste-coloured ceiling tile. She forces them down fast when she hears the classroom door swinging open and Mr Poole's voice booming out towards her.

"All right, you mad scientists," he says. "I've got good news!" There are mutters of excitement and interest from the students who aren't Kieran and Bug. The thing about Mr Poole is he's supposed to be one of the cool teachers. Most kids love his edgy humour and willingness to sometimes cuss in front of his classes. They love his enthusiasm for taking animals apart and revealing their inner secrets. Mr Poole makes no secret of his contempt for Kieran and especially for Bug, but if anything that just adds to his coolness for all the others. Kieran and Bug are not likeable or liked.

Mr Poole is middle aged, medium height, bespectacled, and built like a boxer. He wears his shirtsleeves rolled halfway up his broad forearms. Bug feels strangely envious of those forearms, with their thick black hairs like small antennae. Bug wishes she was strong.

Today, Mr Poole is carrying a big leather thing like a briefcase. Bug wonders what could be inside it, and then, as he carefully places it on top of his desk and begins to undo the latches, she remembers.

*No*, Bug thinks, *oh, no*. She grips the cold edges of her stool and squeezes her eyes shut tight.

"You asked for it, and now I proudly present to you—the Andrew Poole Beetle Collection!" says Mr Poole.

Bug rocks back and forth a little. She'll be okay. She'll get through this. She's being too sensitive.

"Bug?" says Kieran's voice beside her. "Hey, do you need to go out in the hall or anything?"

Bug shakes her head.

"Samantha!" booms Mr Poole. "What's going on back there? Is your boyfriend groping you under the table?" There are gasps and titters from the rest of the class.

Bug makes herself open her eyes. Mr Poole is carrying something toward her and Kieran's table, smiling like he's bringing them both a gift. The something has a wooden frame and a shiny glass front like a painting in a museum, but it isn't a painting. It's a tray full of dead beetles, each insect stabbed through with a silver pin and neatly labelled in minute letters. The beetles are terribly still. Their legs and antennae are like the ink lines of anatomical diagrams. Their wings are all sheathed.

Bug knows other people would think they were beautiful. People who would scream if they saw an insect crawling alive through their house would admire its shimmering colours once it exists only as an object on display.

"Here," says Mr Poole, handing the tray to Kieran, "You two take a good, long took at these, and then pass them back to the front of the room. Don't get your greasy fingerprints on the glass, or I'll smack you." He winks at them, but Bug doesn't think he's joking.

Kieran holds the tray limply. Bug averts her gaze. Mr Poole won't be defeated so easily, though.

"Come on, Samantha!" he says. "*You*, of all people! These are practically your cousins, right? Take a look!"

"Yeah!" someone yells from another table. "Look at your cousins!"

Bug takes a deep breath and looks. There's a beetle with enormous, hornlike jaws, now useless to him. There's a beetle iridescently blue as the sky reflected in a puddle of gasoline. They float against a white background.

Acid starts to rise in Bug's throat. She shakes and makes a little noise. She feels her antennae rise too. They're in the air, waving wildly, brushing Kieran's inflamed cheek through a haze of angry humiliation, feel-smelling something oily and bitter and self-satisfied from Mr Poole.

"*Samantha!*" Mr Poole thunders. "That's no way to behave. If you're going to cause a disruption, I'll have to send you out of the room."

His words are melting into an incomprehensible slurry in Bug's ears. Bug feels feverish and cold at the same time. There's too much sensory data in the classroom now for her to process: she doesn't know what to make of everything she feel-smells through her antennae. She pulls herself from Kieran's side, and she turns a little. Then she lets herself spew rancid citrus-scented puke all over Mr Poole's button-down shirt and hairy forearms. It sprays out of her like she's a busted fire hydrant. The chaos around her heightens and shimmers. It's so overwhelming she actually thinks for a moment that she might die.

Someone is grabbing Bug's arms. Someone is pulling her backwards. Bug realises it's Kieran holding her. She lets him lead her through the door, into the mostly deserted hallway. Kieran keeps his hands on Bug, steadying her. He holds her close and tight.

"I'm sorry," he says. "Fuck. I'm sorry."


"It wasn't her fault!" Kieran shouts, back in the Special Ed. rooms. "He brought his bug collection! Looking at them made her sick, I mean, can you blame her? It'd be like if he brought in a box of

82

aborted fetuses or something! From her perspective, you know? She couldn't help it."

"Samantha," Mrs Metzger says softly, touching the underside of Bug's chin to make her look up, "is that what happened? Did you mean to throw up on your teacher, or was it an accident?"

Bug hates the Quiet Closet. Bug could lie. Bug is a better liar every day.

"I aimed," says Bug, making eye contact. "I meant it." Her voice buzzes, but the words are clearer than they've ever been.

"Well," says Mrs Metzger, shaking her head in sad disappointment.


The Quiet Closet is ostensibly not a punishment. It's supposed to be a place for Special Ed. kids to calm down from mood swings or overstimulation and reflect on their behaviour. Both teachers and kids know the truth, though, even if they don't say it out loud.

Bug trembles as the door clicks shut behind her. Two hours, said Mrs Metzger. Bug has never spent more than ten or fifteen minutes in the Quiet Closet before.

The interior of the Quiet Closet is soundproofed, padded, and entirely, seamlessly white. If Bug reaches out, her palm brushes the back wall and leaves a glistening smudge there. Its nearness makes her claustrophobic. When she withdraws her arm, she's adrift in an endless sea of nothing—nothing but herself and the smudge of her own slime.

Bug screams. It doesn't make her feel any better.

She throws herself to the floor and lies there like she's been pinned, for what feels like forever. That doesn't make her feel better, either, and she gets dizzy from looking at all that nothing. It feels like she's falling up.

Bug curls up on her side in the smallest ball she can, whimpering and lightly smacking herself in the face. That helps a little bit, a very little. She almost thinks she can see the layers of white paint and padding start to take on depth and form around her.

Bug's body feels suddenly bloated and squishy, although she hasn't eaten all day. She twists around to look at it, and finds that she's become a fat, smooth, girl-sized grub. She has three rows of stubby legs that wave in the air.

Around her, the Quiet Closet melts into sunshine and grass. She's on top of the hill behind the school where she and Kieran play their game. The daylight is brutal on Bug's new skin. She has to protect herself from it.

As soon as she has the thought, she feels herself excreting something. It oozes out of her in huge, yellowish globs. She rolls around until she's covered in it, until she can't feel the ground beneath her anymore, until it clouds her vision. Until it's hardening into a coffin.

Bug begins to dissolve. She feels herself turning into soup. There is no Bug anymore. There is organic liquid in a perfect grub-shaped box, sloshing around, reshaping itself, suffused with a vague anticipation.

Time passes. The liquid doesn't feel it. There's no Special Ed., no Quiet Room, no Kieran or Mr Poole or speech therapy or speech or names for minutes and hours.

The liquid starts to reconfigure.

It separates itself into segments that harden and cohere. It forms a glossy carapace. A long, sleek horn. Six strong, thin legs. Two tall, flexible antennae.

Soon, a newborn beetle tears through the hard box that holds it captive. The material crumples to tissue-paper shreds as the beetle emerges, its shell-like armour, its antennae smell-feeling everything the world has to offer. It is bigger than a school bus and stronger than a storm.

With a loud whirring rattle, the monstrous insect spreads its translucent amber wings and...

And falls abruptly back into a human body, whirling, collapsing, scrabbling for purchase on white foam as the door of the Quiet Closet whispers open.

"Samantha?" says Mrs Metzger. She crosses her arms in front of her. "I hope you've been using this time in a productive manner."

Bug blinks blearily. She bobs her head up and down.

"Good," says Mrs Metzger. A bell rings shrill and hollow. It's time to go.


Bug's parents work late and don't like her to be unsupervised, so she gets off the bus with Kieran after school. Kieran's dad doesn't care what Kieran and Bug do as long as they don't interrupt him while he's watching TV and drinking beer in the basement, but Bug's parents don't need to know that.

"Are you sure about this?" asks Kieran. They're standing in Kieran's bathroom, which is very small and smells like iodine. Bug's taken her shirt off; Kieran's not looking at her chest but at her hair. Her hair and her antennae sticking out of it. He's holding a pair of scissors.

"Yezz," says Bug. "Sure." She sits down on the closed lid of the toilet. "Do it now."

"What if I hurt you by accident?"

"Don't care. Cut."

"What if it looks stupid?"

"*Cut*, Kieran."

"You know what Mrs Metzger and them are gonna say. You know what they'll–"

Bug glares, and then Bug laughs. "Kieran, you wusszzz. I'm the emp-er-or, remember? When I say you cut, you cut."

Kieran laughs too. "Can't argue with that, your majesty." He brings the scissors close. They make swishing sounds around Bug's head.

There is no pain. Long curls of dark hair fall to the tile floor, where they lie like dead worms. When Kieran is finished, Bug's hair is shorter than his. She turns her face from side to side as she examines his work in the mirror. The back of her neck feels tender and naked. Her antennae are visible as radio towers in an open field. They're as visible as a pinned beetle on a white background. There's no hiding them.

"You're in so much trouble," says Kieran, but he's grinning. "*So* much trouble. But what do you think? Did I do an okay job?"

Bug nods. Still entranced by her reflection, she lifts her hands and gives Kieran two thumbs up.

# Don't Play With My Heart

## Ray Rhys Phillips

Content Warnings: Transphobia, Misgendering

Author's Note:

"Special Interests" are important to autistic people. They can be broad and mainstream or they can be weird and obscure. Either way, it's easy to say a lot of nerds are autistic and a lot of autistics are nerds. But gatekeeping is prominent in nerd culture, especially against marginalised genders. The pressure to know everything about something, especially when other factors like time, money and/or disability stop you from consuming your special interest as in-depth as some, is so, so wrong.

What makes something a special interest is you saying it is. For me, if there's a single quiet moment in my life, it is filled with games—playing them, watching YouTube, discussing plots and characters with friends. Do I remember all the cheats to the game I've played the most? Hell no! Have I played all the instalments of my favourite series ever? Am I made of money?! The special interest is in the shaking of my bones when a new trailer comes out, in the deep-dives on wikis and noticing a pattern in voice actors. This story is for you, gatekeeping-haters. Keep on being nerdy as hell.

# Don't Play With My Heart

Ray Rhys Phillips

I KNEW I got the job at Reckless Role when I pointed out that the shelf labelled "six player games" had Fury of Dracula on it. The owner of the café, Peter, raised his eyebrows and looked me up and down, focusing on every inch of my being. I admit I felt exposed —the constant eye contact that I was trying to maintain in this interview was burning a hole in my brain to begin with, and I couldn't help but follow his gaze down at my body.

The smile on his lips is what gave the game away. I'd like to think that all my previous responses helped towards the decision, that my ability to make the coffee and my ability to roleplay selling a board game helped too. But this random comment, unprompted, is what did it.

"You're eighteen?" he asked.

"Yes."

"You go to Winston University?"

"Started this term."

I moved to the city only two weeks ago, and I felt like I was already carving out an identity for myself. I had been out as trans before moving away from my family home, and not that it was hostile or anything, but having the complete freedom of adulthood meant that I'd steam-rolled ahead into everything I wanted to do to grow my euphoria. I started wearing my binder whenever I felt like it, got a piercing on my right ear that I quickly started to stim with, and bulked out my wardrobe with comfy, baggy gaming hoodies and soft flower shirts.

I'd spent a lot of money on this new identity. Student loans still had to be budgeted somewhat.

Thank whatever god is out there that the board game café position came up. There was not a more perfect job for me.

"I'm needing cover on Wednesdays and the weekend; does that interfere with any of your lectures?"

I grinned, before looking up and straightening my back. Professionalism still, professionalism. I look him in the eyes. "Don't have a problem with that."

Peter extended his hand. "Welcome to the team, eh…"

"Skylar."

"Skylar, yes. Thank you for reminding me," he said bashfully. I didn't blame him too much. When I had applied online my application came with my deadname attached to it for safety reasons. I wanted to gauge how cool the staff were in any given place before I outed myself. I was pleased to see that the owner himself brandished a bi pride flag pin on his blazer, so I felt safe enough to test the name earlier in the interview. "Are you able to start this coming Wednesday?"

"Of course," I said, shaking on the deal. "You should change the placement of Fury of Dracula soon, though, don't want to get any clientele confused when they go to pick it up and they're one person over."

"That was all part of the test," Peter winked. "That's the sort of attention to detail I've been looking for. It's what we desperately need to balance out the team."

It warmed my heart to hear that. It was my best quality.

Being autistic, there are certain quirks and tricks one picks up, sometimes it's a stereotype, sometimes it's just how that person is. Being good at maths or being able to memorise and recount the entirety of Hamlet, or being able to perfectly capture someone's likeness in a drawing like it was a photo can be the thing that an autistic person is good at. But the key link between these quirks—and any other quirks that work in a similar way—is they often derive from a special interest. The part of my brain that liked to problem solve and organise needed to be fed on a nearly constant basis, and the endorphin hit whenever I succeeded was euphoric.

Table-top games ruled my brain. They were the most unique way of scratching that itch. The different strategies for each game, the building of a character in an RPG, the moment of joy when you looked round the table and saw the concentration on everyone's face, fully invested. It was what my brain needed more than anything else in the world.

In my attempts to mask, I tried to bring this quality into everyday situations. I was always picked up on for being detail-oriented. I learned to pick the right times to bring things up, when to let go and when someone would genuinely appreciate it. Working in this board game café had the triple-whammy of organising stock (tick), making people's coffee orders perfectly (tick), and talking said people through any board game they picked off the shelf and asked me to teach them how to play (tick, tick, tick). I would have to summon back my customer service voice, the dreaded skill I hammered into myself when I worked at Starbucks during A Levels, but my brain would be happy. It would be satisfied.


The first day on the job I came in wearing a Legend of Zelda t-shirt and some slim jeans.

"Nice, Triforce of Courage?" Peter said, looking up from the coffee machine.

"Thought I'd wear it to give me strength for my first shift."

"Like the way you think, you're hired again." Peter reached down behind the counter and pulled out an apron with the café's logo and a metal name tag. "You're on coffee today. We'll make sure you're familiar with the equipment and menu."

I put on the apron, the ribbon tying around my small frame twice. I looked at the name tag, shiny and hard, a black background with silver letters slotted in: 'SKYLAR'.

I rubbed my thumb over the metal. The corners of my eyes prickled. Threatened to give me away as a sappy loser. No way am I crying on the job. *Professionalism. Professionalism.*

I clipped the name tag onto the apron and patted my flat chest with pride.

Coffee orders came in fast despite it being only a Wednesday. I knew that Saturday would be hard mode, so I kept up the pace and got out the orders with accuracy and flair, building up the stamina for it. *Mocha with cream, medium latte, two sugars, oat milk please, black americano, actually can I have a pot of milk on the side? Do you do tea too? Can I have a latte too but no sugar?* My body worked fast and my brain powered up faster. Soon my hands were reaching for the right sized mugs or scooping perfectly levelled sugars without having to exert much energy.

All the more brain power to people watch.

There was a couple that were playing Carcassonne, placing the tiles slowly in between sips of coffee and gazing into each other's eyes. There was a Magic the Gathering group, a mixture of age groups but all at least my age and above, as it was a school day. I'd heard the weekends were lawless, you couldn't go from one table to another without a child throwing a meeple to the floor or jumping because another child screamed in delight when they won. I wasn't particularly looking forward to that sensory overload. I at least had my little tasks to take care of, to occupy myself.

The following Wednesday was a little different but also very much the same. Having survived the increased pressure of the weekend, I decided I did like the job enough to endure masking through the rowdy families. The Magic the Gathering group was here again, with the same line up. There was a couple on a date, but not the same couple, two girls, a little older, who were playing Patchwork.

Then there was the third customer who walked through the door.

"Hi," the boy said. So casual. So normal.

It didn't mean anything to him that my mind was sent whirring out of control. His face was flawless; clear, soft looking skin with the hint of stubble, dark brown eyes that glistened and cute round spectacles that balanced perfectly on his hooked nose. He flicked his dark hair to one side as he waited for me to respond and I could've reached across the counter and punched him for how cute he was being. Was he doing this on purpose? Was he a siren sent to lure me?

I reached for a mug and stumbled. My fingers caught the rim and I yelped as I dropped it and then caught it in quick succession. The blood pounding in my ears meant that I just barely caught the cute-as-hell giggle that this guy let out.

God, strike me now.

I cleared my throat. Cleared my head. Got myself back into gear. "What will it be?"

"Large flat white with oat milk."

"Coming right up."

I turned my back to him to pour the coffee. I bit my lip. No. Silly fantasies were above me. No way was I allowed to picture myself on the other side of that counter, playing a board game with him, judging whether he was as competitive as I was. He was just a cute boy, and there was no telling if he thought I was a cute boy too. Despite my name being right there on my nametag, I still got the occasional "Thank you, Miss" from the clientele.

Once the coffee was poured, the dreaming ended. I steadied myself back on task.

"Enjoy."

"Thanks," he said, scooping it up with one hand. I noticed tucked under his other arm was a big laptop bag. He settled at a small table and brought out said laptop and a few books that were in there too. In a café where most of the appeal was you get to play any board game you want off the shelf, it was weird to see a lone customer. Especially one not even playing anything. Single-player games did exist, after all.

As I shifted through the tables, doing my duty to wipe surfaces and ask players if they were enjoying their games, my eyes wandered back to the mysterious Cute Boy. He'd put on some headphones and bopped his head as he scrolled through something. Sneaking a closer look, I noticed that one of his books was actually a sketchbook, which unfortunately lay unopened the entire time.

He was there for a solid hour. Once he was gone my brain could focus again.


The following Wednesday showed the same pattern. It was comforting to know that the shift would be my time to reset, collect my thoughts and go about my tasks. The fast-paced nature of the weekend and the ever-changing pressure from university was challenging in an enjoyable way, but being on easy mode for one day a week was sorely needed to balance it all out.

Magic the Gathering group in the corner, a few other students I'd seen about on campus arguing over the rules to Catan. Standard. Normal.

Then the Cute Boy walked in again.

*Shit.*

My eyes darted to the clock above the door. He came in at the same time last week, exactly to the minute. Was this going to be part of the routine? If so, I wasn't sure Wednesday would continue to be the respite I sought it to be.

Panic rose to my cheeks. My heart could not sustain this level of stress.

"A flat white with oat milk, please."

He said it like he didn't remember me. That was good. I was just a simple NPC in his life, which he obviously was the protagonist of, being that perfect. The more he treated me as such, the more my body would acclimatise to him being around.

I made his coffee the exact same way, my movements slow and methodical, making sure to hide my shaking hand. No way was I going to break my streak of not messing up. The week before when I almost dropped the mug was the closest I'd come to ruining it.

"Here you go," I croaked, sliding it over. I couldn't make eye contact with him as I rang his order through the till, I just couldn't. I listened out for the beeps of the contactless going through before pressing the right buttons on my end. He made his way to his table without addressing me further.

I continued to hang my head low. No. I couldn't be like this. Not in this safe space that I'd made for myself. Not once had I been flustered by a boy. It was not logical, not beneficial to me in any way. I liked the idea of love, I just thought I'd be strong enough to accept it in my own time, on my own terms. I didn't need the chemicals swirling round in my brain right now, in fact they were hindering my ability to map ahead. I was carefully cruising down the road, solving the mysteries of life that I chose to solve—my gender, my career path—and this damn crush was a massive boulder blocking my progression.

The marbled effect on the counter was starting to hurt my eyes. I'd been staring down at it for a few minutes already, hands balled into fists, squeezing out whatever life was left in the kitchen towel I was holding. What was I doing again? I was cleaning. I was cleaning, then I was collecting mugs, and then I was offering customers advice, and then I was collecting mugs again and then and then and then…

I was halfway through helping an older gentleman who had never been in before but was intrigued to know about the café, giving him advice on what games to recommend to his granddaughter, when the beautiful illustrations caught my eye.

I felt bad for the man, my pitch for Sushi Go was more rushed than it should've been, all because I was distracted by pretty colours.

*Strike me, strike me, strike me.*

I grabbed a cloth and began wiping the table next to him. Anyone paying any amount of attention would know that table had not been used today, but whatever. My motivation was clear.

Cute Boy had his head turned, glasses reflecting the low light coming through the window. He was lost in a daydream, pencil balanced between his fingers like a drummer waiting to bring down their drumstick. Whatever inspiration he was waiting for hadn't hit yet.

I took a peek.

The open page was full of bold, thick marker lines, which at first didn't seem to be anything, a sea of colour that at the very least was pretty. Some sort of abstract art? I turned my head to get a better look at it, maybe the angle was off, the solution staring me right in the face…

"Do you like it?"

My stomach dropped so fast I thought I was going to explode. My face flooded with red hot panic. I didn't have to see my reflection to know my cheeks were like plump, ripe cherries. I hated when my cheeks exposed the roundness of my face, with my short hair and masculine clothes, my cheeks, whether it be from them blushing or me smiling, made me look like a prepubescent boy. Which, I guess I am, but y'know.

I didn't give him an answer. I was not going to play his game, no siren could tempt me when on my own path.

In that moment, the Magic the Gathering guys called me over to settle an argument about a rule for them, and I couldn't be happier to be drifted off course.

When the hour was up, Cute Boy left. Just like he did the week before.


The next Tuesday night, my stomach wouldn't settle. I'd had some lectures throughout the day, and, although talking about some ancient king's effect on history was why I was there, the need to recuperate from being in those massive, densely packed halls was strong. I'd flopped onto my dorm bed, tucked into the corner next to a cluttered desk covered in card sleeves and half-read history books, and assumed that I would go straight to sleep. I was tired enough, wasn't I?

My phone rested on top of all the junk on my desk, playing a multiple-hour podcast of someone's Dungeons and Dragons game. The seven am alarm was still ten hours from now, but I was dreading it.

Wednesday didn't have lectures.

Wednesday was a work day.

My respite.

What was not clicking in my head?

The swirling colours coming off the page, dancing in front of my closed eyes. I tried to block it out, but I couldn't, his pull was too strong.

It was that fucking Cute Boy, wasn't it?

He was coming tomorrow. Same time. Same order. Same table. Never once picking up a board game, just sitting by himself with his coffee, his singular coffee. He could go anywhere else. He could go to one of the many Costas or Starbucks down the road.

The mystery surrounding this boy hurt my head. It was illogical. Why the hell was he there?

The anxiety of confronting that mystery made me feel sick. Pulling my legs up to my stomach, into my chest, I held my breath and tried to calm myself. Is this what they meant when they said love hurts? I didn't want it. I hated the break of the routine I thought I'd set out for myself. I hated that it made me feel disoriented, out of sync with my own brain. My perfect problem solving brain. He gave me a riddle I did not ask for. I did not want to be challenged this way.

I crossed my arms over my chest, pressed my boobs softly into myself. No binder in bed, of course, but the feel of those chubby circles being held flat and tight scratched the sensory itch. My stomach untwisted. The fog in my brain cleared.

Screw him. I was not going to let some boy ruin my perfect routine. I had a job to do, one that I was great at, skilled at.

The next day, he arrived. On time. Same order.

I prepared the coffee as normal, lips held tight as I tried to think about anything else. The most recent Star Wars trailer, which title to go for on my essay, remembering to call my mum soon. Anything, everything. I rolled up my hoodie sleeves after accidentally spilling a few droplets off the side of the mug. The siren would not distract me. I *refused.*

"Here you go."

This was when he would take his mug and sit at that same table, which was always, somehow, free. This was when he would take out his laptop and sketch book and do whatever the hell he did for an hour.

He broke the routine. He pointed at me.

"Winston Uni?" he said, a trace of a smile on his lips.

I glanced down at my hoodie. I'd not worn it out to work before, so he'd never really had a reason to bring up university. But now he could clearly see the embroidered yellow and blue emblem resting against my chest.

My hand reached for it, knocking my name tag loose along the way.

"Uh, ah, yes? What about it?" I asked, fumbling with the name tag.

"I go there! Haven't seen you around though. What do you study?"

I squinted. His smile seemed genuine, this couldn't be some power move on his side, could it? There didn't seem to be any ulterior motives behind those eyes.

Still, I had to play properly.

"History, no reason for you to have seen me, seeing as it's on the other side to the art department."

"What makes you think I do art?"

I fought the urge not to blush so hard I had to break customer service etiquette and stare out the window to hide my face. Plus the eye contact was getting painful. His damn beautiful eyes.

He laughs. "I'm playing with you. I saw you take a look at my art."

"What was that?" I ask, not bringing my gaze back. I hoped he didn't think I was rude. "In the sketchbook. The colours were nice, but I couldn't work out what it was."

"Skylar! Can you help me for a moment?" Peter called for me from out back. A big tower of boxes to unpack leaned against him menacingly. I jumped to action and collected the boxes off him, which were all varying degrees of heavy. Thick cardboard and plastic tokens and the like all add up in weight.

"Anything new come in today?"

"Quite a few new games, actually. A lot of those pre-orders got shipped out at once, as you can see."

"Do you need me to shelve them?"

"Don't worry, I've got—"

"I'll do it. I'll be very efficient."

Peter puckered his lips in thought. I only then realised how tense I was holding my jaw. I must've looked like a desperate sod because he snickered. *Please*, I needed this distraction. I needed to feel in control again.

"Fine, I'll manage the drinks," he said, thrusting a few of the new games into my arms. "Just don't get too distracted out there."

His wink said it all. I took a moment to stare at the floor. What had I become? Even my boss noticed? What the hell did Cute Boy think of my behaviour? Was he aware? Oh God, what if he was aware? All reasonable threads in my head began to unravel, the heaviness of the thoughts weighing me down. I held my breath, held the board games close to me, and felt the comfort.

"You finished organising yet?" Peter called.

"I'm on my way!" I yelped. I caught the teasing tone in Peter's voice, but I was still sure that he was annoyed at me. I had to make it up to him, get my head back in the game.

The calmness that organising the board games brought me was unlike anything else in the world. The energy it takes to work up to organising is a huge chunk of the process, my dump of a desk being the main example of my lack of spoons for such things. But when the job is in motion, it is zen. My eyes laser-focused on the boxes, taking in all the necessary info—title, play time, player limit, these were all factors that helped me shelve the games in a way that made them easiest to access. Despite not seeing most of these games before, my brain absorbed this new info like a sponge.

I was good at my job. No boy could get in the way of that.

"Hello."

"Gah!" I let out, forgetting, for a brief second, there were customers within my safe space. The room came back to me and it had filled up with a few more clientele. The person who had interrupted me was a sandy-blond haired boy with a sea of freckles over his nose.

"You work here?" he asked, his tone stern. "Can you help me?"

I side-eyed past him to Peter at the counter. He was currently swirling whipped cream onto someone's hot chocolate.

"You can order drinks from over there."

"I want a board game recommendation."

I didn't like the confrontation in his voice. There had been some customers who hadn't liked my recommendations in the past, unsure if I was offering the right thing, but they'd always been polite about it. Something about this guy set off something in me.

"Certainly," I said, wetting my lips to feel more human. "Are you playing by yourself? Or do you have others joining you?"

"What would you recommend for a solo game? Particularly one with lots of challenge and replayability?"

"Why don't you try Root? The Mechanical Marquise feature is a lot of fun, and if you haven't played Root before I can walk you through–"

"I have played Root before."

"Right. Of course. Then you'll be able to pick it up very quickly–"

"I have played the Root solo mode before. Tell me something else."

"Um, well, do you like Marvel? There's Marvel Champions and its many booster packs–"

"I wouldn't call them booster packs, a booster pack suggests that it adds extra cards to the game that can bulk out existing decks, like how we describe Magic or Yu-Gi-Oh packs you buy as booster packs. They are separate hero expansions, and that's before you get into the different villains."

"Uh-huh."

"And what about–"

"Callum!"

I finally allowed my breath to escape from my body. When the guy —Callum, I assumed—turned around to answer, I untensed my chest and shoulders and let them flop into place. I didn't like that my body tensed up this way when confronted with a (I presumed) cis man, like I was trying to match his macho, dick-wagging assholery by making myself seem tougher.

"What?" Callum called casually.

Cute Boy responded. "Come finish your drink before it gets cold. We don't have time to play a whole game of something anyway."

Callum looked back at me and then back to Cute Boy. No way. This was far from routine now. I hated it with every fibre of my being.

I followed Callum to their table. It was bizarre seeing this new boy sat in the always-empty seat opposite the man of my dreams.

"If you want recommendations for ten minute games, I can gladly bring something over?" I suggested, my customer service voice crisp and clear. I couldn't help but wince at how high-pitched it was. My shoulders threatened to tense up again.

"Ten minutes?" Callum asked.

"You need to leave at half two, don't you?" I addressed Cute Boy.

There was a hint of red at the tip of his nose. "Uh, yes, I do. But honestly, we're fine. We're just brainstorming."

His sketchbook was out again. It was on a different page, little doodles of geodes and crystals scattered across the spread. They were beautiful; so detailed and so varied.

"What are you brainstorming.?"

"We're working on a board game for a class," Cute Boy said, tapping his fingers excitedly on the side of his mug.

"Marc can't stop talking about it," Callum perked up. My heart exploded all over again. Oh no, Cute Boy had a name now. How could I ever recover from that? It was in there now, implanted in my brain. "There's gonna be different geodes you can dig up in different rock formations, it'll be some worker-placement type game. Marc, show off your biome map you did last week."

"Hey now, I've shown some restraint," Marc said. "This is the first time I'm bringing it up to him."

God, slay me! He used the right pronouns!

Externally, I stayed super still, hands cupped within the folds of my hoodie and apron. Internally, I was freaking the fuck out. Fireworks exploded in celebration, burning down every tower of rational thought left in there. I was dead. A walking dead man.

"'Him'?" Callum blinked. "Oh! Okay."

I bit my lip. The walls came back up. There was never any chance I was passing. I knew it. I didn't even hate the fact I didn't pass, it didn't help that I was small and soft faced. The sting of being misgendered, especially at work, was as expected as the aches of my soles after being stood up for hours. It was annoying, but it was an expected pain.

So Callum's words stung worse than a wasp's sting, having come right after the rush of euphoria from Marc.

"Well…" I grinned through my pain. "If you need a top up or anything else before you go, feel free to call me over…"

"Wait," Marc called. I had already started creeping back towards the counter, but my movements slowed down considerably. His voice had a hold on my soul. "I wanted to ask. I've not seen you at the university's tabletop society, did you know it's a thing?"

My eyes went wide. "Um, uh, kind of."

"I would've thought someone who worked in a board game café would want to join such a society," Callum said.

"Well, uh, I didn't go to the freshers fair because I had a cold and then I didn't want to intrude and then I got the job here that takes up a lot of my time and–"

"Well, why don't you come along to my game night on Friday?" Marc said.

Brain error. Communication breakdown.

"For real?" Callum muttered.

"Why not? It's Halloween, Polly's going to run that Monster of the Week one shot anyway, so it won't interfere with any of the DnD stuff."

I fiddled and tugged at the insides of my apron pockets. The urge to stim right now was high, but I translated my hand-wiggling into fabric-picking. "O-only if you have space. I don't want to intrude."

"You won't. Trust me."

I looked Marc right in the eyes.

"Okay, write down your address and phone number."

Marc wrote it down on a napkin. The moment he handed it to me, my fingers very nearly touching his, I felt like I was levelling up, achieving another objective in life. Not only had I fallen for a boy for the first time, I was getting a cute boy's number and address for the first time.

Marc checked his phone. "Half two. Better get to that lecture."

"See you on Friday," I muttered, thumb caressing the soft napkin.

"See you on Friday." Marc leaned over to shove his book back in his bag and winked at me.

Once they were gone, I excused myself to the stockroom to "get more napkins" and I yelled into the wall.


Marc's house was off campus. It seemed like a typical frat lair, or rather the nerdy equivalent of one. The path to the front door had three pumpkins outside, all of which had been carved with some sort of anime reference. They ranged from a perfectly sculpted 'All Might' face, to a mediocre Leaf Village emblem, to a messy but funny Pikachu meme face. Through the front window I could see a cluttered living room with bottles of beer and half-packed up board games strewn across the floor. I gulped. I knew I was a boy, but why did cis boys have to be like this?

I shook my head. That wasn't fair, unless I was willing to clean my own desk, I'd have to eat my words.

But still, poor board games.

I knocked on the door and Marc answered. The light coming in from the hall bathed him in a heavenly glow. I shook my hands at my sides rhythmically.

"Glad you found us okay," he said. "Come in."

"Bad decision on your part," I said.

"What?"

"To let me in. I'm like a vampire. I'll come and go as I please now. There's no stopping me."

Marc blushed, which triggered the same reaction in me. Maybe I was getting too confident. Over-levelled.

"I'm not actually a vampire," I said.

"I know, I would be surprised otherwise."

"But maybe I am."

"You playing one in Monster of the Week?"

"I've not actually played Monster of the Week before."

"Oh, dude, I'm sure you'll enjoy it. It's a ton of fun, and you can totally be a vampire if you want to. The Monstrous playbook can be all yours."

"I don't know what that means but I'm eager to learn."

He led me into the kitchen. A six-seater table stood in the centre of the room, covered in papers, six-sided dice, and people's half-drunk beverages. Four of the chairs were occupied. Two boys, one with long hair and a brown beard and one with cornrows, sat on the side closest to the fridge. They were in pyjama pants and slippers, so I assumed they were the other housemates. There was one girl sat at the far end, her pink hair tied back into buns.

Then on the other side was Callum.

He scowled at me.

"Guys, this is Skylar," Marc introduced me. "Skylar, you know Callum, this is Polly, our all-powerful GM, this wizard-ass looking dude is Jeramiah, and the cool kid is Russell."

They all chanted "hey" and I waved back awkwardly.

"Can I get you a drink?" Marc's hand was on my shoulder as he asked, which made the whole area burn. Maybe I was a vampire after all, and Marc was the sun.

"Sure, whatever's to hand."

Jeramiah leaned on two legs of the chair and fished out a Coke from the fridge. I held it close to myself, the cold condensation seeping into my hand.

"Shall we start?" Polly asked. I sat on the chair between Marc and Callum. As I settled, he side-eyed me again. What was this guy's deal? I picked up one of the pencils and a few dice, fiddled with them until the rising anxiety in my throat pushed itself back down.

Monster of the Week uses the RPG engine Powered by the Apocalypse, which had become popular as an RPG framework since 2010. I'd listened to podcasts where players ventured through spooky campaigns and superhero worlds following this system, but I'd never experienced it myself. The moment the character sheet got placed in front of me I started taking it all in, remembering the names for the stats I'd heard as I travelled to campus. The idea of springing a new character from the depths of my imagination worried me still. I had to be efficient, the best version of myself. I was in the company of new people. New people to impress.

As Marc mentioned before, I stuck with being the Monstrous, picking the vampire angle.

Callum sucked his teeth.

"You going to be sparkly?" he muttered.

"What was that?" I muttered back.

"Nothing."

I'd heard him.

Marc picked the Mundane playbook, meaning he was the everyman, the Shaggy of the group, who stumbled into traps and saw the weirdness in things that others couldn't recognise. Jeramiah chose the Spooky, Russell chose the Hex. Callum chose the Chosen.

We started the one shot in an abandoned mall, having been drawn here by some weird pull that something wasn't right. We'd heard rumours of a shadowy figure slinking in and out of the—supposedly broken—automatic doors, the haunting creak as they slide open drifting over the town. Callum's character went first, armed with a flashlight.

"My vampire boy, uh, let's call him Flynn, is sneaking behind. He doesn't want to be caught in the beam of the flashlight, and he's also watching our backs," I said.

"Kyle is with you," Marc said. "He's too scared to be up front."

"Okay, so you're creeping through this mall, the plants that were once neatly maintained in the planters have overgrown, there's a few flickering lights that were never properly turned off, the flickers highlight some of the boarded up doors to the shops, the empty metal chairs from the food court."

"Gee… I don't know how I feel about this," Marc said, putting on a cowardly voice that brought a smile to my face.

"C'mon Kyle, grow some balls," Callum announced. "If anyone is going to get to the bottom of this mystery, we are."

I wasn't sure about him using the phrase 'grow some balls', but I fought against myself to let it slide. We were supposed to be in a cheesy eighties horror after all.

Some time was spent exploring different shops, digging through the wreckages for clues. Russell narrated how his Hex character started collecting random cheap tat left behind for his spells and it tickled me. I don't know if it was me mimicking the joy going around or if I was genuinely lost in the nerdiness of everything, but I started to relax. Slouching in my chair bit by bit, I stared at the map of the mall Polly drew, analysing where to go next and what to prepare for, ideas of cool vampire moves playing out in my head.

It was awesome.

Until it wasn't.

Polly slammed her arms down on the table as we entered the underground car park. The sudden noise made me physically lift from my seat. I crossed my arms and tried to shrug it off but I could see that Callum and Marc had noticed. I lowered my face, embarrassed.

"Bam! A gross, gooey sludge that somewhat resembles a man bursts out from behind an abandoned car. It flies between you, scattering you to two sides. Its arm bursts out again to try to grab Flynn. Can you roll me 'act under pressure'?"

The clinking of the two d-sixes in my palm was so satisfying. One of the best sensory details about playing games at the table instead of online. I rolled. With my modifiers I got a six.

"Damn!" I said dramatically. A six was just a miss, a seven would've been a mid-success. I was fully expecting Flynn to be grabbed and me to take an experience point. Failing at something is all part of the immersive experience. But instead Callum raised his pencil and interrupted.

"As the Chosen, Robert is going to jump in front of you at the last minute and try to save you, as any good chosen one would do. I'm going to roll 'protect someone'.

"I… okay," I said, my confidence leaving me. If that's what his character would do, why interfere?

"You rolled a ten!" Polly shouts. "So you save Flynn, but now you are grabbed. Jeramiah, what is Violet doing?"

As the attention in the fight moved away from me a bit, I focused down on my character sheet again. Was there something I was missing here? Why would Callum want to take my thunder like that? I know he was the Chosen, but it felt like he didn't trust me to make a good narrative decision.

"I'm going to bite the weird goo guy's neck to save Robert," I said when it came back to me. Everyone else was cornered fighting off other goo minions, so it was up to me to play back-and-forth with the main guy. "I'm going to 'protect someone'."

"Do you mean 'kick some ass'?" Callum said. "I really think 'kick some ass' is the appropriate move here."

I blinked quickly. "Yes, of course. 'Kick some ass'."

I roll, getting an eight. A mid-success means I do what I set out to do but I get hit in return. I bit down on the gooey, slimy neck of this weird creature, nearly gagging as I explained what it felt like compared to draining someone normal of blood, and got myself thrown off him and bounced into the hard concrete of the car park. Now that Robert had a moment of opportunity, he swung his bat and clocked the guy.

"Yeah!" I cheered for him. "Go Robert!"

"You shouldn't be celebrating like that when you're hurt," Callum said coldly. "It's not good roleplaying."

"Dude, what is your deal?" I said, grabbing the edge of the table.

We locked eyes. The contact was draining me, but I refused to blink or look away first.

"Yeah, Cal," Russell followed up. "I know you like your edgy, grim-dark dudes but you're just being cold for no reason. What gives?"

"Can we go back to playing?" he sighed dramatically.

"Is something bothering you?" Marc said. This breaks into his psyche. I knew that Marc and Callum were well acquainted, having been paired together to work on that board game project. Something about Marc's calm but formal tone got to him, made him show his cards.

Callum scrunched up his face. "Why did you have to invite her here, again?"

Her. The shockwave rippled through me and froze me like a gorgon's stare.

Marc found the words that I couldn't muster.

"*He* is here because I asked him to be."

Callum squeezed his pencil so hard I thought it was going to break. "I don't like the way he's playing. I would've expected better from someone working at Reckless Role."

"Aw, dude," Polly sighed. "Is this about that job again?"

I bit my lower lip. Uh-oh.

"I'm not being crazy about it!" Callum shouted like it wasn't the first time he'd brought it up. The friends in the room all rolled their eyes. "Seriously, I have so much more charm, I've got my barista experience, I've got good customer service. I witnessed her– his customer service myself. You let yourself get distracted by what we were working on, plus you didn't have anything good to recommend to me."

"You were pestering me…" I whispered digging my nails into my palms.

"Let this beef go, okay?" Polly instructed, pointing down at her whiteboard with the mall map on it. "Are we playing or not?"

Callum tutted at all of them. All of us. "Whatever. Yeah. Just ignore my struggles. This is what diversity does to the games industry."

While I sunk down into a smaller ball, Marc was on his feet. "What are you trying to say?"

My heart was in my throat. The low frown, the growl on his lips. God, could he be any cuter? He just needed to push his glasses up his nose and reflect the light like an anime protagonist and I'd swoon.

"Don't worry, man."

"No. Say it."

I could see the drop of sweat coming off his forehead. The shock of being misgendered in such a way was transforming into schadenfreude. I was revelling in his discomfort.

Finally he huffed. "Whatever. I'm going."

He jumped up from his chair and zipped up his hoodie.

"Damn, way to be dramatic about something so stupid," Russell muttered, making me smile.

A hand was on my shoulder the moment the front door closed. "How are you feeling?" Polly asked.

I thought for a moment. Fine? Chill? Empty? I couldn't work it out. There was nothing there and everything there. The shock had numbed any actual hurt seeping into me, but I knew I was trying to recuperate from something. I tried to work out why Callum being angry meant anything to me because, on a surface level, it didn't. I didn't know him. Other than as the intense guy that was with my crush that one time. Thinking back to the café though, imagining him there, pelting me with questions to try to get a reaction, it made my safe space feel invaded.

I took a deep breath. I was not less valid as a board game fan because I didn't know all the answers. I was not less valid for being trans or autistic either. I was not there for diversity points. Peter saw my ability to recognise things, work things out. Did Callum notice Fury of Dracula was on the wrong shelf in his interview?

I put my hand over Polly's to show that I'd accepted the comfort.

"I'll be fine."

"I'm glad," she said, before turning to her map. "The vibes are off now, though. I don't want to run this right now."

"What about some other games?" Marc said. He was running his hand through his hair, looking anxious. Maybe he was feeling guilty about inviting me after what Callum did. I wanted to shout at him. *No, I wanted this since the first moment you came through the café doors.* "Considering you're planning to stay the night, we still need to make it worthwhile."

He was addressing Polly in that moment, but I couldn't help but blush at the thought of staying overnight too. Being able to make the most of every moment with Marc, get to know the real him, the soft, cute boy I'd seen draw board game maps in between lectures.

The night rushed by, full of laughter and victories. I whipped everyone's ass in Root. Polly taught me Mahjong, while also going on an hour-long rant about the iconic nature of classic games. The incident with Callum was but a distant thing in no time, the healing factor of good games and new friends working its magic. This was why I played games. This was why I spent the effort to solve puzzles, to seek them out. The thrill of coming to the right conclusion with people who pose as perfect competition by your side is the best, most fulfilling feeling in the world.

We finished a game as it turned midnight. On cue, the bus back to campus flew by on the main road outside.

"Shit, that was the last one," I yelped, flying to the window like I could've stopped it. Campus was on the outskirts of town, unawalkable unless you were willing to trek through the shopping district and two neighbourhoods in the dark. I dragged my fingers down the window. Shit. Shit. I could grab a taxi, though the anxiety of doing so on my own for the first time bubbled in my stomach. Before I gave in to the idea of downloading Uber, Russell cleared his throat. "You can stay here tonight, no big deal."

I blinked. "For real?"

"You're working tomorrow, right?" Marc asked. I couldn't help but focus on his fidgeting fingers, tapping quickly on his leg. "What time do you start?"

"Not 'til noon," I said, a yawn escaping from me. No way was I going to crawl into an Uber now, I didn't want to fall asleep in the back of some stranger's car. "I will have enough time to go home and change."

"That settles it then," Polly said, ruffling Marc's hair. "I'm still claiming the sofa and I'm a snorer, so maybe not the best for you to sleep near me if you've got work tomorrow."

"I–"

"Do we even have extra bedding?" Russell asked.

"Polly's already nabbing the spare," Jeramiah answered.

"Where do I sleep, then?" I managed to say. My voice sounded small, vulnerable.

They all looked at me. My eye-contact capabilities were now non-existent, I had to dart my gaze around the room. Sleep was creeping on me too, making the whole place blurry and muted. Spoons running out fast.

"Stay in my room," Marc whispered. "You'll be safe with me, I promise."

I couldn't look up at him, but I heard in his voice pure sincerity. I would be safe with him. I knew it. My heart squeezed, ready to burst.

"Get him tucked in then!" Polly said, exaggerating her own yawn. "It's late as hell."

"It's up this way," Marc said, rubbing his hands together nervously. I reached my arm up and let him lead the way. The burning sensation of him touching my side hadn't dampened from the last time it had happened, but it was nice and warm and exciting.

His room was like a hurricane had passed through a paint factory. Canvases with half-finished pieces were propped against the walls. His drawn curtains had blue paint splatters on them. Tapletop miniatures stood in a row on his desk, the finish on them spectacular. His bed was propped against the far wall, unmade, the sheets bundled up like a nest. I felt like he wasn't worried about the security deposit.

"Uuuuuh," he breathed, running his hand through his hair. "If I take one of my pillows and that blanket, I'll sleep on the floor."

"You don't have to."

"I insist." He gestured to the mattress. "You have work. I'm not making you sleep on the floor."

"That's not what I meant." I didn't know if it was still confidence, or some other stat, but something was maxed out and I was feeling brave. Bold. "You don't have to be on the floor."

"But then you'll be on the floor."

"God, strike me," I whispered, blushing at his idiocy.

"What was that?"

"Nothing."

He fiddled with his glasses before deciding to take them off. It was bedtime after all. The air was thick with the tension that must've been obvious to him as well, right? I'd spent weeks fantasising about him, cursing his name for ruining my routine. Now I was here and he was being awkward and it was the cutest shit in the world.

"Um, sorry, but I need to take my binder off."

"Your bind— oh, um, of course. I'll leave for a moment."

He marched out of the room with purpose. I was sure steam was coming from his ears. I turned my back towards the door and pulled my hoodie and shirt off to expose my half-body binder. Despite how safe and sensory wearing one felt, my skin and bones still thanked me when I peeled it off. I looked around on the floor for a safe place to leave it, thought about the possibility of Marc stepping on it, and tucked it under the pillow. Being binder or braless in someone else's house was unnatural, and even more so when I put my shirt back on. The weird lumps were even more obvious than I remembered, obviously his eyes were going to go to them as soon as he came in.

It dawned on me that I didn't really care all that much. The discomfort was unfamiliar, but somehow I imagined Marc would make it feel normal.

He knocked on his door. "Are you decent?"

"Yeah."

He crept into the room. I don't know if it was to add to the bit or he was struggling without his glasses on, but he moved along with his arms out and his eyes squinted. I bit my thumb to suppress my laughter. No, this was a bit. He must've known what he was doing. A cheeky siren trick.

Once he made it to the bed he nabbed one of the pillows and the thin yellow blanket that gathered at the bottom of the bedding pile.

"You don't have to–"

"Shhhh," he hissed. He puffed up his pillow and plopped it one the floor. His large frame followed suit, the blanket just about covering the space between his neck to his knees. "Get your rest. Need it to make that damn good coffee."

I reclined back onto the remaining pillow. "You think my coffee is good?"

"It's addictive."

"I don't grind the beans."

"But you prepare it the exact same way every time."

Someone had noticed. A big win for me.

"Good night."

I twisted over to face the wall. The faint light from the streetlight outside crept through the gap in the curtains illuminating just enough of the wall for me to focus on every detail. Every scratch, every blemish in the paint. Places where Marc had scuffed up against, more things for his landlord to pick up on. For such a gentle boy, he had a skill in creating mess.

I could hear his breathing. In. Out. In. Out. Loud. I wondered if he was asleep already. Could he hear me breathing? Was he as distracted as I was?

I couldn't go to sleep. My mind was reeling. The world was too loud, too full of things to pay attention to, to work out where they were coming from. Mysteries to solve played out in my head; the answers to the universe; life and death. It scared me sometimes. My brain needn't work those things out and yet it attempted.

Audio stimulation was my respite. I never fell asleep without a podcast or a playlist or a YouTube video. How could I get away with that here? I hadn't brought my headphones.

I tossed over to the other side. Marc's shadow lay down below. His eyes were open, shining through the haze.

"Can't sleep?" he whispered.

"No."

"What do you need?"

The question threw me. There was nothing he could summon up to make me more comfortable, that's not what I needed, but the fact he wanted to help sent tingles down my spine.

"I…" I gulped. "I can't go to sleep without audio stimulation."

I awaited the laugh, the comment about how childish that was. How hard was it to just fall asleep? Couldn't you just tune out the sounds of the world? The puzzles in your head?

Instead his eyes shone, unblinking. He brought his phone to his face and the brightness of it blinded me. When I acclimated to the sudden light I noticed that he had some earbuds nested in his ears. He unplugged them and rewound whatever he was listening to.

"This okay? I won't be offended if you think my music taste is bad."

A song started playing out loud, first the bass kicked in and then the guitars. A gentle rhythm filled the room and I could not be more in love. He understood. Oh God, he understood.

I hid the excitement on my face in the pillow. "That's perfect."

"I'm glad."

He put the phone on the floor next to him and let the song play out. It jumped to another song with a similar vibe. My eyelids finally started to feel heavy. I curled my fingers into the sheets, kneaded the fabric like a satisfied cat. My mind was settling now. The quiet was coming, all puzzles and mysteries complete for the night.

We both turned back over at the same time.

"Do you wan–"

"Do you want t–"

We both interrupted and then shut up at the same time. I squeezed the sheets tight, fighting with myself to not chicken out of this.

"Do you want to date?" Marc asked before I could get there. His words were quick, breathless.

If I could find my words again, I'd be breathless too. This boy had been in my head for weeks, scrambling up all my solutions, being predictable in his unpredictability. Not only did he not care about my autistic quirks, he understood them; not only did he see me as a boy, he liked that. He was cute and cool and smart and had stolen my heart.

I knew that had been his objective all along.

"Yes," I gasped. "Let's do it."

He sighed, maybe from sleepiness, maybe from relief. "Wanna go for coffee sometime? I know a good café."

# The Doll in the Ripped Universe

Jennifer Lee Rossman

Content Warnings: Gender Dysphoria, Anxiety, Ableism, Mention of Menstruation, Misgendering

"The Doll in the Ripped Universe" first appeared in Spoon Knife 4: A Neurodivergent Guide to Spacetime, published 2019.

# The Doll in the Ripped Universe

Jennifer Lee Rossman

THERE'S A RIP in the universe.

Not a big one, not like a proper wormhole or anything. Just a little frayed edge, like the cushion on my Aunt Carol's sofa.

I found it on my seventh birthday.

The rip in the universe, that is. The rip in the sofa, I found that when I was five, and kept poking at it until it was big enough for my favourite Polly Pocket doll to fall in. And because I was too afraid to reach in and get her, too afraid of touching the stuffing and crumbs and whatever else might have fallen in, she's still in there. I keep making my aunt promise never to get rid of the sofa, because as long as the doll is in there, I haven't lost her. She's always there, waiting for me to have the courage to reach in and get her.

But back to the rip in the universe.

Someone had decided my birthday would be princess-themed. That somebody was not me. I wanted dinosaurs.

Technically, I didn't want a party at all. Too loud, too many people I didn't want to talk to. So after cake and presents, while my friends were playing with my new toys, I snuck out to play by myself in my aunt's backyard. No one noticed.

I sat in the grass in my pink dress with its itchy lace sleeves, and had a grand time quietly lining up dinosaurs in chronological order. Then, just for fun, I did it in reverse chronological order.

Oh, yes. I am a *rebel.*

And then my parasaurolophus vanished. Just slipped right through reality and poofed out of existence.

So of course I poked the rip. That's what I do.

I poked and picked at it, tearing it until I could see straight through to the other side. It looked just like my Aunt Carol's yard, but it was winter. All snow and bare trees and uncomfortable jackets made of vinyl that squeaked when you moved.

I didn't want to fall through into a world of jackets, but I did want my dinosaur, so I sat and waited.

A hand popped through a moment later, setting my plastic parasaurolophus right where it went in reverse chronological order.

Then a man peered through the rip.

I waved, and he almost started crying, so I stopped waving and hid my hand in the folds of my dress.

"Did I do something wrong?" I asked.

The man shook his head. "Never. You remember that, okay? Nothing about you is wrong."


The rip in the universe went away after that. I knew it was still there, the same way I knew about the little doll in the sofa, but I didn't go looking for it and the man didn't come looking for me.

I knew I wasn't supposed to talk to strangers, but I didn't like to talk to family even though I was supposed to, so I figured it all evened out in the end.

I don't think with the same logic as other people. Never have. When I went to middle school, I thought maybe they would teach me how to be normal. How to make eye contact and talk about the weather, how to hug without my skin trying to throw up, how to play with the other little girls even though they always played wrong.

I really liked dolls sometimes, but everyone wanted to brush their hair and change their clothes, and that ruined them. Dolls only have so much hair, and it never grows back. And if you play with the clothes too much, the seams will rip.

No one else my age had tantrums, but I just wanted my toys to last forever.

Sometimes I think about that Polly Pocket in the sofa and smile because she never had to endure the torment of all the people who were supposed to be my friends. She's lost, but she's safe.


My aunt had to pick me up from school again for fighting. It wasn't my fault.

The girls wanted to paint my nails at recess, even though I didn't want to be pretty, even though nail polish makes my soul itchy. And it was hot out and my socks were too tight and my brain short-circuited and I couldn't make the words come out.

I told the principal it wasn't me, but I've always been bad at lying.

And the purple glitter on my nails matched the purple glitter on the arm of the girl I scratched.

So to Aunt Carol's backyard I went, to wait for my mom to get off work so she could be loudly disappointed in me again.

That's when the universe ripped open, and he showed up. It was winter again in his Aunt Carol's yard, but he wasn't wearing a coat. He asked me what happened, and I told him. Yeah, he was an adult, but he was an adult with blue hair, and my brain decided that meant he wasn't scary.

He frowned while I talked. I realise now that he was empathising with me, not that I was doing something to make him sad.

"Listen," he said softly. "You shouldn't have scratched that girl, but you know that. It's just hard to act the way people expect you to act, especially when people expect you to be quiet and polite and—" His eyes dropped to my pants, which had begun life as My Little Pony pants but now had Iron Man logos sewn over all the ponies. "—feminine."

I nodded, too afraid to interrupt him. No one had ever understood me like this before.

"Your mom's probably gonna yell at you tonight. She doesn't understand that you're not acting this way on purpose." He reached through the ripped universe and handed me a pamphlet, still covered in perfect little snowflakes.

"'Autism'," I read aloud. It sounded familiar; I was pretty sure a boy in my class was autistic. But I wasn't anything like him.

"Trust me," said the man with blue hair, and I did trust him. "Autism looks different for different people, especially people raised as girls. Read it and see what you think."

When he waved goodbye, I noticed he wasn't trying to make eye contact.


I think my aunt thought she and I had a special connection because I always ran to her when I was upset, but really, the rip in the universe in her backyard just seemed to know when I needed to see him.

He showed up when I got my first period, and I know it sounds creepy to talk about that with a grown man, but he was the only person I knew who would get it. My mom said it was beautiful and natural, my classmates said it meant I was a woman now. They were all wrong.

"I think it's an autism thing," I told him, even though that didn't feel totally right. "I don't like my body doing this. I know you don't know what it's like, but—"

"Don't I?" he said, and I looked at him for the first time. *Really* looked. At his soft jawline, at his figure beneath his winter tank top.

"You have boobs," I blurted out. Maybe that was rude of me. Okay, it almost definitely was, but I couldn't always stop myself from saying the things I thought.

He looked down. "So I do."

"But you're a boy." I paused. "Right?"

"Right. But I was born with a body that wanted to grow boobs. I even thought I was a girl for a while, but it never felt right. So I've decided I'm a guy."

He explained it in simple terms, but I never felt like he was talking down to me.

This conversation was like pulling at a rip inside of me. It was a tiny rip, like the one in my Aunt Carol's sofa, and I didn't know what was hiding in it, but I knew it was safe in there, whatever it was. No one could ruin it, no one could call me weird for the way I wanted to do things, as long as they couldn't see it.

But I couldn't see it either, so I poked at the rip a little. Just until it was big enough to see inside, down among the stuffing and lost toys.


My Aunt Carol is getting rid of her sofa.

I sit on it for the last time, poking at the hole in the cushion.

It's been years since I saw him, the man inside the rip in the universe. Maybe I'm too old for imaginary friends, or maybe I don't need him anymore. Have I ever told him about the doll I lost down in the hole, or how I've always been too afraid to reach in and get it?

He wouldn't be afraid of crumbs and cushion stuffing. He's brave and confident. Maybe that's why I've dyed my hair blue: to subconsciously absorb some of his personality.

I don't even remember what the doll looked like, only that she was my favourite. I don't want her to go to the dump, but I don't want to take her out, either. She's safe in there; if I take her out, expose her to the world, something might happen to her.

But he would reach in to get her.

I tug at the fabric, the old threads tearing with a satisfying scratching sound, and I reach my fingers inside.

All of a sudden, bits of information start to fall into place and it's like I'm reaching inside a little rip in myself, where I've been hiding the things I don't want to touch. It isn't stuffing and crumbs, though.

It's the way I cringe when people call me a beautiful young lady, that I always thought was some autistic quirk. It's the dread of my body's cycle making me cry at silly movies when I want to be tough.

It's the tiny scribbles I make in my journal, when I'm safe and no one can see, where I call myself John and then cross it out real well just in case.

My fingers touch the hard plastic doll and I pull it out.

And it's a boy, like me. A little plastic boy with blue hair.

Holding the doll close to my heart to keep him safe, I run outside. It's snowing but I don't stop to put on a coat.

I go straight to the rip, but it's so small, I can't even see through it.

A shiver goes through me, and not just from the cold. I know what I'll find if I poke the universe, but I'm afraid. If I open that hole, if a plastic parasaurolophus falls through, then I'm all alone.

I lose him, my role model, the only person who understood me. It'll just be me from now on, trying to find my path on my own with no one to turn to, no one to tell me it's okay to be weird, that it's okay if the person I want to be differs from the one on my packaging. That the world might not accept me but that doesn't mean I'm doing something wrong.

Who will tell me it's okay to be me?

But who will tell me if I don't? I'm strong today because I had him guiding me when life hurt the most. Maybe I don't need him now, but I definitely needed him then.

So I poke the rip in the universe, like I poked at the rip in my Aunt Carol's sofa all those years ago, until it's just big enough to fit a toy dinosaur through.

I set the parasaurolophus back where it goes—reverse chronological order.

There's a rip in the universe. It's just a little one, but I can see my younger self through it, a scared little autistic boy in a dress playing with dinosaurs at the princess party he never wanted.

And I tell him he isn't doing anything wrong.

# On Belonging

## A.R. Vale



Author's Note:

Since I was a child, I found myself drawn to stories about boarding schools, drawing Malory Towers characters in my school journals and watching The Worst Witch over and over. As someone who always felt like an outsider, like someone who didn't belong, the sense of community and belonging expressed in many of these stories appealed to me. While not all of Enid Blyton's works have aged well, for a kid who felt he didn't belong anywhere, Malory Towers felt like home.

I had a lot of ideas for what I wanted to write for this story, but in the end, Eli and Arthur's story felt right. These are characters I started writing when I was just a kid myself, who have grown and developed as I have. I wanted to tell the story of how they met. This is a story about being a kid who feels like they don't belong, about generational trauma, and most importantly, about magic and werewolves. The kind of story I loved to read when I was younger.

One last note: while it isn't explored in depth, Eli experiences pathological demand avoidance (PDA). PDA is common amongst autistic people. It's a condition in which anything that feels like a demand is overwhelming and paralysing. It's a condition that's affected me my whole life, and one that affects the way Eli thinks and experiences the world.

# On Belonging

A.R. Vale

DAD ACCOMPANIES ME all the way to the school gates. Even first formers don't have their parents hovering over them the whole way; they drop them off at the station just like everyone else. It might be my first year but I'm fifteen, going into the fifth form. This is embarrassing. Except, standing there in front of the metal gates, the impenetrable stone walls looming over us, I'm glad he's here.

"Are you sure?" He asks for what must be the gazillionth time.

"Yes, Dad, I'll be fine," I lie.

Other kids walk by, burdened by bags and suitcases and heavy coats, glancing curiously at us. Like I said, it's not normal for a parent to come all the way to the school gates. It's also pretty much unheard of for a new student to be starting in fifth year.

I force myself to smile up at Dad. I asked for this.

Dad's always been protective. So much so that he decided to homeschool me for most of my childhood, convinced it wouldn't be safe for me to attend Oak House, the UK's best school for magic folk (supposedly) and his old school.

He didn't want me to go. I'm pretty sure he still doesn't. If I asked, he'd take me home right now, no questions asked, and we'd forget about this whole thing. But this is what I want. It took months of begging to let me go to Oak House. Months of convincing him to let me introduce Eli to the rest of the world. And now I'm here, I feel sick.

Remind me: why did I think I was ready for this?

I glance down at my shaking hands then up at Dad's anxious smile. He doesn't make eye contact. We don't do that.

I throw myself into Dad's arms and squeeze tight around his waist. He goes tense and still for a second before embracing me. He hugs me as tight as he can, just the way I like to be hugged, tight enough to squeeze the anxiety out of me. I reluctantly pull away, setting my face as I do. I have to be strong for him. He's already lost a lot and he's been terrified of losing me ever since Mum died.

I pick up my bag and nod at him, not trusting myself to speak. He smiles.

"Call me—as often as you like. I'll be back to see you at half term and, if you want to see me on a weekend, let me know. And if you change your mind, I can be here in three hours to pick you up. I promise. I will."

I nod my head again. If I try to talk, I'll definitely start crying.

I don't look back but I can feel his eyes on me all the way to the school gates.


I look through the gate, squinting through the overgrown trees and shrubbery at the crumbling manor house beyond. Beside the main gates is a smaller gate through which a line of students are disappearing. And I do mean that literally. Once they step through, they're gone. You can't see them on the other side.

I knew about this of course. The school isn't in this realm, the gate to this old abandoned manor house acting as a portal to the real Oak House in the Beyond. Still, a pulse of anxiety runs through me as I approach the front of the line. My brain creates a non-stop feed of everything that could possibly go wrong from the portal breaking down when I'm halfway through and cutting me in two, to me tripping over and face-planting in front of the entire school on my first day. There's a possibility I may have a slight problem with anxiety.

There's one person in front of me now, a teenage girl with a pair of long black braids, warm brown skin and a bejewelled pink suitcase. She flounces ahead of me, barely bothering to look away from her compact mirror as she steps into another world.

I take a deep, steadying breath, and step through after her.

If I didn't know where I was going, I'd have thought I'd tripped and hit my head and that this was a nightmare. I stand in the courtyard of a mansion that looks more like a fortress surrounded by hundreds of young mages and magic folk. Above us, a lightning storm rages across a purple sky, bathing everything in an eerie violet light.

The others all seem to take the Beyond in their stride, most of them spend eight months of the year here after all, with the exception of some smaller students—first years, I'd guess—who seem as overwhelmed and awestruck, if a little more excited, as I am.

I've only visited the Beyond twice before. The magical realm that exists alongside our own is not a safe place for a child to wander. The only reason they can have a school here is because the walls and warding spells protecting Oak House are some of the strongest in the realms. The only way to get in or out of the Beyond is by portal. Portals can be created by mages or occasionally occur on their own, rips in time and space that just appear one day but will seal up on their own so long as they're left alone. The wards stop both kinds from appearing in Oak House without authorisation.

Something knocks into my back and I stumble forward, turning to see someone has stepped through the portal behind me.

"Get out of the way." A pale blonde girl sneers at me. I stand there blinking at her, trying to think of how to respond. Why is this place so loud? "Are you slow?" She asks. It's a rhetorical question.

I turn away, no longer wanting to apologise, and not sure I could say a single thing with the thick bile blocking my throat.

My eyes dart around, looking for somewhere safe to sit and calm myself enough to think straight. There are so many people now, the courtyard getting more and more packed with every passing moment. I push my way through the crowd until I reach a wall. I look up. It's massive, larger than the walls in the mortal realm were, made of black stone with runes carved into it at regular intervals.

I sink down to the ground with my back against the wall, curled up to make myself small. I've made a mistake. I need to go home. I look for the portal but it's impossible to see through the crowds. I'll have to wait for the place to clear a bit then figure out how to get home. Maybe there is an adult around who can help me call Dad. This is a school after all, there have to be teachers somewhere.

A plan of action formed in my head, I sit and wait. I try not to be too conspicuous when I cover my ears with my hands to block out the sensory overload of three hundred people talking over each other in a confined space, but I needn't have bothered. No one's paying me any notice.

My eyes shut tight and hands over my ears, I don't notice when someone does approach me. I don't hear them speak to me at first either. A hand touches my shoulder and I flinch back, hitting the wall, my eyes fly wide open and I look up at the person standing over me.

He's a boy, about my age, maybe younger, with dark brown hair cut short and dark-rimmed glasses. There's something familiar about him that I can't place. He's speaking but I can't hear him with my hands covering my ears still.

A frown forms on his lips and he releases me, crouching down and pulling something from his pocket. He spins in a circle, low to the ground, and I see that it's chalk. When he completes the chalk circle, he mutters something under his breath and I feel a pulse of power in the air around us. He looks back at me, smiling, and gestures to his ears. He wants me to take my hands away.

I hesitate but figure that the only way to be left alone is to cooperate for now. I remove my hands from my ears and am met with silence. I look around in shock.

Outside the circle, teenagers are still crowded, chatting and shouting, but I can't hear them at all.

"Neat, huh?" I look back at the boy when he speaks. "That has to be one of my favourite spells; 'circle of silence' is what Mum says it's called. Dad usually calls it the 'finally some peace' spell."

He's grinning. A wide smile where I can see his perfectly straight teeth. They look like the kind of teeth you see in magazines. It makes me suddenly very aware how misaligned and oddly shaped mine are. You can't exactly go to the dentist with teeth like mine.

"I'm Arthur, by the way," the boy continues. I nod.

He's quiet then, looking at me. Continuing to smile. Like he's waiting for something.

Oh, right.

"I'm Eli," I squeak out.


Arthur decides to stay and chat with me for a bit. That is, he decides to stay and chat at me. I'm not really in a talking mood but he doesn't seem to mind. He clearly has a lot to say. He talks about magic, and school, and sharks (a lot about sharks) and I don't think he realises I'm not fully listening.

A figure appears behind Arthur, blurred slightly by the shimmering circle. I wouldn't have noticed them amongst the crowd if it wasn't for their sparkly purple dress. They are hovering around the edge of the circle but there is nothing else that stands out about them.

That is until they slide a foot forward, the toes of a glittery shoe smearing the chalk. There is an almost audible 'pop' as the circle is broken and the spell dissolves. The sound floods back in all at once. My hands fly back to my ears, trying to block out the sudden influx of noise. It's somehow worse now after a moment of reprieve.

Arthur looks up at the person who broke his spell. A young-looking girl with long dark hair and light brown skin wearing a glitzy, purple outfit. She looks like Arthur, if he was shorter, grumpier and covered in glitter.

Arthur turns to her and it looks like they're arguing about something but I can't hear them with my hands blocking my ears and it's not worth the sensory overload to listen in on whatever they're fighting about.

The girl turns to look at me. She stares at me so long and so hard that I have to look away but I can still feel her eyes on me.

"I know you," she says, loud enough that I can just barely hear her over the background noise and through my hands.

'No, you don't,' I want to say, but I can't make my mouth form the words.

"What are you talking about?" Arthur replies, raising his voice, "I've never seen Eli before, so how could you have?"

"No." The girl doesn't look at Arthur. I shift uncomfortably under her gaze. "I do know you! I've seen your face before in Mum and Dad's old school photos."

I frown. What does that mean? How could that even be possible? There is no way I could be in her parents' old photos.

She continues while I am trying to process what she has just said. "You're Marcellus Riven's daughter!"

I feel sick to my stomach. I don't know what feels worse; the way she said my father's name like it was a swear or the fact that she said 'daughter'.

I know I don't look that masculine yet, but I had hoped that I at least passed a little, even with blond hair down to my shoulders, my slight face, and my big eyes. I guess I was wrong.

"Ivy!" Arthur hisses. He stands up and turns to the girl. He's short. She's nearly as tall as he is.

"Well she is!" Ivy replies huffily.

My eyes sting. My throat burns. I can't take this anymore.

Leaning heavily on the wall behind me, I pull myself to my feet.

Ivy and Arthur turn to stare at me. Their faces are almost identical except for Arthur's thick-rimmed glasses.

My legs are jelly. I grab my suitcase and stumble away into the crowd. I think I hear a voice calling my name but I can't hear clearly with my heartbeat pounding in my ears and I'm not turning back now..


I sit on a hard wooden bench in the school office. The bench would usually be uncomfortable but right now it's grounding. I've finally stopped crying but that may just be because I'm too dehydrated to keep producing tears. I want to go home.

"You can't leave," says the woman standing over me.

I clench my fists, sharp nails digging into the flesh of my palms, and force myself to look up at her face.

"I'm sorry—" She looks down at her notes. "I'm sorry, Eli. The portal to the mortal realm has been closed and it takes a lot of magic to reopen it. Unless it's an emergency, you cannot go home today."

I want to scream that this is an emergency, that I need to get out of here right now. I don't belong here and I need to go home. But I'm pretty sure that's not what qualifies as an 'emergency' in her mind.

My eyes burn but there are no tears left for me to shed. The woman sighs and crouches in front of me.

"Listen, we get this a lot from first years," she says—I don't point out that I'm significantly older than the first formers she's talking about. "Have something to eat then go up to your room and sleep on it."

I don't want to go to my room and sleep on it. It's not even my room and I don't want to be here full stop. I want to go back home as soon as possible.

But the words won't come and there's nothing I can do. The woman stands over me with her hand out. She's waiting for me to stand up. I stare at the floor. I want to stand up, it'd be easier if I just stood up, but my brain is screaming at me that I absolutely cannot stand up, that I must not do the thing I am being told to do.

It takes an embarrassingly long time for me to force my feet beneath me. It's easier to do what I'm being told to do when I've waited long enough that it no longer feels like a demand. I pick up my suitcase, it feels heavier than it did this morning or even when Dad left me at the school gates.

The woman—I'm not sure if she's a teacher or just someone who works in the school—leads me up through a maze of hallways and staircases. I glance out the windows when we go by them. The sky is still storming, violet and indigo.

The dormitories are large, wide open rooms that make me feel exposed. The room that is not my room is a long space with a row of beds lined up against either wall. Each bed has its own side table, wardrobe and dresser. All of them are filled with other people's things except for one. It's in the corner. Thank god. I don't think I could

135

stand to be in the middle of the room. I wouldn't sleep at all until I got home.

The walls are plain apart from the decorations the other boys have put up: posters, photos, one bed has a pride flag over it. That makes me feel at least a bit safer.

"Get some rest and unpack. The other children will arrive soon and then you'll go down to dinner. They can show you where to go."

I sit down on the bed and pull my legs up to my chest. I'm dreading when the other kids will arrive. I don't want to be around other people right now. And I don't want to think about eating anything. I'm not going to unpack though so I'll just wait here with my thoughts until I'm able to leave and go home. Home to my actual bedroom with my blankets and my books and my posters of my favourite things. It's the place where I feel safest in the world. Not here. Not in this large, open room surrounded by other people's beds, other people's blankets and their favourite things. This place isn't mine at all. And it's cold. I pull the plain grey blanket off the bed and wrap it around my shoulders.

I am broken from my reverie by voices outside in the hall. My whole body tenses as the door opens and a group of teenage boys step into the room. They stop and stare when they see me curled up on the bed.

I hate this. It's the thing I dreaded the most even before coming here. No privacy. Sharing my space with a bunch of strangers. Never being alone or having space to really breathe.

"Eli?" A somewhat familiar voice asks. And no. No. No. No. No.

I cannot deal with this right now. Not after I embarrassed myself storming off like that earlier.

Arthur steps forward, a gentle smile on his freckled face. He approaches me like you would a cornered animal. That's fair. That's how I feel right now, like I might lash out and bite anyone who comes too close.

I won't really.

Probably.

"Are you okay?"

I don't answer. Of course I'm not, but I've learnt that people don't like to hear the truth when they ask questions like that. Arthur glances round at the other boys.

"I guess this means you'll be rooming with us, huh?" He changes the subject. I so appreciate it.

"No," I force out.

Arthur tilts his head to the side like a confused anthropomorphic owl.

I shake my head but I'm not saying anything else. I can't. Talking to anyone is hard enough when I feel this awful, let alone to a bunch of strangers.

"Don't waste your time," one of the other boys says, walking across to one of the beds and flopping down on his back. "He obviously doesn't want to talk to you."

Arthur looks down at his feet. Suddenly I feel bad even though I didn't actually do anything to him. I look away. Easier to stare at my knees than deal with whatever I'm feeling.

"Well," says Arthur, "we're going down to dinner in twenty minutes so we can show you where to go."

I don't want to eat, but it's easier to not say anything than to explain myself and deal with the potential argument. I don't acknowledge what he's said. He gives me a long look, before turning back to his friends, leaving me to my quiescence.

I watch them. It's odd. I've never been around this many kids before. It's weird to see how teenage boys act together when there are no adults around. There's a lot of talking and a lot of swearing. At one point, the boys start wrestling with each other. There are a lot of sex jokes too, which I don't love, partly because I have no idea what they're talking about. They're talking about girls and boasting about their experiences. I'm a trans boy who's rarely ever had friends, let alone a girlfriend. Also, I think I might be gay. Not that it matters. Who'd want to date me?

Arthur is more reserved than the other boys. I wonder if that's how he usually is or if he really is upset about me not talking to him. It's nothing personal. I'm the socially isolated weirdo, not him.

A bell rings after fifteen minutes. It's a loud, echoing chime that sounds throughout the school. I jump at the first sound but quickly settle when I realise what's happening.

The other boys start grabbing their things, slipping their shoes back on and heading toward the door. Not Arthur. He tells the others to go ahead and steps toward me.

"Hey," he says.

My eyes flick up to his face then quickly dart away.

"You're not getting ready to go."

I don't respond.

"That was the dinner bell."

It's obvious what he's trying to communicate. I get the feeling he's not going to leave without an explanation at least.

I squeeze my eyes shut tight. "I'm not hungry."

"You need to eat," Arthur says. "You'll feel better if you eat."

Agree to disagree.

He sits down heavily on the bed beside me and I restrain myself from flinching.

"I know it's hard, it took me a while to adjust to being at Oak House too. But once you settle in–"

"I won't." I cut him off.

He looks at me with that owlish head-to-the-side look again.

I guess I should explain.

"I'm not going to settle in. I'm going home in the morning." I don't make eye contact. I don't even look in his direction.

He sighs heavily. "Oh." He says, then; "If this is about Ivy, what she said…"

He leaves the thought hanging in the air between us. Ivy. His sister. The girl covered in purple glitter.

"It's not." I close my eyes. It's easier to speak when I'm not looking at him. When the lights and colours aren't constantly assaulting my eyes. "Not just that." I amend.

"Then what?" he asks.

"Just…" Just what? How do I even put this into words? I don't think in words, it's all just images and feelings in my head. Whenever I speak, I have to try to translate all of that into words other people can understand. It's difficult, especially when I am looking for exactly the right words to describe something and they don't seem to exist in the English language. "I don't belong here." I settle on.

"Of course you do!" Arthur says. There's more confidence in that statement than I think I've ever felt in my life. "You're a mage, aren't you?"

I cringe.

"What?"

I open my eyes to glance at him. "Not a mage." I wish I was a mage, it would be simpler if I was a mage. Dad was a mage but he got bitten by a werewolf in his late teens and there was a fifty-fifty chance I'd inherit lycanthropy. Fate flipped a coin and I grow excessive body hair, fangs and claws every full moon. (Better than the other monthly change my body goes through, I guess.) "Second generation werewolf."

"Oh." Arthur says. Yeah, oh. It was within out lifetimes that Oak House started letting in non-mages for the first time. Werewolves and other magic folk are still fighting to be accepted and understood in magical society. Being a trans, autistic werewolf really feels like I'm fighting the rest of the world on three fronts. And losing.

"You're still magical. All magical folk belong at Oak House," Arthur says definitively, like believing it hard enough will change the rest of society's attitude toward people like me.

There's a long silence. Arthur doesn't say anything, just stares at the opposite wall. I can't read his facial expression, can't say what he might be thinking right now. I think—I hope—that maybe he's done with this conversation. But then:

"Are you– was Ivy right? Are you Marcellus Riven's son?"

"You know about my dad?" I ask, not wanting to know the answer but unable to stop myself asking.

He looks away across the room, thinking maybe. And I realise why he looked so familiar. I recognise that face, a face I've seen constantly in newspapers and on magazine covers: Nathan Locke: The Chosen One; The Man Who Saved The Magical World; The Most Powerful Mage of His Generation. Take away the freckles and age him twenty years and Arthur is the spitting image of his father. His father who my father tried to murder.

"Kind of," he finally says. "Dad doesn't like to talk about his past much but you hear stories. Mostly from other people. It's hard not to."

I nod slowly, processing this. "My dad's the same. He– he doesn't like to talk about his past. I think he's ashamed." (He should be. Neither of us say it but I imagine we're both thinking it.) "It's hard to get away from it all. People in our village talk when they think we're out of earshot…"

Arthur laughs. I don't know what's funny.

"Sorry," he says, still grinning at me. I don't think he's sorry at all. "Just… never imagined I'd be bonding with the son of my dad's childhood enemy."

I'm still not sure what's funny about that but he has a nice smile, cheeky and a bit lopsided. And I absolutely cannot be developing a crush on Nathan Locke's son.

"You should stay," Arthur says, his expression serious again. "I know you might feel like you don't belong because you came late in the year and you're not a mage and your dad is who he is but… but I like you. And if you don't stay, we might not get the chance to become friends."

The biggest downside to being the palest person I know is that everyone can see when I blush. I feel the heat rising to my cheeks and turn my whole body away.

"It's not that easy."

He sighs, but doesn't fight me on it.


In the end, I don't go down to dinner. Instead I stay in the dorm room, talking with Arthur and sitting in contented silence with Arthur.

At one point, he goes down to the dining hall and comes back with two mugs of soup and a plate of bread rolls. He hands me a mug without a word and I do end up drinking it. Food is difficult. Mealtimes feel like a demand. Something I have to do. And that makes my brain not want to do them. But a mug of soup in a silent dorm room with someone who isn't even looking at me, but seems to like my company, is easy.

I wish everything was this easy.


The first time I went to the Beyond, I was only five years old and it was an accident.

I woke up in the middle of the night. The house was dark and silent. Shadows stretched up the walls of my room, long fingers reaching for me in my bed.

I stumbled out of bed. A plush toy shark clutched close to my chest.

The corridor seemed to stretch on for miles and the ceiling was so far away I could see nothing but blackness above me.

Cold moonlight lit a path before me, coming through the gaps between the curtains, as I made my way to Mum and Dad's room. I could feel the shadows following me in the darkness.

The door creaked open, slow and heavy, and I was filled with a sense of dread for what was on the other side.

The room was empty.

I turned slowly, afraid of what might be following me, but it hid before I could catch a glimpse of it.

I didn't dare look behind me again as I tiptoed down the stairs. Down and down I went into the black night, my bare feet cold on the wooden stairs. I daren't let go of the bannister in my left hand or the little shark in my right.

When I reached the bottom of the stairs, the back door was wide open, looking out onto the woods beyond.

I felt drawn out there despite my mind screaming at me to stay inside where it was safe. It didn't feel safe inside though, not with the shadows right behind me.

I stepped out into the dark forest, walking through the woods. There was a light up ahead, bright and white. I didn't realise in that moment my shark slipped from my hand. I couldn't have kept hold of it anyway. My fingers were changing.

I walked toward the light. As I did, my senses sharpened further until they were almost unbearable. I fell to my knees, no longer able to stand on two legs. The colour drained from the world as I walked forward. A familiar smell was in the air; old books, dark chocolate, and fur. It smelt like Dad.

I came to a pond. Surrounded by reeds and long grass, the full moon shone reflected in the water.

I walked toward it, I couldn't help myself.

I found myself in the centre of a lightning storm. When I turned around, I could no longer see home.


I wake to find my hair damp, lying in an unfamiliar bed. I am terrified for a moment that I am still in the nightmare. Until I see the other boys surrounding me, hearing Arthur snoring lightly across the room.

I rock back and forth until I calm down.

That night, when I was five, was the first night I fully turned. Dad found me, curled up crying on the ground in the Beyond. Apparently a portal had opened beneath the surface of the pond in the woods behind our house. It's rare for portals to the Beyond to open up on their own but it happens. In my lycanthrope form, my magical senses were heightened and I was drawn to the magical realm.

I hadn't stopped shaking for hours afterward. Dad didn't let me go all morning and didn't let me out of his sight all week. I'm still not sure if that was for his sake or for mine.

I still get nightmares about it.


They aren't able to send me home the next day. "It takes a while to recuperate that kind of magic," they tell me. I go to the start of term assembly with the rest of the fifth form. Arthur sits next to me, and even though he's talking to his actual friends, it's a comfort to have someone I like there.

The day after that, they tell me they can't send me home. The people who need to authorise it aren't available. I go to classes. I meet some of the teachers. The school isn't big so the same kids are in all my classes. Arthur is always there, always smiling, always kind. I'll miss him.

On the third day, they tell me I still can't go home. I'm starting to despair at this point. I miss my home and I miss my dad. Arthur being there helps, but it's not home. I learn a bit more about the boys in our dorm. Most of them are mages but there are a couple of other magical folk. Dominic is a selkie, he's a handsome boy with shoulder length dreads and a short, stout frame. Zaid is a half-elf with dark hair, dark eyes, and light brown skin. He's got a wildness about him that both scares and excites me.

After four days, I can't help but think the school doesn't care about me. It's not fair. I just want to go back home. I am paired with a girl named Vivian for a history project. She's curious. She asks me lots of questions about myself but she doesn't seem to be unkind about it. I decide to ask her about herself.

"Are– are you a mage?" I blurt out.

Vivian raises an eyebrow at me.

"No." She says. She doesn't make eye contact. I realise she hasn't tried to make eye contact the whole time I've known her. "I'm a changeling."

"A changeling?" I repeat. I've read about changelings before but I've never met one.

"I was raised by non-magical parents until they found out I was a faerie who was swapped at birth." She fiddles with a strand of mousy brown hair as she flicks through the history textbook in front of her. "They thought I was autistic, before they found out I was a faerie child. Turns out I'm both."

No wonder I like her. I've always gotten on better with other autistic people.


One week after arriving at Oak House, I finally get called to the office. A woman comes to get me from the last lesson of the day. I think she might be the same one I met on my first day but her hair and clothes are different so it's hard for me to tell.

She tells me that they will be contacting my father tonight and reopening the portal in the morning. I need to pack tonight. I'm finally going home.

When I get back to the dorm room, Arthur is waiting for me. He's sat on my bed and his face pulls into a warm smile when he sees me.

A heavy feeling solidifies in the pit of my stomach.

I'm going home. I'm leaving.

I open my mouth to speak. I don't know what I'm going to say but I'm saved from finding the words when Vivian bursts into the boys' dorm. To my surprise, she walks straight past me as if not even seeing me.

"Arthur," she says, sounding slightly out of breath. "Did you hear?"

Arthur frowns. "Hear what?"

"It's Ivy. She's missing."


I don't know why but, when Arthur runs out of the dorm room, I follow. Arthur doesn't question why I'm with him. I guess we are friends so it makes sense that I'd want to help.

I'm not sure where we're going until we get there. I follow him through the maze of corridors, and find myself standing in another dormitory similar to our own. Three girls who all look about eleven or twelve stand around a familiar woman.

The woman from the office turns to face us as we burst into the room.

"What happened?" I flinch at the volume of Arthur's voice and I'm not the only one. The woman visibly jumps before regaining her composure.

"Arthur Locke." She says his name slowly.

"What happened, Miss Ravencroft? Where's my sister?!"

The woman, Miss Ravencroft, looks between the two of us.

"Arthur," she says again, "…Eli."

"Vivian said Arthur's sister is missing. We need to know what happened to her," I clarify. Arthur is anxious and not communicating well. I know because I've been there. I'm no good at speaking up for myself in front of people but it's easier somehow when it's for him.

Miss Ravencroft openly stares at me. I don't think she's heard me say that many words in a row before.

"She was boasting," one of the girls speaks up before Miss Ravencroft can. Arthur's head whips around to face her and so does mine. She's on the shorter side, which makes sense given she's eleven, with wild, curly hair surrounding her round brown face and two curved rams horns peeking out between the ringlets.

"Ivy kept saying she's just as good as her dad, that she'll be a really powerful mage someday."

I notice Arthur roll his eyes in the periphery of my vision. I get the impression she says this kind of thing a lot.

"Kelly challenged her. Said if she was some powerful mage she should prove it."

One of the other girls, a thin-faced child with long orange hair, pale skin and a sharp nose, looks away at that. Kelly, I assume.

"I just wanted her to shut up, I didn't expect her to actually do it," she murmurs.

"Do what?" I ask.

"Go outside the walls."


The second time I went to the Beyond, I was ten.

I remember that night so clearly. It's burnt into my mind. I'm shocked I don't see it every time I close my eyes.

I remember sitting in my parents' bedroom, on my mum's favourite rocking chair next to the bed. I held Mum's hand as she slept beside me. I listened to her soft breathing as I dozed off in the chair. When I woke up, the room was silent.

I blinked my eyes, looking around in confusion. Mum was still there. She lay peacefully in her bed.

Sometimes, since she'd gotten sick, she would sleep so deeply you couldn't wake her, completely still apart from the subtle rise and fall of her chest.

Beneath the sheets, her chest did not move.

I stared in shock. I did not want to believe it.

I reached toward her, my small, pale hands shaking her arms, her shoulders, desperately trying to rouse her.

I don't remember saying anything but I must have made some kind of sound. Dad burst in, his eyes panic-stricken. He pulled me off of her, calling my name—not my name, the name he knew me by. I started screaming as he restrained me. Usually he could hold me tight to his chest and I would feel comforted, grounded, but in that moment, his touch felt suffocating. All I wanted was to break free, to get away. I fought him off. I don't remember it. I remember afterward, the scratch marks on his cheek, the bite mark on his hand left by my sharp werewolf canines.

He let go and I fled. He called after me but I didn't turn around. I couldn't breathe, couldn't think. I just wanted to get away.

I ran out of the house and into the cold rain, bare feet on cobbled streets (I never did like shoes).

This time, when I found a portal to the Beyond, I knew what it was. Sitting at the end of an alleyway, a rip in time and space. It was like static electricity in the air. My hairs stood on end as I approached it. When I touched it, put my hand through, my fingers vanished, I could still feel them.

I wanted to get away. To escape whatever reality awaited me at the house, in my mother's bedroom. I stepped through the portal.

The sky was violet. I hadn't seen it last time; wolves are colour-blind. Stars shone far above in the purple sky, tiny dots glittering. The ground was warm and dry beneath my toes.

I was amazed. Astonished. Stupefied. I wished I had a thesaurus to properly put my feelings into words upon seeing this place.

I wandered for what could have been hours or minutes, feeling the soil beneath my toes, looking at the stars high above me in the sea of purples. I didn't realise I'd been crying until I ran out of tears.

That was when It appeared. It was humanoid in form but stood on four long, thin limbs. I could see Its silhouette ahead of me, Its head turned to one side as if curious. I stopped walking, watched as Its head turned, then continued to turn, all the way around until it was the right way up again.

I took a stumbling step backward. That was when It moved.

It was fast for something with so little grace. Its limbs skidded clumsily under Its spindly body, slipping on the soft ground. But It was approaching, getting closer and closer. I turned and ran.

I could hear Its footsteps on the ground behind me but I didn't dare look back. I heard a soft growling sound and nearly tripped as my feet got caught on the too-long legs of my trousers.

I could barely breathe but I could hear Its heavy breathing behind me. I didn't stop running, even as the tightness in my chest became near unbearable. Then I felt it; the portal up ahead. Static electricity in the air.

I knew It was right behind me, but I didn't look back until the last moment when I stepped back through the portal. The last thing I saw in the Beyond was a set of long, needle-like teeth just inches from my face.

I'd thought it was strange to be in the Beyond again when I'd arrived at Oak House. I think I'd have been more freaked out by it if it hadn't been been for all the noise and the crowds.

Standing outside the walls of Oak House, it really hits me. I'm back in that place. Lightning flashes across the purple sky above me and I try not think of the nightmares as I follow Arthur further away from safety.

Miss Ravencroft made it absolutely clear that no one was to follow Ivy out into the Beyond and there would be serious consequences for anyone who did. We'd both nodded along as had the first formers, but, as soon as we were out of her sight, Arthur made a break for it. And, of course, I'd followed.

I don't ask how he knew where to find the door hidden behind a statue of some great mage from ages past and a tangle of overgrown vegetation. I may have been at Oak House a week but he'd spent five years of his life here. Plenty of time to uncover some of the school's secrets.

We won't have a hard time finding Ivy. That's the thing about the Beyond: time and space work differently out here. If you go here with a goal in mind, you'll find your way. Just pick a direction and start walking.

As we walk, the landscape changes, from a desert of grey-blue sand under a purple sky, to thick trees. A forest of black wood and yellow leaves. I hear something rustling in the leaves above us but I don't dare look up. It feels like we've been walking for hours when I spot something sparkling amongst the underbrush. I reach down and pull it free.

Arthur turns to see why I've stopped and his breath hitches when he sees the sequin-covered purple cardigan in my hand.

"It's Ivy's," he says.

I nod. Who else could it belong to?

"We must be getting close," he says.

I bring the cardigan up to my face and inhale.

"What are you doing?"

I look up at Arthur, realising that it must look pretty weird that I'm sniffing his sister's clothing.

"The scent," I say.

He gives me a blank stare.

"I can track her."

"Oh," he says. "Werewolf stuff."

I can't help but smile a little. Werewolf stuff.

I take another big whiff of Ivy's cardigan. She smells of flowers, and raspberry shampoo and self-assurance. Then I close my eyes and turn in a slow circle, focusing on the scents around me. There are all kinds of confusing scents in this place, but most of them distinctly non-human. I tune those out, along with Arthur's scent (gummy bears, two-in-one body wash and shampoo, and an undertone of anxiety). I stop when I find a trace of artificial raspberry and start walking in that direction, leaving the path behind. Arthur follows, unquestioning.

The scent grows stronger as we go further into the forest, where the trees become so thick, we have to squeeze between trunks and watch the ground to keep from tripping up. Then I hear a scream.

I freeze. Arthur freezes. Then instincts kick in.

Arthur runs toward the sound, pulling something from his jacket pocket as he does so. I remain in place. Not from fear. I can feel my body shifting, bones moving beneath my skin. There's a hot sensation, like my blood is literally boiling. Then I black out.

When I come to, my vision is in grey-scale, I'm closer to the ground and I'm running. I follow the scents, Ivy and Arthur somewhere ahead of me, and the sounds of Ivy's screams.

I find them standing in a clearing. Ivy back to back with her brother, looking around frantically. Arthur doesn't see me but she does. The moment her eyes lock onto me, she shrieks again in fear. Arthur whizzes round and his eyes widen. He doesn't scream though, just stares at me. Then his shoulders seem to relax. He recognises me, even in my wolf form. I'm surprisingly touched.

I have less than a second to dwell on that thought before something else catches my eye. *It's* behind them. I watch, frozen in fear as It approaches them, long, spindly legs moving clumsily beneath Its body. The thing from my nightmares.

I take a step back, my tail falling between my legs. Cowering.

Arthur turns around, just in time to see It diving right at them. He throws himself to the side, knocking Ivy down in the process, both of them tumbling to the forest floor, just feet away from where It now stands.

It looks at me. I've not seen It so close before, could never make out the cold, grey eyes. Then it turns back to the Locke siblings.

*No. Please, no.*

It begins to walk toward them again.

Arthur stumbles, drawing a chalk circle on the ground around them, but he's scared and he's slow and the thing is getting closer with every second.

It takes another step toward them.

*No.*

It bares needle-sharp teeth.

*No!*

I move.

I'm sprinting forward before I let myself overthink it, placing my body between It and my friends.

A low growl forms in my throat as I stare up at It. I make eye contact, four grey eyes meeting.

It makes a strange hissing sound then takes a step back. I take a step forward, baring my canines.

It turns and walks away.


Arthur, Ivy and I walk back to the school together. Ivy is much quieter than when I first met her. Arthur wraps his arm around her shoulders, the image of a protective big brother.

"That was so cool." He turns to me. I'm back in my human form now. As soon as It was out of sight, I'd slumped in exhaustion and turned back, the adrenaline leaving my system all at once. Now, I feel like taking a ten hour nap.

"What?" I whisper, my voice strained.

"You." Arthur grins.

"What?" I repeat. Surely, I heard wrong.

"You! Chasing that thing off! Saving us. I didn't even know werewolves could turn when it's not a full moon."

"It works different in the Beyond," I say. I don't know how to process the rest of what he just said.

"I didn't know you were a werewolf," Ivy murmurs. It's the first thing she's said since we left the clearing.

"He and his dad both are." Arthur turns to her.

I wait for her to say something about my dad. I couldn't blame her. But she doesn't. Instead she just says "huh," and keeps walking.


Miss Ravencroft threatens to have us all expelled the second she sees us. I can't really argue that. We did disobey a direct instruction from a teacher and everyone knows 'don't go outside the walls' is rule number one for students of Oak House. Instead, she lets us off with a warning and sends us straight to our dorms for bed.

"Eli," she calls after me. I glance at Arthur, who shrugs, then turns to leave. "Eli, I wanted to let you know that your father has been called and he will be outside the school gates to collect you after breakfast tomorrow morning."

Oh.

I'm going home.

In all the chaos, I had forgotten.

It'll be nice to go home.

I think.

I pack my bags before breakfast. There's not much since I never really unpacked. The other boys notice them, stacked neatly at the end of my bed, but nobody says anything. Nobody except Arthur.

"You're really leaving?" He asks.

"I guess," is all I can think to say.

"I'll miss you," he says.

"I'll miss you too," I say, and I mean it more than I ever expected to.

"Thanks," he says.

"For what?"

He laughs. "For last night. For saving us. And for being my friend."

I cock my head to the side like an owl. Like Arthur does. "You have lots of friends."

"Not like– Not like you. Not friends who'd risk their lives to go into the Beyond and save my little sister."

"Oh."

There's nothing more I can say.


When I step through the portal, back into the mortal realm, Dad is waiting for me as promised. He smiles when he sees me, a look of relief.

I stop in front of him, setting my suitcases on the ground and throw myself into his arms. He stumbles backward, but I don't let go, holding as tight as I possibly can. He runs a hand through my hair. "That bad?" He asks.

I pull back and look up at him. "No," I reply, surprising myself. I glance back at the house, at the side gate with the portal to Oak House, at Miss Ravencroft, who steps through the portal behind me.

"I think…" I think of Arthur, of Vivian, of Dominic and Zaid, and even Ivy. I think of sitting on my bed, eating soup and rolls, and walking back to school, through the Beyond, after facing the creature from my nightmares.

*"You should stay," Arthur said. "I know you might feel like you don't belong because you came late in the year and you're not a mage and your dad is who he is, but… but I like you. And if you don't stay, we might not get the chance to become friends."*

I turn to Dad, then back to Miss Ravencroft. "I think I want to stay."

# Those That Came First

## Miles Nelson

Content Warnings: Mild Teasing, Isolation and Loss, Contemplation of Social Justice and Climate Change, Exploration of a Long-Dead Civilisation, Drinking Water from Live Animals

Author's Note:

Hello everyone, Miles here!

I just wanted to take a moment to share how excited I am for you all to read the following story.

As some of you may already know, "Those That Came First" takes place in the Riftmaster universe; a series of books that started with my debut novel, appropriately titled *Riftmaster*. Despite its place in a larger universe, this story can be read without the context of the originals. My hope is that "Those That Came First" will introduce old readers to a new world, and new readers to my signature flare and beloved characters.

Even though I, as an author, am trans and autistic, Riftmaster's main character, Bailey, is cis, straight and neurotypical. Assuming that his mentor is the same, it comes as a shock to him when his assumptions are proven wrong. "Those That Came First" takes place before this reveal, three months into their journey together. It shows a side to the story you'd otherwise never get to see; the Riftmaster's perspective before they've felt the need to come out as trans and autistic.

And so, without any further ado, I'm proud to present my story.

Hope you enjoy!

# Those That Came First

Miles Nelson

BAILEY SLUNK AFTER his mentor along a narrow mountain path. As his boots fell silently against the stone that was worn smooth, he had the uneasy feeling that he wasn't the first to walk this way.

Against the ominous hum of the wind, he considered his unbelievable yet undeniable luck for what felt like the hundredth time. *Only he* could have ended up in this situation; kidnapped by the universe and dropped unceremoniously onto another planet. Ending up hopelessly lost in the infinite cosmos as he plunged haphazardly between dozens of hostile and terrifying new worlds.

And *only he* could somehow end up finding the only other human who had managed to survive a life like this.

Bailey froze as his mentor stopped ahead of him, the cloaked figure still among jagged boulders that were streaked with roiling veins of copper, sickly-green.

For a moment, the Riftmaster listened to the shrill whine of the wind among the wreckage.

*What have you heard?*

Bailey's heart beat faster and he hunched low, knowing they could be seen by anything circling the wine-red sky. This world seemed, so far, as empty as it was cruel, but he still didn't trust it. He couldn't even tell if the skeletal grasses poking up around his feet were dead or alive, but at least they were something.

Seemingly satisfied, the Riftmaster let out a breath and then crouched. Bailey watched him test his fingertips on some grass, then pluck a clump from a vein of copper. Bailey slowly approached his mentor's back, looking questioningly over his shoulder.

"For kindling?" Bailey asked.

The Riftmaster looked up sharply, and Bailey flinched at the suddenness of it. His mentor blinked as though still surprised to find another human standing beside him.

The shadows beneath his eyes made his expression seem hollow in the half-light, skeletal despite his rounded cheeks. His explosion of freckles looked like blood splatters. Only the upright prickle of messy hair and the blink of ash-grey eyes betrayed any emotion.

"Yes, that's right." The voice that answered him was high-pitched and hoarse with disuse, but familiar. "Or maybe food. We can see when we find somewhere to hide."

Bailey nodded, shoulders relaxing and the Riftmaster turned away.

"...That said... this is no place for surprises, Rifthopper," his mentor added, eyebrows rising and a smile tugging at his cheek. "I almost took you for a carnivore."

Bailey glanced his way. Though the Riftmaster's voice was edged with humour, there was no laughter in his eyes. "I'm sorry, Riftmaster."

The Riftmaster's smile faded.

Bailey looked back the way they had come.

The long, jagged pathway looked no more inviting than it had any other time. But at least it was out of the wind.

Ahead of them though, miles of barren plain sprawled, a cruel gale billowing clouds of dust from the cracked, scorched earth.

Bailey swallowed, wishing that he was somewhere—*anywhere*—else.

Especially home.

It felt like a lifetime since he'd last seen Earth. The memories alone made his heart ache in a way that still felt uncomfortably raw.

Lightyears away from everything he knew and loved, Bailey had spent the last three months being whisked from world to world at the cruel and unpredictable whim of the Rift.

Yet that was nothing compared to the Riftmaster's five-thousand years.

In the half-light, his mentor's face was ashen, deep grey eyes leeched of their usual light. Red curls of uneven hair whipped his cheeks. His eyes held the same cool look that Bailey suddenly realised was anticipation. He squinted against the grit carried on the wind.

Against the faintest hint of sunlight, Bailey realised what his mentor was looking at. Rising sharply from clouds of sand stood a twisted tower. As the dust cleared, only for an instant, Bailey saw the horizon take shape into an uneven array of orderly lumps. It took a moment for him to realise what he was looking at, shivering in the fog. Miles of distance betrayed what he could only assume to be a city.

The Riftmaster stood, ready and poised to step out onto the wide, bare plain. But once they started walking, there would be no going back.

Bailey was tired. The wind whistled in his ears, and he wasn't ready to fight for every step.

"When do you want to stop to eat?"

The Riftmaster glanced back with an expression that was something between a smile and a grimace. He held out the clump of grass. Bailey didn't think it would be very nutritious. "I was hoping to find something a little more appetising than this."

"It… Isn't it poisonous?"

"Probably." The Riftmaster smiled, an expression dusted with irony and tinged with the faintest hint of pride.

"Riftmaster… You're smiling as if that's a good thing!"

"Caution is always a good thing. If we don't find anything else, we can always eat what we have preserved."

"And then?"

"We press on. The city could be a good place to start. With any luck, it was built next to a water source."

Bailey grimaced, eyeing the waterskin his mentor always carried at his belt. It was almost half empty. "And if it isn't?"

"We can only try."

Bailey gritted his teeth and looked out across the plain, black hair whisking in the wind. It had grown since he'd left Earth. "No food. Hardly any water. Burning sand, hell-red skies and now the ruins of some long-dead civilisation. I don't think this place could get any worse."

The Riftmaster scoffed, wagging a finger at his apprentice. "Rifthopper, the situation can always get worse. Don't tempt fate."

"You'll get us through it though, right?"

"I sure hope so!" The Riftmaster offered him a lopsided grin. "But no promises."

They wandered between boulders that Bailey now speculated might have been hewn into sharp angles by ancient tools. The Riftmaster's quiet footsteps seemed to barely skim the path. When the duo finally dropped onto level, cracked ground, the Riftmaster peered out towards the forlorn horizon and paced unsettlingly. In the relative shelter of the rocky mountainside, Bailey saw grit and sand whisking along the wide, flat plain. Sharp shards bounced across an empty void.

Silence reigned. By the time the Riftmaster finally stopped pacing, Bailey stared into the distance with resignation. On level ground, he stood a head above his diminutive mentor, but the Riftmaster's pride made him feel about ten feet taller.

"I don't like this," Bailey said. "Have you ever seen a world like it before?"

"Unfortunately, yes."

Bailey expected his mentor to elaborate. But in this case, he seemed strangely distant. The Riftmaster pulled his fur cloak tighter around his shoulders, shielding himself from the wind. "We're going to have to walk in the open for a time. Do you still have your mask?"

"From the Mountain-Dwellers?"

The Riftmaster nodded. "It'll protect us from the wind."

Bailey hesitated, fumbling at his belt for a moment. Finally he withdrew an ivory mask, shaded by a bright pink cowl. Its visage was modelled after the Mountain-Dwellers, a goat-like species from a planet of bitter cold; back there, oxygen-rich herbs stashed in the muzzle had helped to prevent altitude sickness. Like the pink fur cloaks around each of their shoulders, it would help protect them from weather of almost any severity.

After an approving nod, the Riftmaster donned his own, and crept out onto the open plain. Bailey hesitated, then followed. The wind hit him like a wall, and although they both braced against it, it was like wading through honey. Bailey saw the Riftmaster crouched low. He copied the stance, his breaths deep and long.

The Riftmaster glanced back across his shoulder, checking Bailey's progress.

Sand hissed around them, and a hollow fluting sound rose distantly from the crumbled ruins.

"You know," his mentor yelled cheerfully, "I've heard instruments that sounded far worse than this wind. If I heard this playing in a Riftworld tavern, I'd probably dance to it."

Bailey looked up, trying to figure out if the Riftmaster was joking or not.

"From the sounds of it, you'd dance to anything," he called into the gale.

The Riftmaster laughed. "You're probably right!"

The distance to the city was further than they had thought. With no days or nights on this world, there was no way to estimate the time. Bailey's steps faltered as his muscles ached from straining against the wind. Since leaving Earth, he had become stronger and fitter, but his endurance still had a long way to go.

The inside of Bailey's mask was coated with perspiration, small eye holes limiting his vision.

Finally, a shadow fell upon them. Bailey looked up to see the tower looming somewhere beyond the mist. But by this point, even the Riftmaster was flagging. Despite his short stature, his mentor's endurance was something to be admired. For every stride Bailey took, the Riftmaster made two. In the months they had known each other, Bailey had never seen his mentor tire.

Until now.

They struggled on as capes thrashed at their backs. Bailey breathed hard, focusing on the ground at his feet.

Step by step, he kept pushing onward. But something felt wrong; somewhere ahead of him, the cracked earth ended. Beyond that, there was nothing.

Bailey took another step forward, straining to see.

No more than a metre ahead, the ground fell away into what might have been an abyssal moat.

Bailey looked up at the Riftmaster, but his gaze was on the ruins, his focus on how close they were to shelter, to safety.

"Riftmaster!"

Bailey lurched forward and grabbed his mentor's shoulder, yanking him back. The Riftmaster looked down over the edge into a terrifying drop.

They both stood for a moment, heavy cloaks shuddering, shoulders heaving. Bailey's mentor stared down into the dark that had very nearly ended him. And then he swallowed, looking up into Bailey's worried eyes, shadowed with exhaustion.

"Well done, Rifthopper."

"Are… are you alright?" Bailey asked, breathing heavily.

The Riftmaster gave the slightest nod. "I've almost died in far worse ways," he said, though his tone of voice belied his humour. "But this would have to be the most embarrassing."

"You can tell me about those later," Bailey said. "I… I don't think now is the time for a story."

"No, no. Probably not." His mentor's expression cheered abruptly. "On the bright side, I think we've found a water channel."

Bailey said nothing, breaths hot and thick and echoing within his mask.

"…Bailey?"

Bailey glanced down, abruptly realising he still held the Riftmaster with a dead man's grip. Their gazes met, and the Riftmaster replied to his unspoken question with a slight nod. Slowly, he unhooked his fingers.

His life was worth the bruises.

"I just hope we can find a bridge soon."

The ruins loomed, tall and broad. The duo followed the dry canal along its snaking way, watching long-fallen structures pass. In some places a coating of black fuzz still covered the stone at the very bottom, where water must have flowed until quite recently. Finally, they found a narrow walkway across the canal, and entered the city in single file.

It was empty. Although Bailey had never really expected to find life here, his stomach still sank.

Some of the buildings had collapsed, looking like cracked eggshells in the dark; but most seemed built for this sort of weather, still standing stoically against the sandstorm. Rivulets of copper stuck out where stone had worn away. They examined ancient doorways in a weird procession of shapes and sizes. With each one, Bailey prepared to see someone watching them, hackles rising.

Then he deflated when there was nobody there.

Finally, they emerged into a narrow walkway between still-standing buildings.

Bailey swallowed as he paused to peer under another empty arch. "Do you think we're really alone?" he asked. His voice felt painfully loud in the silence that was only broken by the keening wind.

The Riftmaster looked around tentatively. He shrugged. "I doubt it. If there's shelter to be found among the ruins, there will be something living in it."

Bailey didn't ask any more questions after that.

As they pressed deeper into the foreboding darkness, Bailey's breaths grew short and clipped. The Riftmaster's hand fell to the knife sheathed against his thigh.

Finally, he beckoned Bailey through a narrow stone archway into a building that might have housed someone far taller than themselves. It had taken him a long time to settle on this particular ruin. There was another entrance, a smaller one, that led to another narrow side-street, and the roof had begun to crumble but was mostly intact. There was no way they could be cornered here, and the smoke from their campfire could escape and disperse.

The Riftmaster assumed the duty of setting up camp, using their cloaks as curtains to hide the camp from prying eyes. He hummed along to the howl of the wind as he carefully arranged their possessions beside the meagre fire. His expression flickered in surprise when Bailey helped without being asked.

He took his mentor's knife carefully from his hand, and struck it against a flint bead his mentor slipped from one of his necklaces. As the spark caught hold of some dry grass and flared into a greenish-hued flame, Bailey finally let out his breath in a heavy sigh.

Only then did he look around.

Rivulets of copper shone faintly in the firelight, marking the mortar joints between puzzle-like blocks of grey-brown stone. It gave the otherwise empty room a vague implication of style.

Very little of the previous inhabitants seemed to remain. But Bailey felt their ghosts all around him.

As they took turns drinking from the waterskin, Bailey settled with his back to the wall, forlorn and exhausted but unable to sleep. Sharpening his knife with long, slow rasps, the Riftmaster watched him, but said nothing.

Finally, Bailey spoke. "I… never thought I'd see a place like this," he said.

The Riftmaster glanced up, blinked.

"Like what?"

"Like a city," he said. "Only… it's so dead, so empty."

The Riftmaster tilted his head. "I suppose it would be quite a shock. But you've met sentient races before, like the Mountain-Dwellers; you know they're out here."

"But this… this isn't a sentient race. This *was* a sentient race."

Bailey paused, opened his mouth, then closed it again. *I worried about this,* he wanted to say. *About change. Extinction. About my kind slowly killing the Earth.*

"I don't know what happened here, but it feels…" Bailey trailed off. He brought his knees up to his chest. *Too close to home.*

He rested his chin on one knee.

Bailey heard a rustle as his mentor shifted positions. His expression was sombre as he knelt at Bailey's side. "Don't cry," he said gently. "We need to preserve water."

Bailey looked up, opening his mouth to protest until he saw the Riftmaster's expression. Then he sighed and said nothing.

"This is only one city. There's a big chance these people still live on, somewhere warmer and wetter."

Bailey slowly lowered his legs and looked away for a moment. "Riftmaster?" The tiredness in his eyes had returned. "When you lived on Earth, did anyone ever worry about the planet? And what humanity was doing to it?"

"I don't recall. My memories from back then are… fuzzy."

"I'm sorry… I forgot it had been so long."

The Riftmaster shrugged. "It's alright."

There was a long pause before the Riftmaster finally spoke, tone tentative. "Remind me, Rifthopper. You decided it was easier to hold onto hope of going home one day, didn't you? So why not hope that your people might surprise you when you do?"

Bailey didn't answer, the silence chokingly thick. He stared into the greenish fire that crackled in the dark. *What if they already have? What if this is Earth?*

Finally, despite the tightness of his throat, he spoke. "You must be missing the stars."

The Riftmaster took a moment to consider, moving back to the fireside. He patted the space next to him. "I'm not sure if missing them is the right word," he said with a smile. "I know they're always there." He sheathed his knife and settled back, resting his weight on his palms.

Bailey shuffled over to his mentor, tawny skin sickly green in the firelight.

"But… I do feel quite lost without them. I like to know my place in the universe."

"Do you know the names of all the stars?" Bailey asked.

The Riftmaster shook his head. "I only remember a few from my time on Earth."

"Maybe you should start naming them yourself."

The Riftmaster grinned.

"I'll leave naming things to you. I have too many memories, too many routes and foods and routines. There's not enough space in my head for much else!"

"If you say so."

"Though…" The Riftmaster dropped his voice to a conspiring murmur, and winked. "I do make up my own constellations sometimes. I try to pick out the shapes of creatures from different worlds."

"Aliens?"

"No. Not aliens." The Riftmaster smiled. "We're the only aliens here."

"Oh, right." Bailey nodded, and flushed red. "I forgot about that. Sorry, Riftmaster."

The Riftmaster turned back to the fire, grey eyes watching the flame flicker and dance. "How about you get a bite to eat and some sleep? You look exhausted."

"Will you keep watch?"

"Of course. I don't trust this place any more than you do." The Riftmaster peered out into the empty street. "You'll have to come up with a dastardly name for this place when we leave."


The Riftmaster jolted awake from a shallow slumber and found that the wind had ceased its fervent whine. The first thing they noticed was a lingering pain in their shoulder: bruises from Bailey's vice-like grip.

The second thing they noticed was that something was wrong. They blinked around at the scattered possessions, strange surroundings, and the fire that had since burned down to ash. *It's not like me to fall asleep while on watch.*

They blinked a few times, steadying their thoughts.

*Bailey...?*

The Riftmaster shook their head, staggering upright, and lurched over to the curtained entrance of the small, round dwelling. They couldn't see much of the street where it wound around a labyrinth of small stone houses. Bailey was nowhere to be seen. The Riftmaster backed further inside, darted across the ashes, and looked out the other door.

They heard his footsteps before he appeared around a bend, hair dishevelled and face troubled.

"Bailey!" they hissed. "Why didn't you wake me?"

"S-Sorry! I wasn't going far, and…" He hesitated, but only for a moment. "I thought it might injure your pride."

If there was one thing that the Riftmaster could say for the young man, it was that he wore his heart on his sleeve. Their shoulders relaxed.

"Waking up on watch duty injured it regardless!" they said, expression softening as they held the curtain aside. "But that doesn't matter. Something's wrong. What's wrong?"

"I…" Bailey rubbed a bristly cheek, glancing away from them as he moved to the fireside. "I was wondering if you'd help me figure out what happened here," he finally said. "This building is empty. The others seem to be too." He paused "There are no bodies. If the people left in a hurry or died, there would be something left behind. So, what happened?"

The Riftmaster took a moment to consider. Between the clinging feeling of their parched throat and a low growl in their belly, they had more pressing concerns. "Survival should always be our first priority," they said. "The answer won't mean anything to us if we die trying to find it."

"Er, well," Bailey stammered. "It was just a silly thought–"

The Riftmaster held up a hand to silence him, shifting their legs into a more comfortable position as they settled at the fireside. "…But, when our waterskin is full and food stored, perhaps." They tipped their head slightly. "But tell me something, Bailey. Why?"

"Wh… Why?"

"Many different alien tongues have some variation on 'curiosity killed the cat', and in a place like this, why should we care?"

Bailey took a moment to think. When he spoke, his tone was tentative. "What if the thing that drove them out is still here?" he asked. "This could be the only place for miles that has water and shelter. If it's alive, it would have a reason to stay."

The Riftmaster's eyes gleamed. "Just the answer I was looking for," they praised. "Even if I know you're lying."

Bailey looked away as they stood, stretched, and began to pack. Finally, they held the curtain aside, revealing the city looming beyond.

"Come, then! We'd best get foraging and watering out of the way if we're going to beat the weather. I'd like to find a place for my garden, too."

Bailey hesitated, looking at them questioningly.

"Perhaps you should take the lead."

Bailey's eyes widened, hair standing on end. "In a place like this?! Can't you teach me somewhere a bit less…" He hesitated. "…Hostile? Hot? Dead?!"

"This life we lead won't often give us a choice, Rifthopper." They grinned at his stricken expression. "Don't worry. I won't let you get us killed."

"Where should I take us?"

"Where do you think we'll have the best chance of surviving?"

Bailey thought for a moment. "The canal was still damp. We should try and find the source."

The Riftmaster nodded approvingly.

Soon after, the duo padded out of their shelter and headed into the labyrinth, leaving only the remains of a fire behind. To help learn the terrain, the Riftmaster gathered the ashes, and made scuffs on the tumbled walls to mark their path.

Without the crushing weight of the wind, the Riftmaster felt light and agile, clambering over tumbled walls and up onto the sloping domes of the buildings to look out across the cityscape. From here, it seemed to go on forever; the great, tall tower marking its centre and judging them from the clouds.

It didn't take long to discover the small, flat creatures spread out on the stones, taking advantage of the thin sunlight and the break in the wind. Wavering feelers appeared to filter nourishment from the dust, their bodies mottled brown for camouflage. Stuck in place and unprepared for predation, the most difficult part was prying one from the roofs of the dwellings.

The Riftmaster checked for a mouth and found the creature's underside clung to their palm like gecko feet. It didn't *seem* poisonous, but they would need water to know for sure.

Their journey continued its tedious and winding route, picking around small dwellings and rubble. In the meantime, the Riftmaster realised that the creatures would cling to almost anything.

Bailey's expression was severe as he stalked ahead, fists clenched, and pace determined.

The Riftmaster waited until there were a few metres of distance between them, and then hurled an unfortunate creature. It stuck fast to the back to Bailey's cloak. They stifled a snort, peeling another from its perch. Unused to having time to spare, they turned it into a game. Time would tell how many they could stick to their apprentice without him noticing.

Transporting the creatures would be a lot easier from that point on.

Bailey was not amused when he finally noticed the extra weight and discovered the host of passengers clinging to his back, but the Riftmaster cackled like a hyena.

"Think of it as another lesson for you, Rifthopper—always watch your back!"

After a while, Bailey finally caved in and allowed himself a tiny smile.

When they reached the edge of the ruins, their path joined the canal. As yesterday though, the waterway was too deep to jump into, and its sides were smooth with the waterflow. The creatures that Bailey had dubbed 'slapjacks' had taken residence there, swollen round with water and algae.

They pressed on, hoping that the still-damp canal would eventually lead them to its source. But the trek was long. Before they reached its end, they could stretch their water supply no further, and their water pouch finally ran dry.

"Before long, we might need to chance a leap," Bailey said, sounding resigned.

"Or we could cut up our cloaks and make a rope ladder," his mentor pointed out.

"But then, what if the next world is cold?"

"We'll just have to deal with that when we get there." Although their voice was even, the Riftmaster was about as eager at the prospect as he was. "We won't always have the luxury of planning ahead. Sometimes you need to make sacrifices in the moment."

Sometime after, the duo reached another narrow crossing that spanned the dry canal. Keeping low, they darted across.

Barren wasteland lay on the other side; but at least from here they could see foul weather approaching.

As they followed the waterway around the boundary of the city, they found themselves passing over a low, crumbling wall that enclosed a wide area of the plain. Bailey spotted a shelter that looked like an upturned bag, rumpled but round. Unlike the rest, boulders scattered this section of wide-open plain.

Here, the canal's sheer side became a gentle slope.

"I think this must have been a corral for animals," Bailey said. "The canal has a bank so they could drink."

The Riftmaster beamed. "It must have been!"

Curious, Bailey moved towards the shelter, while the Riftmaster trotted towards the waterway's sloping bank. A few paces later, they were called back. "Riftmaster? You're going to want to look at this."

The Riftmaster approached with a measure of caution.

Beside Bailey was a jagged boulder, but as they drew nearer, the texture became smooth and shiny, and they could pick out different segments, the foremost of which possessed two symmetrical holes. At some point, the realisation hit them that this was the huddled husk of some great creature. Six-limbed, smooth, and streamlined, the wind curled over it even now. It was curled with its back to the wind, hollow with age. The Riftmaster lifted their head, peering around them at other boulders. The more they looked, the more they seemed to see; beasts of burden that had lived out their days in a dried-out corral.

"They must have died of old age," the Riftmaster said. "If the water had receded, they could have entered the canal and escaped.

"I'm not so sure," Bailey said, gravely. "Some of them have wounds."

With his boot, he shifted what the Riftmaster had taken to be a part of the dead thing. Another exoskull, narrower and with two immense curving horns, turned over. Sand poured from its empty eye sockets. Bailey knelt and pulled a rusted copper blade from beside it, leather straps breaking away from the body beneath the sand.

Bailey dropped the blade at his feet.

They had found the city's inhabitants.

"Bailey? We should move on."

Bailey seemed torn, hesitating. Something wrestled with the ache for water that they knew he needed just as much. They knew that thirst would soon win out, but they felt concern growing. Was this answer so important that he would risk death to find it?

"Bailey?"

It seemed the encouragement was enough.

"Let's keep on moving," he said finally. "We need to find water."

He turned his back on the shelter and the fallen creatures, although his mentor's gaze lingered for a moment longer, thoughtful.

"Do you think we could use these?"

Bailey paused, looking hesitant. "What for?"

"Depends what we need. It seems quite sturdy, but we don't need more armour or souvenirs."

*A strip of leather could make this into a find shield*, they thought. But shields were cumbersome, and not always as useful as they seemed. They eyed their apprentice, thoughtful.

Catching their gaze, Bailey's expression matched theirs. "Perhaps we could use part of the exoskeleton for a cooking pot?"

"Yes, could be! Let's see!"

The shell was hard, but slightly bendy. Curved, and cool to the touch. Years lying in the sand had failed to wear it down, but it was surprisingly light. The Riftmaster weighed it for a second in their hands before tucking it under an arm.

They waited as Bailey trotted ahead of them, and then hurried down into the canal, sliding only briefly on a film of algae beneath their feet. Stagnating puddles surrounded them. The Riftmaster eased a swollen creature from the rock face with their knife and offered it to Bailey. He held it for a moment, looking more than a little bit uncomfortable.

The Riftmaster set down their satchel and brought out three clay bowls, and three small pouches. They beckoned him over. "Settle by me. I'll take the lead for now."

The Riftmaster took a small pinch of blue flower petals from the first pouch and showed him how to grind it into a fine powder with the pommel of their knife. Then, the Riftmaster made a small puncture wound in the creature's side, and warm water flowed free. They let a little bit drop into the bowl, and thought for a moment before speaking.

"The blue herbs detect acidity and alkali," the Riftmaster explained, their expression growing distant. "A little bit of either is okay, but you don't want to drink anything that will burn. If it fizzes, turns red or dark blue, avoid it like the plague. If it turns purple, then it may be some form of venom. But you'll need the red herbs to know for sure."

As they spoke, the Riftmaster's eyes lit up.

They had repeated this lesson many, many times; both for themself and others. The Riftmaster's expression grew slightly wistful. Even after so long, they could recite it almost without thinking. And they knew that for Bailey's sake, they'd need to repeat this many times more.

But their patience was limitless.

Bailey nodded, but they gave him another moment to let the information sink in. Then they sloshed the water around to stir it.

"What do you think?"

"Er… looks good to me? It's slightly blue, but not dark."

The Riftmaster nodded approvingly.

For the red herbs, they allowed him to grind the powder and offered a similar explanation.

"What do you think, Rifthopper?"

"Hm? Oh, it seems clean, right?"

"So far, yes! But you mustn't skip the final step. This one is for dissolved minerals. Listen for the fizz, this time. It's a good thing."

From the last pouch they removed a black leaf. They crumbled it in their palm and showed it to him before adding it to the final bowl.

It fizzed lightly on contact, and then their shoulders relaxed.

"Did you get all that?"

Bailey nodded.

"Good. Now how about you test our dinner?"

Now that they knew it was safe, they lifted their knife and slit open the creature.

Clean, filtered water flowed free; they drank it straight from the source, much to Bailey's horror, and their amusement. There wasn't much, but for now it would be enough.

Wiping a smear from the corner of their mouth, the Riftmaster offered him the wriggling creature.

The new cooking pot worked like a charm, and as their broth boiled, Bailey helped to filter water from stagnating pools and muddied hollows.

The Riftmaster set a covering of leather across the cooking pot, letting the condensation slowly fill the waterskin over time. He kept an eye on the sky as the wind began to echo in low moans over the fallen city. While their start on this planet had been shaky, Bailey found himself slowly relaxing now that the waterskin and their bellies were full.

It was his turn to keep watch while, after a half-hearted protest, the Riftmaster fitfully slept, tossing and turning by the fireside. In the quiet, that feeling of discomfort came creeping back. He knew that he needed to find answers before the Rift whisked them away and the opportunity was gone forever.

Like an eternal watcher, the tower loomed, the wind howling about its curves.

He could see it in his mind's eye, like bubbles blown in stone, or a thousand little domed clay houses stacked haphazardly on top of each other, an eldritch palace fit for an alien king.

Who had lived there, and what had happened to them?

Bailey didn't know if he would ever find out, but he knew he would have to try. The Riftmaster wouldn't understand; he had been away too long. Although Bailey liked to think that his mentor cared about the planets he visited, he didn't think the Riftmaster liked to dwell on what might have been.

The Riftmaster lived in the now, and never looked back. The name that he'd used on Earth was useless, long forgotten by all but him. Instead he favoured a name that could be spoken in any tongue. With a small clench of guilt, Bailey remembered the joy flitting across his face as he found fascination in life and nature. But he never spared a moment for those long gone. Just as leaving a world severed his connection to it, death was an end.

Skulls were just skulls to him; bones just tools to be used. He had made Bailey's armour from the hide of a fellow Rifter, as he told Bailey stories from its homeworld with wonder and reverence.

The Riftmaster didn't know what came after death and had made it clear that he didn't plan on finding out.

But Bailey wanted to know what had happened here. Only then, he felt, could this place finally put its ghosts to rest.

Even so, the Riftmaster's question bothered him, itching in the back of his brain like a flea. Why did he care? He had never been here before, and never known its creatures or its people. It was nothing like Earth, he told himself, or anything else he had ever known.

But what if the inhabitants here shared Earth's fate? What if there was something he could learn, something he could do?

Even if Bailey never made it back, he knew he had to try.

Bailey rested his chin on his knees and waited for his mentor to awake, brows knotted and knuckles clenched around his knees.

When the fire had burned down to ash, the Riftmaster finally cracked open his eyes, and stretched. Bailey was on his feet before he'd sat upright, their belongings already packed. The amusement in the Riftmaster's eyes died as he saw the expression on Bailey's face. He quickly stood.

The Riftmaster didn't know what he was looking for. He didn't know why Bailey cared. But he would follow without question.


Bailey led the way at a speedy trot along the canal, the same way that they had plodded the night before. There had been a substantial argument before Bailey finally conceded that it would be best to keep following the waterway.

At first, Bailey wanted to go back the way they had come, returning to the ruins and heading for the bulbous tower. But the Riftmaster was unwilling to forgo stable food and water supplies. Besides, he'd reasoned, when they reached the natural end of the canal, they could make camp and continue the search from there.

Much to Bailey's relief, the towering walls did not remain impassable forever. The further they walked, the wider and shallower the waterway became. Deposits of bricks and broken debris made Bailey confident that it would be possible to climb back out. Finally, they reached a dead end, where an ancient dam still leaked the tiniest trickle onto the ground. Although the drainage valves looked to have been out of use for many, many years, a few leaks had sprung from shallow cracks near the very bottom. Thinking of the stagnant pools, Bailey didn't think much water would remain on the other side.

The Riftmaster slapped a creature onto one of the cracks. Somehow, it succeeded in blocking the flow.

"There—fixed," he joked with a lopsided grin.

Bailey couldn't resist a smile. His heart wasn't in it, but he knew the Riftmaster was only trying to help. "Those creatures swell up when there is water—but we keep finding them on the roofs! Do you think the dam might have burst?"

The Riftmaster looked thoughtful. "I think it's more likely they store water when it rains and save it for the drier months. Creatures that live in the water permanently would have dried out a long time ago. Plus, the city would bear signs—there are no algae or weeds sprouting, or sedimentary deposits. It's as though the people here…"

"…just vanished." Bailey finished.

The Riftmaster nodded. He glanced around. It was relatively sheltered here, with access to clean water and food. Then he looked back at Bailey questioningly.

*No*—Bailey thought, with a sudden surge of triumph. *Not a question, a test.*

"This place is too enclosed to make camp. If we were attacked here, there'd be no way for us to get out."

"So…?"

"Let's… ah… how about we do some gardening?"

The Riftmaster's eyes sparkled. He opened up his satchel and held out one of his herb pouches.

"Let's bring some life back to this place."

The soil was thin, but enough. They worked together to till a small section of hardened sediment and bury the seeds.

In a few days, the seeds would burst into small blue flowers, which in turn would make the soil safe for the rest.

When they had finished, the Riftmaster looked around at the shallow walls of the canal. He padded over to a wall on the city-side, but the nearest handhold was just out of his reach. "Bailey? A hand?"

Bailey hurried over to assist him, cupping his hands. The Riftmaster stepped into his palms and a moment later, was over the edge. Soon, Bailey was being hoisted up as well, trying to hide his surprise at the strength packed into his mentor's stocky body.

Soon, the pair sat together beside the dry canal, looking at what might have once been a wide, slow moving pool. By following the waterway, they had found their way into the very centre of the city. Bailey looked up, found the bulbous tower stretching above them—and realised that, despite changing direction, the canal had led precisely where they wanted to be.

They could look out to see the channel threading through the ruins, and the tumble of tiny dwellings seemed to go on forever. A billowing sandstorm crept across the distant plain.

Bailey allowed a moment to admire the view. Then he turned away.

He set a slow pace, wandering cautiously around the perimeter of the tower, and the homes sprawling from its base.

Although time moved slowly on, this world seemed trapped in perpetual stasis. The sun did not rise or set. It just hung there, looming like a broken clock face. Bailey lost track of how long he walked.

He did not enter the tower at first; he wanted to look inside the smaller buildings, almost exactly the same as those on the outskirts.

Here, Bailey found the first signs of unrest.

First he found belongings, packed to go; satchels, saddlebags, pouches crammed with preserved meats and long-withered leaves. The still, dry air had kept it all dusty but unchanged. The Riftmaster eyed the weathered bags with some interest.

"We could take one?" he suggested. "You've been needing a satchel."

"Riftmaster…" Bailey sighed and shook his head. "Not this time."

The Riftmaster shrugged, expression downcast. "They would probably be brittle with age, anyway."

Though many buildings were empty, the closer to the tower they drew, the more evidence of life Bailey found. Evidence of beings that had once tried to escape but were unable to.

In the next, a forlorn exoskeleton lay crumpled next to its belongings. Bailey slowly and painstakingly looked through them, hoping to find some indication of what they were fleeing from. Yet the artefacts, which must have meant so much to those long dead, meant nothing to him.

Finally he sighed, shook his head, and stormed out.

The Riftmaster watched him from some distance away. His expression was unreadable, and he said nothing as Bailey moved on to the next crumbling ruin.

He dug into a leather satchel and drew out a scrap of chewed, dusty red linen. Painstakingly, he unfurled the tattered fabric. Strange, scattered markings might have been a form of writing once. After spending some time trying to decipher it and a mystified shrug from the Riftmaster, Bailey returned it to the pile, and pulled out another. This one looked like an art piece, at first; the red dyeing was fainter, older, with blotches of watery copper-green. It was just as meaningless; but even so he squinted at the stylised knots of lines and pathways. Eventually, he realised that it was a map. Markings Bailey had thought were glyphs, seemed to represent the city buildings. He spotted the canal looped around the city with water spilling out onto a green-dyed plain.

The corral was marked with tiny symbols of six-legged beasts.

The buildings stood in joyous disarray, clearly marking this city, and one or two others as well. He could see the mountains from where he and the Riftmaster had come, their path marked with copper paint, and the dammed lake set into a crater above the city, perfectly round. The path continued along the plain to the next city, then the next, before finally looping back in a perfect circle.

But there was no tower drawn on the map.

Bailey looked out of the rounded doorway, and saw it looming over them, an amalgamation of the city buildings below. What could possibly lie inside?

The Riftmaster popped his head into the building from where he kept watch. Seeing the fabric, he tipped his head. "Find what you were looking for?"

Bailey sighed and shook his head. "Only more questions," he said, hauling himself to his feet and holding up the map. *I'll take nothing else, but the Riftmaster will appreciate this.* His knees clicked, stiff from kneeling.

Finally, he made his way out into the open. He wound his way between buildings, reminded himself what he had found in each one:

*Two bodies, packed belongings. Letters. A waterskin, I think, and leather ropes.*

*Empty.*

*A sleeping roll on the floor of that one. One small bag, empty except scraps of linen and… some kind of pen?*

*A copper blade in here, and copper plates. No bags.*

*Same for that one. And that… and that.*

The homes were sparsely decorated, except for the shimmering mortar joints. It leant them an air of impermanence, although they had clearly been built to withstand the sandstorms and the wind.

Finally, Bailey found himself standing before a great arched entranceway, leading into a huge, circular hall. He looked up and saw the tower directly above him.

He wasn't sure why, but his heart beat faster.

*I may find nothing within*, he reminded himself. *So why does it feel like all my efforts have been leading to this?*

Bailey turned away and found himself trapped by the Riftmaster's concerned gaze. "You don't need to do this, you know," his mentor said gently.

Bailey shook himself and stepped over the threshold.

The tower hall immediately felt different. Intricate patterns of copper made it feel strangely opulent and exoskeletons draped in chainmail lay dutifully where they had fallen either side of an arched doorway. The Riftmaster stepped over the remains without looking twice, stopping only to pick up a chainmail shawl.

"Riftmaster!" Bailey hissed. "Put that down!"

The Riftmaster's brows raised and he glanced down. "They don't need it anymore."

"Still!"

The Riftmaster breathed out a small sigh, then dropped the garment on the ground with a clink. "It would be too noisy for our purposes, anyway," he mumbled, and moved on.

The Riftmaster said nothing as Bailey searched, but peered into dark corners and corridors, always keeping a hand on the pommel of his knife.

Bailey padded the length of the room, looking for traces. His feet whisked up curls of dust, and revealed the shimmer of polished stone, likely, brought in from somewhere else.

This hall at least had furniture, strangely rounded like everything else and gilded with copper. In one room, he found a hole in the ground that might have once been filled with water from the canal, although the contraption attached to it was still as alien as anything else.

*A fountain, perhaps? Or was this a kitchen of some kind?*

Either way, the permanent features were something new; Bailey had noted that every building except the tower was completely empty of furniture.

*Either way, the people in this tower seem to have had running water.*

There was not much else he could glean here.

Bailey slowly made his way through an arch and onto a tightly curving spiral of stone. The ceiling above stretched off into abyssal darkness lit faintly by shafts of red light.

"Bailey!"

He glanced back.

"We should go. I don't want to get stuck or cornered!"

"Stay here if you like," Bailey said. "I'll only be a moment."

Up and up and up the pathway wound. Bailey's footsteps echoed and soon he was gasping, his hair growing shiny with sweat. The pathway became narrower, its curves tighter, and he glanced down to see the ground dozens of metres below. Without a barrier between him and the fall, he gulped back the vertigo and forced himself not to look again. But still he pressed on, with the Riftmaster walking close behind him, brows knotted. Finally, an opening loomed ahead.

Bailey stepped out and into an empty room, decorated with copper tapestries of the city.

A single exoskeleton slumped beneath a window arch, drapes of blue-dyed linen threaded with copper beads.

Bailey stepped up beside the ancient remains and looked out to the distance. He saw nothing but the empty horizon, clouds creeping across the sky.

"There's nothing here," Bailey said, the disappointment in his voice tangible. "Perhaps we should try looking somewhere else."

"Bailey…" the Riftmaster said gently. "Maybe it's time to stop. You'll never know the full truth."

Bailey turned to face his mentor. "But if I don't, who will?"

"Bailey… this isn't your world."

"If you don't care about this, why did you come with me?" A sharp jab of indignance made Bailey's voice shrill. It startled him.

The Riftmaster's expression clouded. "I might not care about finding answers," he said as he moved towards Bailey's side, voice gentling. "But I care that you're hurting yourself by trying to find them." The Riftmaster didn't look at him, watching the sandstorm slowly drift by. "I wouldn't be here if I didn't."

Bailey opened his mouth to speak, but no sound came out. He swallowed, and suddenly felt his heart tighten. "What if this is Earth?" he said, voice small. "You said that time is fluid, out here; in the Rift."

"It's not Earth, Bailey. You've seen the skeletons."

"But Earth could become this, one day."

The Riftmaster said nothing. He looked up, and just for a moment, their eyes met.

Bailey swallowed and clamped his eyes shut. "This place feels like home again, and not in a good way." He opened them again, gazing through tear-blurred vision out at the deep red horizon. "This planet, it's everything I was afraid of: hot and deserted, its people dead and skies cloudy with dust." He glanced down at the slumped, linen-draped exoskeleton beside him. "But no-one important would do anything about it. I remember being one of thousands of voices clamouring to be heard, but no-one listening. And now that I'm gone..."

"You're just one person, Bailey. Don't think of that responsibility as wholly yours."

Bailey looked down, tears shimmering on his cheeks. "I tried picking rubbish from the beach, but more would turn up the next day. The weather was getting nicer, but that's because the world was getting hotter. Soon, it will be like this." Bailey let out a deep breath. "Even if I do make it back to Earth, what if I'm too late?"

"Bailey, you can try as hard as you want, but the weight of an entire planet is too much for one person to carry. Sometimes, what you're doing just won't be enough. And that's okay." The Riftmaster sighed. "Some people back on Earth would call me callous, but sometimes you need to be selfish. Take care of yourself first. Do you understand?"

"Riftmaster…"

The Riftmaster reached up and, after a moment's hesitation, patted his apprentice's arm. "All that matters now is that you're alive, and that you're still taking the time to care. Sometimes, that's enough." He looked out again over the labyrinth of stone, the winding pathways that were so small from up here, like insect tracks in the dirt.

There was a momentary pause.

"For now, just look at this place, Rifthopper. Look at the view! If nothing else, at least you'll have a story to tell your apprentice, one day."

They glanced each other's way for a moment, before the Riftmaster looked back out over the city.

Bailey looked exhausted. He spoke as if he didn't quite believe his own words. "That's… that's true." But as the light fell on his face, hope glittered in his brown eyes. A long silence reigned between them. "Riftmaster?"

"Mh-hm?"

"I'm sorry I said you didn't care."

"That's okay, I… understand. I've been alone a long time. I forget that not everyone thinks like I do."

Bailey dipped his head. "How about we head back to camp? We can gather food, harvest our herbs, and then," he glanced out to the horizon. "There were other cities on the map. Perhaps the others will have more for us."

The Riftmaster smiled.

"Sounds like a plan. We don't want to outstay our welcome."

The Riftmaster stepped aside to give him room to move. As they took their places side by side, Bailey noticed the Riftmaster's shoulders relax, and he looked happy at the opportunity to get back to their usual routine. "With any luck, the Rift will take us to somewhere prettier, next time," he said.

Bailey nodded, glancing at his mentor out of the corner of his eye. Before stepping onto the twisting walkway, he felt a flicker of bemusement.

*I've told you about my life, about Earth. You know everything right down to my deepest fears. I have no secrets—but after all these months, I feel like I don't know a thing about you. Not your Earth name, not your history—not even the name of your last apprentice.*

Sensing Bailey's stare, his mentor looked up curiously. "What?"

Bailey let out a breath. "It's nothing," he said with a small smile.

After a moment's hesitation, the Riftmaster smiled back. The expression seemed to hide nothing away.

*You don't need to tell me anything,* Bailey finally decided. *As long as you keep us both alive, I suppose I don't have a choice but to trust you.*

Bailey shook his head to dispel the thoughts and stepped out into the lead. But as he did so, the Riftmaster let out a stifled snort, and Bailey realised that a single hapless creature still clung to the back of his cloak.

# Mizmor L'David

## Dorian Yosef Weber

Content Warnings: Deadnaming, Blood, Violence, Animal Death, Referenced Past Ableism and Transphobia, Brief Mention of a Dead Parent (Father), Unsafe Binding

Author's Note:

I feel so lucky to get to share this story about Jewish trans and autistic identity with you all. In the current political climate, tensions are high between trans people and many of our communities, and Orthodox Judaism is no exception. It's exhausting to never know whether or not your own people have your back, or even worse, to watch them turn away from you when allies are so crucial. Now more than ever, it's crucial to both claim the often little ground we have in our traditions as well as carve out spaces in the stories that have been passed down for generations. Autistic and/or trans people have always been important, valuable members of their communities. We have always been here, and we always will. I hope this story can be a testament to that in the face of all of the people in power who treat us like we're lesser.

# Mizmor L'David

Dorian Yosef Weber

I HEARD WHAT the people in town said about me when they didn't think I was listening. They said I had a dybbuk clinging to my back. If that was true, then dybbukim weren't nearly as bad as people made them out to be.

My dybbuk never made me hurt anyone, or lie, or say cruel things. And even when I did things that no one else in the shtetl did, it was never anything scary. But when I flapped my hands, or rocked back and forth, or slapped my palms against my skull, I heard what they said.

*"Dybbuk."*

If dybbukim were real, and I did have one attached to me, then I learned one thing about them that I had not seen written in any book yet: they did not frighten sheep.

Every morning, I woke with the sun, washed myself, and rewrapped my chest in the fabric that I used to flatten it during the day. I had begun doing this a month ago. The idea had come to me after I tore up a shirt I had worn through, meaning to use it for rags, and somehow ended up with long strips instead. I had never been comfortable with my breasts, nor dresses, but I was happier now that I had begun wrapping my chest underneath the men's clothes that I bought from Yaakov, the town's tailor.

Usually, I then opened the sheep pen that hugged the side of my house and drove my flock onto the rolling field that my family's cottage squatted on. I had inherited the small, cosy building after my father died and I took up his shepherd's crook. The wood of the heavy staff was lightened by the sun and worn smooth by my father's hands. It was beautiful, and pleasant to touch.

But every so often, there was a morning when I first visited the beit midrash in the synagogue to trade the book I had finished reading for another. There were already boys studying there last time I had stopped by, sitting in pairs with Talmud volumes that I had tried and failed to read propped up in front of them. They had stopped outright whispering about the "girl in pants" in the beit midrash when I entered by now, but there were still glares shot my way as I went to the back corner with its more accessible rabbinic books.

Yaakov, as usual, sat nestled back in the corner farthest from the door, flanked on either side by bookshelves that flared out from him like wings. He was the only boy I ever saw study without a chavruta. He looked up and smiled as I approached.

"Hello, friend," he said. He always called me things like that, never using the name I had been given as a child that the other people in the village called me. I was fairly sure that he knew who I truly was, but neither of us ever talked about it. I didn't care much what I was called; it made little difference what my name was when I was alone in the fields with my flock. Still, the gesture was kind of him.

"Finished that book already?" he asked, gesturing at the volume under my arm.

"Yes," I said as I put it back on the shelf and grabbed a new one that didn't look familiar. I tended to enjoy anything I found back here, and even if I did not, I could still entertain myself by raging about it to my flock.

"Your sheep is doing well," I told him as I flipped through the new book I had chosen. I skimmed the text until I was sure that I hadn't read it before and, once satisfied, I hugged it to my chest. "Her lamb is growing quickly too. The two of them are very healthy."

Yaakov was one of the few people who didn't roll their eyes at me when I brought up their livestock.

"Oh, I'm so glad!" He beamed. "I have you to thank for that, you know. You care for the sheep well. I've seen you with them. They all adore you."

A surge of warmth burned through me at his words. When I was younger, I hated feeling happy or excited because of the way that it seared through me, scalding me from the inside out.

Yaakov had sat with me during my father's shiva and told me about someone he'd met during his apprenticeship who had worked through their feelings through textures and movements and vocalisations. My father hated it when I did anything like that as a child, but after he died, I could do what I wanted. The next time I felt overwhelmed, I let my body move in whatever way it wanted to, and found that when I didn't suppress the physical expression of my emotion, I radiated my joy into the air around me. Now that I knew what I'd been missing all along, the heat that remained in my veins could simmer down to a bubbling, cosy warmth.

I brought my hands up to my shoulders, flapped them like fluttering bird wings, and grinned.

Yaakov smiled back. He had once said that he liked seeing me happy and using the strategies that he had helped me reclaim.

"They love you very much," he said again. "They can tell how much you care for them."

"Good," I said. I lowered my hands, tapping the pads of my pointer and middle fingers against my thumb in rapid succession to work the last sparks of joy out of my system. "I should go let them out to graze now."

"Have fun," Yaakov waved as he hunched back over his Talmud. "If you want to talk about the book, you know where to find me."

I nodded and left. Yaakov knew more than me, and I was often intimidated by it. He was always kind, but it was still sometimes embarrassing for me to talk to him about my learning. He was often in the beit midrash but, if he was not, I would occasionally go to his home tucked on the edge of town, and we would learn together on a bench nearby. I never entered out of consideration for the laws of yichud, but the outside of the house was small. Yaakov lived alone, like me. Sometimes, while on my way to see him, I heard people in the street murmuring among themselves about the fact that he was a bachelor at his age. I could tell by their tone that this was supposed to be a bad thing, but I didn't see why. I was engaged to a man that my father had chosen for me just before succumbing to his illness, but I didn't think there was anything wrong with being alone. My shidduch had asked me the night before to come by his home that evening to talk about something he did not specify, so I could ask him about it then. But before that, I had to let the sheep out to graze.

I walked my practised path through town back home, tapping my crook against the ground as I walked. It was a beautiful day. The sheep bleated impatiently as I let them out, but they stayed near me as I walked them out into the open grass. After they had settled and begun to graze, I sat on the slope of a hill and began to read.

The book was more mystical than what I usually read, but it was intriguing. I was only a few pages in when one of the sheep approached and nudged me. I closed my book on my finger to keep my place. I made quiet kissing sounds at the ewe and scratched the soft patch behind her ear with my free hand.

"Hello, Chrain," I murmured as she slumped down beside me. There was no shochet in town, and moving sheep was too much hassle, so my town just traded all of our wool and fabric for meat instead. That meant I got to raise my sheep with the luxury of naming them all without fear of losing them. Chrain always had been a sweetheart. She lay by me for almost the entire day, only trotting back to her flock a few times to graze a bit more or relieve herself. I leaned my back against her as I read, and she didn't seem to mind.

When the sun began to set, I whistled and rounded the sheep back up. They were a bit rowdier than usual now that their bellies were full, but they let me guide them back into their pen with minimal nudging from my crook. When they were all settled, I said goodbye and went back into town.

My shidduch's house was at the edge of the town square. It was over twice the size of mine. I took a deep breath as I approached his doorstep. I had never enjoyed scheduled conversations if I hadn't already been told what we would be talking about. When I didn't feel as much like I was about to vibrate into pieces, I knocked on the door.

When he opened his door, Ezra's form was a familiar one. He was a short but muscular man, built like the blacksmith he was. I couldn't help but silently prefer Yaakov's slender tailor's fingers to Ezra's large, square hands.

He scratched at his dark stubble and looked at me.

"Tova," he said, and I felt my face twitch. He had been the first and only person who I had outright told that I hated my birth name. He had shouted at me at first, and now he said it every chance he got.

I nodded in greeting at him, eyes fixed on his left cheek.

"How are you?" he asked.

"Fine."

Ezra was breathing deeper than normal, and his shoulders were tense. He hovered in the doorway, shifting on his feet. I was hungry, and wanted to get this over with already.

Ezra took a final heavy breath and spoke. "I know I promised your father that we would marry, but I think I speak for both of us when I say that this is no longer..." He clenched his jaw and swallowed. "A functioning arrangement."

I blinked at him. "Alright."

He studied me, as if I were a beast about to pounce. "I do not wish to marry you any longer."

"That's fine." It made little difference to me. I had told him that I did not like my name, that I did not like going to the synagogue to pray during the Sabbath the way the other wives did, and that I did not want to bear children. With each confession, he would shout insults at me until I ran off into the fields, falling to my knees and rocking back and forth until I felt like myself again. If that meant that he did not want to wed, that was fine.

"I have met another woman," he said, still watching me out of the corner of his eye. "We wed the day after tomorrow."

I started. "How long have you been planning this?" I asked, beginning to feel the first semblances of outrage. The two of them had to have met some time ago if the wedding was set to take place so soon. How had I not known?

He opened his mouth to answer, but was cut off when a voice spoke behind me.

"Ezra," it asked pleasantly, "who is this?" I turned to face whoever had spoken.

"Speaking of my future wife," Ezra chuckled. I barely heard him as it suddenly became much harder to breathe in the crisp night air.

I met the gaze of a woman exactly my height in a pleasant, modest dress. Her long, dark hair was tied back in a scarf, as if she was already married. She was lovely, but I couldn't stop staring in horror at her face. I knew that aquiline nose and those pillowy lips, that small mole on the right cheek. This woman was me, or who I would have been if I had not shorn my curls close to my skull and begun hiding my wide hips underneath formless pants and tunics.

"Hello," the woman said over the ringing in my ears. Her smile was genuine, and it showed her gums exactly the way mine did. A crooked canine poked out between her lips. My tongue went up to probe my own identical tooth. "You're the shepherd, aren't you? My name is Tova."

"Isn't it funny?" Ezra said. I did not look at him. I felt cold despite the warm night air. "She just passed through town recently, and–"

"Are you alright?" Tova asked, head cocked like a bird.

I just kept staring at her. I realised that I was shaking. All of a sudden I was horribly aware of the sensation of my shirt against my back, and the confinement of my shoes, and the smell of stew cooking in Ezra's neighbour's kitchen. Or maybe it was coming from his own home, and he was making something to send off with Tova before the wedding day.

"I'm fine," I choked out.

"You're welcome to come to the wedding," she said, lips pursed in a pretty, concerned little pout. "It's two mornings from now behind the shul. Any friend of Ezra's is a friend of mine."

I had never been good at knowing when people were lying to me. But when Tova spoke, I was certain that she was being entirely honest. I would at least know a lie on my own face.

"Alright," I said. I could feel something deep inside me that was ravenous to see the life I could have had: myself, as a beautiful woman, marrying the wealthy blacksmith and being swept off into a lovely household of challah and shabbat candles that I could finally share with someone else. It felt like I had agreed to attend my own funeral.

I squirmed in my clothing and knew that I couldn't stay here any longer. I pushed past Tova as I fled. I heard her and Ezra shout behind me, but I ignored them as I ran out into my fields, flying so quickly that I stumbled when my feet couldn't keep up underneath me.

As soon as I was free of the shtetl's streets, I fisted my hands in my shirt and tore it off over my head. As I reached my home, I unknotted the fabric wrapped around my torso. The pressure of it usually comforted me, but right now I didn't want anything to be touching me. It felt like I was on fire.

I tore off my shoes as soon as I was inside, pressing my toes against the floor as I undressed the rest of the way. I went to the bed and sat on it, tucking my feet up underneath me and grabbing the strap of tough leather I kept at my bedside. I began gnawing on it, rocking back and forth and letting my hands dance through the air like two flames.

Ezra had to have seen how similar Tova was to me. Where had she come from? I didn't care for Ezra in any romantic sense. I only agreed to marry him to go through with a promise I had made to my father, but I couldn't help but feel insulted by seeing my double brought into Ezra's life to replace me. He had been closer to my father than I had been, and the two of them had never been very kind to me. It had never bothered me until this moment.

I kept gnawing on my leather as my movements slowed to a stop. I didn't feel as if I needed to tear off my skin anymore. My muscles hurt; I must have pulled something as I had writhed. I winced as I stretched out my shoulders. Maybe I was really possessed. Maybe there was a dybbuk inside me that was making me see a similarity between Tova and me when there wasn't any at all, and now it was sending me through monstrous throes of jealousy.

I grimaced as I eased myself to my feet and prepared to go to sleep. I had exhausted myself, and I would need to keep the sheep out for longer tomorrow to make up for the morning they would spend penned up while I attended the wedding. I whined as I felt discomfort well up within me, and my head twitched to the side a few times in response. I tried to distract myself by thinking about my sheep as I lay down and closed my eyes. I missed having them crammed inside the cabin with me the way I did during the coldest winter months. I still needed a name for the new lamb that Yaakov's sheep, who I called

Knish, had birthed this past spring. I finally settled on Knish bat Knish as I fell asleep, because it made me laugh.


The night before Ezra and Tova's marriage, I woke to the sound of something walking outside my cabin. I sat up immediately and listened to the sound of its steps. The gait was so quiet that I couldn't tell if it was animal or human. I slowly crept to the window. I was no stranger to waking in the night and making sure that my sheep were safe. Wolves always waited to strike until the shepherd was asleep.

When I saw that the thing outside was shaped like a person, I sighed in relief. It was always exhausting to beat away wolves with my staff in the dead of night and I was already tired from watching the sheep so late. The figure was walking in the direction of my flock though, and I tensed, ready to go out and confront a thief. But they kept walking past the pen and toward the treeline where the field gave way to forest.

I watched until they disappeared into the trees, and then quietly crept out of my cabin to follow. Usually, I didn't care much about the goings-on of other people in town. But I was on edge from meeting Tova, and whoever this was, they had passed through my land. I wanted to see this through.

There was silence from the woods until I reached the treeline. When I was close enough to reach out and touch the nearest trunk, there was a loud, awful squeal that echoed through the clearing. I froze. I knew the sound of the wild boars that lived in these woods, and that was the sound of one in horrible pain. The cry cut off with an unnatural abruptness, and then there was silence but for the gentle hooting of an owl.

I don't know how long I stood there, but eventually the same footsteps that had awoken me earlier approached from somewhere within the shadows between the trees. I tucked myself behind a trunk, cloaking myself in darkness, as the mysterious figure emerged from the forest. I couldn't see anything but their back as they walked away from me. But a little ways out, they paused and turned their face to their shoulder, head tilted up as if they were scenting the air.

From their profile I could make out two things: it was Tova, and the entire lower half of her face was covered in blood.


It seemed as if the whole shtetl showed up to Ezra and Tova's wedding the next morning. That wasn't a surprise; I could imagine that Ezra breaking off our engagement and marrying a strange girl from another town was causing a lot of talk. Tova was a common enough name, I supposed, but I wondered if anyone else noticed the striking resemblance she bore to me.

On my way over to the women's side of the crowd, I spotted Yaakov arriving on the men's side. He waved, but didn't smile. I was not in a mood to talk to anyone, especially Yaakov. I hadn't slept at all after seeing Tova, bloody in the moonlight, run through the fields back into town. I was exhausted, but I had said I would attend this wedding, so that was what I would do. I sat towards the back, cradling my crook to my chest, and my neighbours thankfully gave me the usual wide berth.

When Tova appeared in her white dress, I heard gasps and coos. She smiled bashfully and ducked her head as she walked to the chuppah. I couldn't help but stare at the way the gown fell over her waist and underarms. I could see the hint of breasts in the way that the fabric draped across the plane of her chest, and I shifted in my seat, tugging at my top in a useless effort to hide my curves. Seeing their exact copies on someone else made me feel like I was about to vomit.

I thought again of the state I had seen Tova in last night. She didn't seem to be wounded, so the blood must not have been her own. I wondered if I should tell someone about what I had witnessed, but dismissed the thought. Her relationship was none of my business.

The nissuin was perfect in every respect. Ezra had his eyes on Tova as she circled him. His gaze was soft, and he wore a small smile that nevertheless reached his eyes. He had never looked at me like that.

The couple drank from the same cup, Ezra gave Tova her ring and the ketubah was read. I couldn't help but admire its intricate decoration as it was held up for the audience to see. It must have taken weeks to illustrate. Ezra had been hiding Tova from me for weeks.

I wasn't angry because I wanted to be the one under the chuppah, but it was humiliating that he saw me as someone who wasn't even important enough to inform about his new engagement. I was easily confused in regards to the finer intricacies of conversation, something Ezra had never hesitated to remind me of, but this was straightforward. Ezra was just a coward.

I sat silently through the sheva brachot, and a glass was brought out and set on the ground beside Ezra. When he stomped on it, the sound of the crunch sent a pleasant tingle up my spine. I tried to focus on that as the crowd shouted "mazel tov!" so loudly that I felt as if their voices echoed against the blue dome of the sky.

Ezra and Tova turned and stepped out from beneath the chuppah, and I rose from my chair, preparing to leave. As I stood, Tova looked at me and smiled. Then she was gone. There was no slow vanishing; it felt as if I had only blinked and then Tova had disappeared.

In her place crouched a lioness.

The crowd around me screamed and fled. I didn't see where any of them went. My feet were rooted in place as shoulders brushed past me, their owners running to safety. I just stood, frozen, watching Ezra and the beast.

It took Ezra a few seconds to register the disappearance of his wife's shadow where it had been cast against him, and a few more to realise what had happened. By the time horror began to dawn in his eyes, the lioness roared and pounced on him, wrapping her front legs around his torso and burying her teeth in the crook of his shoulder. In every drawing of the Lion of Judah I had ever seen, the artists had never conveyed just how large lions' paws were.

When Ezra had been knocked prone in the dirt, he started to scream.

The lion pinned him down, holding his shoulders down with her paws, and she roared in his face. I could see the blood welling up where her claws dug into Ezra's muscle. It stained his black, spotless wedding clothes in dark blotches that slowly seeped into more and more of the cloth. He didn't stop screaming as his voice went raw, his body writhing like a reptile beneath the feline.

The lion changed again, this time back into something humanoid. Clawed hands dragged Ezra back to his feet and clutched him so his back was pressed against the thing's featureless, mottled grey chest. It turned so that they both faced me, and I could take in the monster's whole form.

Uncloven hooves led up into legs with knees that bent backwards. Its limbs were long and thin. It didn't have a nose, just two nostrils, and its lipless, smiling mouth was full of fangs. It stared at me with hooded, startling blue eyes that were almost identical to a human's. But the way this thing held itself had not changed. This was still Tova, but she was no woman.

She was a sheyd. A demon.

I shivered. I knew the Deuteronomy verse about women dressing as men. An "abomination," it said. I had gone to Yaakov weeping when I had first read the verse, but he had reassured me. He told me about the psak that rules that the verse forbids pretending you're someone you aren't in order to deceive others. It protects against lascivious behaviour, but I was just being who I was.

Ezra had told me that the way I dressed was unnatural and dishonest, except I wasn't lying to anyone, and Yaakov had told me that I was still a good person, but now a sheyd was here for me–

"You broke your vow," the sheyd snarled, face turned in towards Ezra, eyes still fixed on me. Ezra whimpered as it dug its claws a little deeper into him. "You swore to provide for a man's child, and you did not. You broke the engagement in secret to serve your own lust, and did nothing to provide for the one that you abandoned." Ezra was openly weeping now.

I took a deep breath and let the sheyd's words settle within me. It was not here for me. It was here for Ezra.

"Tova," he whimpered, wrenching his torso side to side as he fought the sheyd's hold. I could tell that the struggle was hopeless from where I stood. Ezra had always been the tallest man in the room, but the sheyd was a little over a head above him, and its arms looked to grip like iron despite its sinewy build. "Tova, please help me."

I took a step toward the two of them. When the sheyd said nothing, watching me with unblinking eyes, I took another. And another.

Ezra sobbed in relief as I approached. I watched his meaty, calloused hands clench and unclench. He had always loomed over me while reproaching me if I flapped my hands or didn't catch a turn-of-phrase that seemed to be instinctively understood by everyone but me. He didn't look so imposing now.

I stopped when Ezra's yarmulke was at my feet. It must have been knocked off when he'd been bowled over by the lioness. I had never enjoyed looking into people's eyes, but I met Ezra's gaze now. His expression was pleading, but I didn't know what he wanted from me. The bite on the side of his neck was still gushing blood. I realised as I looked at him that I didn't know how old he was. He was only a few years older than me, a little over twenty, but I didn't know the exact number. This was the first time I had ever felt that he looked young.

I broke eye contact, and bent down. I picked the yarmulke up off the ground and pressed it to my lips. I held it there for several heartbeats, and then straightened. I put the yarmulke on my head, and looked at Ezra again. For the first time, I knew my name. I tilted up my chin.

"My name," I said, "is David."

Ezra's face twisted in revulsion, and he opened his mouth to speak. Before he could say anything, the sheyd's wings spread with a leathery snap and it took off into the air, still clutching Ezra. He cried out, and I watched in silence as the sheyd flew away with greater speed than any bird I had ever seen. I did not move until their silhouettes disappeared over the horizon and the echoes of Ezra's screams and pleas had faded.

"So," a voice said behind me, "David."

I turned around and saw Yaakov peering around the corner of the shul.

"Yes," I said, and shook my excitement out of my hands with a motion like I was flicking off water after netilat yadayim. I hadn't realised how nice it would be to hear someone say my name aloud.

Yaakov approached me slowly, glancing hesitantly up at the sky as he emerged from the shadow of the shul. I braced myself, ready for him to shout, to tell me that he did not want to see me again. I just hoped that he would let me keep watching over his sheep.

"Well, David," he said, tilting his face up toward the sky and propping his hands on his hips, "I think this means I'm going to need to rethink all of the learning I've done about sheydim."

I couldn't help but laugh.

Yaakov smirked at me, glancing over out of the corner of his eye. "Feel free to come by the beit midrash if you want to read about them together. Now, if you'll excuse me, I think I need to sleep off the emotions that Hashem is graciously allowing me to keep down until I am alone."

He turned toward his house, walked a few paces, and then stopped.

"That yarmulke looks good on you, David," he said over his shoulder. He spoke my name with tender reverence, as if it was something he relished saying. Now that I had heard my name on someone else's lips, I wasn't sure how I had lived so long without it. "You look like yourself."

And, with that, he left.

I shook my hands a few more times and whispered my name to myself over and over. I felt a bit of guilt as I looked down at the blood on the ground that Ezra had left behind. My head snapped to the side a few times as I whimpered until the feeling lessened enough to be tolerable. I could see what Yaakov had meant about his feelings. I looked away from the dark brown spot where dry dirt had turned into sanguine mud and began walking back towards my home. There was nothing that I could have done before or could do now. It was not my concern what punishments Ezra brought down upon his own head.

I said my name a few more times as I made my way through the eerily silent streets and felt sunlight filter through my chest as I stomped my feet. Once the buzzing in my nerves had died down, having sufficiently been deposited into the ground by my heavy steps, I began to run back to my cabin. It was already late in the morning, and I needed to let the sheep out.

# The Ghost on Oxford Street

## Riley Swan

Content Warnings: Depictions of Gender Dysphoria, Autistic
Meltdowns, Alcohol Use, Homophobia, Transphobia, HIV/AIDS,
Suicide, Murder, Death

Author's Note:

Once you tear through the gritty flesh of this story, you will find a
tender, beating heart—this is my ode to autistic, trans mascs, trans
fems, and lesbians. I am so grateful to be in community with you.
Sending all my love.

# The Ghost on Oxford Street

Riley Swan

IT SUCKS TO spend sixty dollars on a binder only for wearing it to feel like actual death. Excitement had followed me like a trail of pixie dust when the doorbell rang, and it glistened on my skin when I ripped the package open.

Now, standing in front of my full-length mirror, a dark cloud has settled over me, this miserable thing showering me with cry-baby tears. They stain my red cheeks, and I have to look away from my own reflection.

When I can't see my ridiculous chest, I pull the ridiculous flesh-toned fabric off, ditching it in my overflowing laundry basket. The sports bra I slip on is much more comfortable.

I can look in the mirror again, seeing my short brown hair and chubby thighs, and not feel like tearing off my own skin with blunt nails until everything bleeds.

That's the thing about being both trans and autistic—the pieces don't fit.

It's a harrowing thought to have. Especially on my birthday.

My phone buzzes in the back pocket of my denim shorts. I pull it out, and a smile blooms on my cheeks when the screen lights up. Thank god for good morning texts from Killara (or, as she's listed in my phone, 'love of my life').

Love of my life: good morning, my wonderful garnet! happy birthday!!! i love you, and im going to kiss you eighteen times as soon as i see you. until then, have an awesome day :)

Me: thank you, baby, and i can't wait to see you <3

At least I have that to put some pep in my step. It makes me feel a little more alright when I slip on the biggest hoodie I can find. It's in a bright shade of pink and my chest is still starkly outlined by the fabric, but Killara is always a good distraction from the pain.

Whatever. I want pancakes for breakfast. Extra syrup. And whipped cream.


Killara walks through my front door in the late afternoon, this glorious being in a yellow sundress, with her coils of dark brown hair wrapped up by a white scarf, and it's the best present of all. I pointedly ignore the blue, pink and white gift bag in her grip. It's better than the pile of unwrapped presents sitting on my bedroom floor (though I'm still eternally grateful for them, of course).

"You're wearing pink," she says in lieu of a greeting before kissing me on the forehead.

Darkness settles in. *It looks bad. She'll think you're not trans enough. You're just a girl, Garnet. You're not actually non-binary. A non-binary person would never look like you. A non-binary person would never wear pink—*

A hug pulls me back into the light. Killara's warmer than the sun that brushes across my face, crossing over the threshold through the open front door.

"Happy birthday," she whispers, giving me one last squeeze.

"Thanks," I force out as we pull back, and even after two years of dating, we do an awkward dance to close the door and saunter down the hallway to my mess of a room. "So, uh…"

"Garnet," she sing-songs, dragging out the word like there's a river on her tongue, only to pause as she dramatically falls onto my bed. "Come, sit next to me."

I stare at her from the doorframe where my hip digs into the wall. The sleeve of my jumper is wrapped around my fingers, traipsing across the skin in a soothing pattern over and over until it's tingly and numb.

"Okay," I say, gravitating toward her, crossing my legs once I'm sitting on my mattress.

She smiles. It's this gorgeous thing, bright and real, pulling at her cheeks. I'm forced to stop ignoring the multicoloured gift bag in her hands now because she pushes it into my lap, positively glowing.

We have this tradition of getting each other a dozen little gifts. This year there's a whole pile. A strawberry-scented candle. Fluffy bed socks. Silver hoop earrings. A book on Australian LGBTQ+ history. My favourite chocolate in a mega-block. A gift card for the cafe around the corner. Then, my personal favourite, a handmade card, covered in scrap paper, crayon drawings, stickers, and whatever Polaroid photo Killara deemed worthy of being front and centre.

But this card is thick, bulging in the middle. I open it, and the perfect scripts begins with 'Dear Garnet', and ends with ' Love, Killara', though all I can focus on is the pin taped to the centre of the page in the same colour scheme as the gift bag.

Blue, pink and, white.

The transgender pride flag.

In the centre is a thick white stripe, and etched into that blank line are blocky, black letters: 'THEY/THEM'. Something hot and sour slides in my throat, and I have to bite back tears. My grip tightens around the card and I have to drop it before I rip the treasured thing.

Killara is watching me, tentative, hesitant, and I basically jump into her arms. I've never held onto her so tight. She believes me. My openly transfem girlfriend believes me. My queer activist girlfriend bought me a book on LGBTQ+ history, and then gave me a god damned pronoun pin.

I'm non-binary. Killara believes me.

It doesn't extract all the anxiety and paranoia and fear from my body, but when I say, "I love you," and Killara says it back, something lightens in me.

When no one else sees me for who I am, at least I know Killara Jackson always will.


Just because I prepared for clubbing over a month in advance, doesn't mean I'm *ready*. The Love Club is a place that is so dark and so bright at the same time, flashing a dozen colours and blasting what feels like five hundred different beats at once. There's a progress pride flag on the wall above the bar though, which soothes the fire in my gut just a little.

I'm here with my friends. In a gay club. It's on Oxford Street, for fuck's sake! I'll be fine. Just keep my earplugs in, and stay off to the side with the tables, and I'll be fine.

Killara and I sit in a booth while the rest of the group goes to get shots.

My girlfriend won't drink. Her mum had a history of addiction, and she doesn't want to risk it. I'm not sure how my autism will handle even a drop of alcohol, so I'm not drinking either.

We're here for the experience, mostly. It's so wonderful to be in a place plastered by LGBTQ+ history. Even the lady at the bar, with the tattoos and moles and ponytails, is donning two pins: the lesbian flag and her pronouns. It's so safe here. A haven.

"Look at that," I say, head tilted upward, as I point at the wall over our table. "So cool."

Killara's joy radiates off of her as we stare up at lines of framed photographs, all in faded black and white, age clear in the grainy quality of each person's smile.

The first is an image of two Indigenous men holding up a sign that reads 'GAY RIGHTS ARE HUMAN RIGHTS' in wonky, painted letters. Beneath it is printed text in a serif font, so small I have to squint to read it. My heart pulses hard against my ribs when it registers. 'Sydney Mardi Gras, 1978.'

"Holy shit," Killara whispers, mesmerised. "That's… that was the *first* Sydney Mardi Gras. And it's *two Indigenous men*. Holy shit."

I've never heard her voice so threadbare, vulnerable and wet with the beginning of tears.

My whole body aches at the sight of any LGBTQ+ pride at all. I can't imagine how it must feel for her to be seeing people just like her existing in our history, loud and proud on the streets, and now on the wall of this gay club.

We link hands across the table as our eyes scan over the rest of the images. A sapphic couple kissing. A butch lesbian with a buzzcut in steel-cap boots. Quite a few more images of couples and groups holding signs and banners with various activism quotes. There's one, third from the right on the very bottom row, of a short, fat person holding up a sign that reads 'BREAK THE BINARY'. I'm not sure what their gender is. Not that it's good to assume, but I've seriously never seen someone so androgynous-looking according to society's standards.

The image is dated 1986. Apparently, their name is Chris.

There's a slam on our wooden table that shakes Killara and me apart.

"Shots, baby!" yells my friend Micah, voice high, before throwing what must be a mouthful of vodka back into his throat. "Nice."

He's unfazed by the alcohol, smiling under the pink lights, and I can't help but admire how the shade beats down on his dark skin and bright dress in a way that makes him look like a model.

Killara and I's other two friends and Micah's friends from Queensland, all take a shot too, in varying degrees of excitement: from mild displeasure to being totally pumped. Killara and I laugh and watch, merely bobbing our heads to the music.

We have a good time. Really, we do.

Until everything falls apart.

Killara disappears to get us both new cans of Coke, and this horrible, hyper-pop song starts, eating through the speakers with its electricity. It's strong, and well-received on the dance floor. The crowd becomes a mosh of drunk dance moves under a glittering disco ball, rainbow lights coming from every direction. My brain hates it.

My entire body feels like it's being stabbed at with a dozen knives, scratching at skin and veins and heart, and I need to get the fuck out of here before I explode.

With my hands clawing at my ears, pushing the earplugs further in, I slide out of the booth and to my knees. There's liquid on my face, wet and cold, and then it's on my tongue too, salty and sad.

The skin of my legs feels raw now, and I have to stagger away from the tables, further from the relentless rhythm, into a dark hallway that honestly feels like a weighted blanket. It leads to three doors, all covered in tacky posters and stickers, and I feel like the protagonist of a middle-grade adventure novel.

Which door do I take? Which one will lead me to my destiny?

Away from the worst of the noise, I reach for the stim necklace tucked beneath my shirt, slipping it between my teeth. Then I wipe my eyes, fingers coming back wet with tears. At least my vision isn't so blurred now.

I look at the three doors again.

They're just bathrooms.

Women. Gender Neutral. Men.

The decision-making parts of myself all conflict with one another. My legs simply carry me through the door in the middle.

Inside, I immediately lean against the door, slumping downward until I hit the floor, bringing my knees to my chest.

My chest, which is… not what it usually is. Where I always find bundles of fat weighing me down, I find nothing but hard bone wrapped up by soft skin, hidden by the layers of my clothes. I can't believe it. My legs go right back down so I can touch it with my hands, make sure it's real.

All that's under my touch is a flat chest. I can't believe it.

Not even bothering to check if anyone else is in here, I lift my shirt to look at my body. There really aren't any boobs there. Or even scars from some form of surgery. It's as if that part of my body never stretched out and re-formed itself at all.

I shove myself off the floor, breaths panting out of me still, and go to reach for the door handle, utterly spooked, only to find nothing there. It's just a wall.

A quick survey of the small bathroom, lined by three old stalls and a singular sink, tells me there isn't a door in here at all.

My eyes flutter shut, air flowing into my lungs as I count to ten, so the fired-up feeling in my stomach stops simmering like a pan pulled over a stove's low heat.

When I open them, standing before me is a short person with a pitch-black mullet, body half ducked out of the stall furthest away. They're a bit faded, fake. When I squint, I can see right through them, reading a few legible words on the sticker tacked onto the door behind them.

My eyes widen as my body stills, and I awkwardly reach up for my chest, like someone seeing me without it is too new, too different, too intimate.

"Cool," they say, voice croaky, like a teenage boy during his first week of puberty, "isn't it, bud?"

"What the fuck!" I shriek. "Who are you?" I wave at their body as it fades in and out before me. "How are you here?" I gesture at what used to be the door behind me.

"What," I whisper, and I finally notice that my voice is much deeper now, "the *fuck*."

"I'm Chris," the person says. "Chris Voskanyan." Then they come out from behind the wall, standing before me in all their five foot two glory, with a round belly and the coolest suit I've ever seen. "To answer your other question; I'm always here. Have been since 1986." A smile spreads across their cheeks. "The real question, Garnet, is why *you're* here."


After another near-explosive meltdown in the literal escape room I'm trapped in, which the person in here with me apparently hasn't left in over three decades, I desperately need to pee. When I do, the anatomy of my lower body has changed too. It's the same as it was before, but with some… developments.

This is the first club I've been to, but it's certainly a weird one. I'm not sure how I'd even compare it to others, even if I only ever attended them through the eyes of fictional characters.

When I come back out, Chris is waiting for me, leaning against the edge of the sink. I sneak in right beside them, washing soapy bubbles and water over my hands, then lean against the other edge. I cross my arms.

"Why am I here, then?" I ask. "And who told you my name?"

"You only have so much time here, Garnet," they say. "Let's not waste it on random bullshit. There are much grittier things to dig into."

"Like why I'm here?"

Chris laughs, hearty and real. It sounds like what you'd expect from a father after tucking you into bed, only to be the one told a fairy-tale instead of reading one.

They turn to face the mirror, perfecting the stray hairs of their mullet, and ensuring their bright purple button-up is tucked into their dress pants. "Yes," they say, almost more to their own reflection than me.

It's like searching for needles in a haystack, but with my hands tied behind my back and a blindfold over my eyes. "Dear god, just tell me–"

I'm interrupted by a sound like tumbling bricks as Chris swipes a single finger over the glass before us, and the room transforms, making me stumble to the ground.

This is my worst birthday ever.

Except I'm not on the ground. I'm in a plastic chair.. One of those rickety old ones they shove aside for kids to use as spares when one mysteriously disappears from the English classroom.

Chris is beside me in a chair of their own, still in the same suit, but their hair now pulled back into a man bun and a chocolate muffin in their hand. They hold it out in my direction.

"Want one?"

I'm too focused on all the others sitting in our circle to answer. All of them are dressed in suits or other manly clothing, just like Chris, chomping down on chips or sipping cans of beer. On the wall behind them is the rainbow flag. Like, the original one, designed by Gilbert Baker.

There's the softest scent of cigarette smoke lingering in the air, and a low hum of eighties pop music coming from somewhere to my right.

When I look back at Chris, their entire muffin is gone, but they're holding another two. They extend one to me, and then the other one to the person beside them. "This is Jordie, Love, and Mateo," Chris says. "We're in 1982."

"Um." I swallow hard. "Hi?"

The three people before me—a girl that looks like Chris, an Indigenous boy with a shaved head and painted nails, and a person wearing a denim jacket with the Gilbert Baker pride flag and the Argentinian flag painted onto either sleeve—offer welcoming waves.

"Nice to meet you, Garnet," says the girl, Jordie, "We've seen so much about you."

After swallowing a mouthful of warm chocolate, I say, "What?"

"We've been watching you," Love says, then clarifies: "not in a creepy way." He smiles. "But we knew you needed our help. The same way we did when we were your age. It's not easy being queer in Australia. It's not easy being queer at all."

"I mean, yeah," I say, eating more of my muffin. "But that doesn't explain why I'm currently *in 1982*."

Chris sighs. "I knew you'd be a hard one," they say.

I go to ask more questions, because I may as well live up to that assumption, but Chris is already swiping their finger in the air like a mime, perfectly pressing against an invisible screen.

Chris disappears.

Everything around me changes. Everything but Mateo, who still sits across from me, now on the opposite side of a long table, surrounded by a dozen other strangers. A massive platter of empanadas takes up the space between Mateo and me, hands reaching in from every direction to grab at them. There are choripanes to the left, and matambre arrollado to the right. Everyone laughs and talks and sings as they dig into a meal made for too many people to count.

Mateo smiles across the way, reaching for an empanada. My eyes flicker over a patch near the bottom of their jacket: ZE/HIR.

To my surprise, ze splits the empanada in half with a clean snap, handing me one piece, beef threatening to spill over the edges. "Here you go," ze says.

I take it happily, chomping down, pleased to find the delicious, tangy flavour isn't tainted by the chocolate I inhaled what must have been seconds ago. But then I remember the flat feeling of my chest. The rules don't apply to the club bathroom, and it makes sense. I don't know where I am, exactly, but it's got a bit of magic to it.

No one talks to me specifically, but I'm not excluded either. There's a flurry of conversation passing around the table, as everyone passes down bowls and sauces and drinks and further laughter, further joy.

That is, until the foxhole radio on the kitchen counter crackles, before a deep, old voice booms from the massive speaker over top of the circular dial.

"According to a newly published report by the United States of America's Centre for Disease Control, also known as the CDC, there have been five new cases of Pneumocytis Carinii Pneumonia among young, healthy men in Los Angeles. Two of them have died, and the others are in unstable conditions.

"In the past year, we've all become accustomed to the new form of pneumonia, and the links it has to the homosexual lifestyle expressed in the United States of America. But today, we mourn our beautiful Australian lands, which have been tainted with the first case of this Gay-Related Immune Deficiency, which many also refer to as GRID. This homosexual disease has been killing men for a year, and now it has come to Sydney too. We do not know how long we have until it takes this young, healthy man's life, a man who was believed to be completely normal by his family until his recent diagnosis. I'm sure they will mourn him as we mourn our country, once unaffected by something so evil, now falling prey to the beast that is homosexuality."

This once boisterous and welcoming house, is now replaced with silence, like someone's just died and this is the funeral.

It's 1982, and people *have* died.

No one else in this room knows it, but I do. Today marks the beginning of an epidemic in Australia. People have died across the water, and now people will die here too.

As vile as the man on the radio is, he's right about that. It will take lives.

Everyone looks at Mateo as tears stream down hir cheeks, and then I remember the flags on hir denim jacket, letting them burn into my eyes. Hir whole family knows; ze doesn't fit into the norm, and now people just like hir are contracting something that kills them.

They don't even know the gritty details. They don't know about all the deaths that will come, rising in numbers, and the horrible things people will say and do. They don't know about the protests that Mateo will likely attend, risking hir life just to be there. They don't know about David Wojnarowicz's slogan: 'IF I DIE OF AIDS – FORGET BURIAL – JUST DROP MY BODY ON THE STEPS OF THE

FDA.' How it could apply to the person they love, all the way here in Australia.

Still, the entirety of them move around the table until they're all bunched up to the left and right of Mateo, behind hir, anywhere near hir, as close as they can be. It's generations of love, from ages ninety to zero, with all different shades of sun-kissed skin and emotions etched into their features from so long feeling them.

I watch, almost distantly, like I'm sitting on a couch and this is my television screen. Tears build up in the corners of my eyes, soppy and wet and insistent. So I let them fall.

"We won't let anything happen to you, Mijo," says an older woman with wrinkled brown skin and gorgeous curls, reaching out to rub her thumb over Mateo's salt-streaked cheek. "No matter how different you are, we won't let anything happen to you. We won't stop loving you."

A young boy reaches up to hold Mateo's other cheek. It's so messed up seeing such a young child supporting someone so much older than them. Likely an older sibling. It's *so* messed up.

My stomach curls in on itself, and I fear I'll vomit the empanadas right back up, until the scene freezes before me, and Chris steps in from my right. They reach a hand out over Mateo and hir family, and I open my mouth to protest, to beg to stay, but I don't even get the first word out before they're swiping a single finger and everything is fading to black.


When I come to, Chris is gone. Again. So is Mateo.

Now with me is Love.

He's not sat across from me—he's to my left. We're both sitting in small, squishy chairs, with miniature wooden tables hovering over our laps. In front of us, hundreds more people file into the room, taking their own seats in front of a massive whiteboard. The date is etched in the top corner with a marker: '27/09/83'. Time has moved along. Or maybe I have moved ahead of time.

The lecturer is an old white man, and he scribbles things on the board for everyone to see as he talks about The Catcher in The Rye, a book I'm surprised to remember I've actually read.

He asks questions about the main character, Holden Caulfield, and people raise their hands to answer them. *His wants were… While his need was… The development he made serves…* on and on and on.

Love doesn't talk to me at all, too engrossed by the lecture, taking down every note he can. Beside his split-open notepad is a decaying copy of the book itself, curling at the corners to reveal yellowed pages, tearing and softening at the edges, several pages marked by dog ears and receipts. It's so well loved. Love loves this book. Love loves to love this book.

Then, the old man at the front of the class speaks with a shaky, wrinkled voice. "And can someone explain to me Holden Caulfield's ideological stance?"

Love lights up, eyes widening with brightness and teeth jutting out in a genuine grin. He raises his hand without hesitation, pale brown skin raising into the air, nails painted a pitch black that's already chipping away.

"Holden Caulfield's characterisation and development arc, as well as the novel's overall plot, are all perfect examples of non-conformist ideology."

The large room is silent. It trickles in slowly, getting impossibly quieter every second.

"Go on," the lecturer says.

"One of the reasons that many people dislike Holden's story is the amount of swearing in it, but I believe that's done on purpose. It's a semiological representation of his inner ideology, which is that belonging to society is a waste of time. He swears. A lot. He calls himself…"

Love scrambles for his copy of the novel, flipping to a page covered with stripes of yellow highlighter and pencil-scribbled words. "'The most terrific liar you ever saw in your life.'

"When he says all he wants to be is the catcher in the rye, he says…" Love does some more flipping, now to page 101, and with every change made to the old pages I feel more deeply just how adored this book is by him. "He says, 'I know it's crazy, but that's the only thing I'd really like to be.' Which almost directly translates to knowing he doesn't fit in the norm, but not caring, because that's exactly what he wants."

The room feels heavy when Love stops speaking. The lecturer clears his throat.

"Well," he says gruffly, "you have done a thorough reading."

Love nods enthusiastically, holding up his lovingly destroyed book. "Yes. It's my favourite."

Then the class moves along. No one tells him he's right or commends him on his efforts. No one asks any questions or adds to the topic at hand. They merely move along to a crappy ideological understanding of Animal Farm.

It's a subtle kind of hate, but it still turns my insides. Especially to see a man as extraordinary as Love this quiet, face pulled back into nothing but a jaw lock only I can notice thanks to years of my own teeth grinding when I'm actually so angry I could burn down a building.

Then people start whispering slurs. They take one look at his red-painted lips and the Mary Janes on his feet and words slip off their tongues, sharp and dangerous, beginning with F, or P, and then another F. Boys giggle and girls roll their eyes, and it's all directed at the person sitting beside me.

Then, fifteen minutes into the lecture, a boy walks in. His skin is glistening white and his hair even whiter. He's in full punk get up— denim jeans covered in political patches, a leather jacket with the classic silver studs, massive boots I dream of wearing but would fall over just trying to stand in.

I may be a lesbian, but he's the kind of guy I can look at and think 'wow, he's hot.'

And, oh fuck, *'wow, he's hot'* guy is walking right our way, toward Love and I, and then he's falling into the seat next to Love.

This girl with too-straight blonde hair is staring back with an obvious grimace, a seat in front of the hot guy. I laugh when Hot Guy squints and kicks his feet up on the empty spot beside her.

"Call Love another word like that," he says, "and these boots will cave in your face."

That wipes away her grimace, sending her attention back to the lecturer as he rambles away.

No one even dares to look Love's way again.

Another thirty minutes later, the lecture splits in half to make way for a quick toilet break.

People file out of the room in flurries of conversation, likely to get coffees instead of actually taking a piss, until the only people left in the gigantic space are the three of us at the back.

Hot Guy leans over Love to extend his calloused hand, and after a moment of staring at his guitar string scars in wonder, I take it, squeezing softly.

"I'm Kit," he says, "Gay man, proud crip, future teacher. Nice to meet you."

"Crip?" I raise a brow.

"Me and my disabled friends reclaim the word," he says, pulling up one pant leg to show a prosthetic leg. "Everyone hates me for being disabled either way, may as well like myself for it."

I nod, looking down at my fingers where they intertwine, rubbing against each other so I don't freak out about the new person I'm talking to.

Kit's so openly, happily gay *and* disabled. It's such an impossible reality for me in 2022. I can't imagine it in the 1980s. For Love and for Kit. They make me want to try. They make me want to–

Chris appears and swipes the world away.


The third time around, I open my eyes to the sight of Jordie, who is visibly Chris' sister. This time though, Chris doesn't disappear into thin air—they stay with us.

There's not much time to ask questions or make observations because I've been dropped smack in the middle of a Mardi Gras parade. I'm not sure what year, but it's an early one. Likely before the tenth anniversary even hit.

People are wearing pride flags like capes. Every third couple holds up a sign with a slogan they invented on their own. Bodies covered in dark hair with beards on their faces wear dresses and crop tops, and large chests are covered by shirts and blazers that could only be found in the 'men's' section.

I've been to pride before. Once. But it didn't feel like this. My body has existed amongst all these others for a mere few seconds, and they already feel like family.

All these people are living in the age of the AIDS crisis, the age of a hundred homophobic hate crimes, the age of Australia in a state that still criminalised gay identities and is yet to legalise same-gender marriage for decades. All these people are suffering greatly, but I've somehow never seen smiles so wide. We're walking on and on, but all I hear is excited chatter and genuine cheers.

To my right, Jordie and Chris have their arms intertwined. She holds up a sign that I can't read except for the word 'lesbian', but I trust it's something good, while they wave a miniature Armenian flag.

"So," Jordie says, waggling her eyebrows as she bumps her hip into mine like we're old friends. "You havin' fun?"

When I lift my hands to flap them, I find I'm holding my own sign. Upside down, I can't read it all, but I know it has the word 'binary' on it, which is cool. *Very* cool for a deeply-confused-and-ashamed-about-their-non-binary-identity guy like me.

I offer a show of joy so big it squeezes my eyes shut and my cheeks out wide instead, as I nod aggressively. "The most fun time."

Jordie seems so glad. Her lips thin out when she offers a close-lipped smile, and I just stare at her, thinking about how pretty she is. How familiar that prettiness is. The tied-back hair, the mole above her lip, the tattoo on her neck. An Armenian lesbian woman, marching down Oxford Street with pride.

We walk as a group of three for what feels like forever, the sun setting overhead until it blends into darkness, some stores on either side of the road closing while others begin to open.

Clubs and bars, mostly. Is it still illegal to enter The Love Club underage if I technically wasn't even born in the 1980s? Surely, that's some kind of loophole. A way to trick the system.

We're right outside The Love Club, I can tell from where it sits on the corner and the street sign that's bent to the left, but it isn't called that. It's called Yellow Brick Road, and a sparkly pair of red shoes sits to the right of the words on the sign. People are whispering and giggling about being 'friends of Dorothy'.

I don't care what the rules are. I walk into Yellow Brick Road with Jordie and Chris.

The place is different inside, all the decorations from The Love Club older and not so overtly queer. The menu is simple, printed onto white wood instead of a dozen designs etched in with rainbow chalk. But the layout is the same. The booth I was sitting at with Killara is in the same spot, and after we all grab cans of Coke, we gravitate to it. I slide into the spot where I last saw Killara. No one else can sit there.

Jordie sips up her drink through a patterned plastic straw. "Is it working?" she asks.

"Um." I take gulps of my own drink. "Is what working?"

She merely smiles as she continues to suck up her Coke. Chris eyes her from the side, playing with the top of their own can, not actually drinking it.

Now that we're not so in the middle of a crowd, I can notice that again, even here, they're not actually here. Not for real. Their light brown skin is translucent—I can see the back of the chair through the fluff of their cheeks. Their actions are stuttered, blending together. Even here, in the 1980s, at the fucking Sydney Mardi Gras, Chris Voskanyan is a ghost.

And then, as we all sit and discuss our in depth opinions on The Wizard of Oz, they come back to life. Their body fills in, and their voice sounds more real.

Across the club, they make eye contact with someone at the bar, and after a few seconds of communication through nothing but facial cues, each of them leaves their seats, walking one at a time to the bathroom.

There's no gender neutral one in the middle, I find as my eyes trace their bodies, entering the door labelled 'Men'. I want to be mad about it, but I'm too happy. I want to be mad about it, but there's a bang. And a scream. And this time when everything goes black, Chris isn't there to make it all feel okay.


The rest of what I see is more like a movie. You know the montage that plays when the main couple falls in love, or when the protagonist's parent dies, or a girl with cancer slowly slips from time? Yeah, it's like that.

Mateo gets diagnosed with AIDS. I see hir in hospital. I see hir with hir family.

I see Mateo at hir funeral.

Love's boyfriend, Kit, commits suicide. I see Love in the hospital after he attempts too.

I see Love at his funeral after the doctors can't save him.

Chris is murdered by a man in the bathroom of a gay bar. I see the moment when their loved ones realise no one is coming to help them. I see Jordie scoop them up off the ground and weep, begging for them to come back, even as they bleed out over her dainty fingers.

I see Chris at their funeral, a place where everybody mourns their loss.

I mourn it now too.


Yellow Brick Road shapes back into its modern rendition: The Love Club.

No one is in the bathroom with me. Not even Chris.

But when I look down, my body is back to normal. *Normal.*

My chest is back, and the feeling in my pants isn't so weird.

"Huh," I say, when I find that the door leading out still isn't there.

My voice has returned to its natural, feminine state.

I don't know how to feel about any of it.

On the wall in front of me, there are a billion posters plastered over one another, advertising things ranging from a day to three years old. One of them, tucked away in the top corner near the roof, is a photo of Chris.

*It's the photo from the wall by Killara and I's booth.* Painted there in black and white ink, is Chris Voskanyan, a wonderful person, holding up a sign that reads 'BREAK THE BINARY'. It's Chris. *The* Chris. And it's the sign! *The* sign. I held that sign. I fucking held it.

My heart swells, pounding against my ribcage, reminiscent of my first pride and the time spent with Jordie and Chris at theirs and the moment Killara first kissed me and–

A clatter behind me has me spinning on my feet, and there stands Chris.

"You understand now," they say, like a truth. "Don't you?"

They don't even have to say it. I know exactly what they mean.

"Yeah," I whisper. "I do." Then, to my own damn surprise, I open my arms. "Can I hug you?"

A tear slides down their fading cheek as they push themself into my arms, their body the same size and shape as it was in the year that they died. Maybe I'm just as familiar to them.

"Thank you," I whisper into the eerily cold skin of their neck. "For everything."

But when I open my eyes, they're gone, and the door has returned.

I sprint out into The Love Club, searching through the crowd for Killara, finding her instantly. She's antsy under a bright white spotlight, eyes flitting every which way as she fiddles with the ends of her hair. When she finds me though, it stills. The world tilts on its axis.

We push into each other in seconds, another warm hug encompassing me, making me feel safe and loved and *proud*.

This time when I speak into a person's neck, it's loud and unashamed.

"I'm non-binary!" I yell.

Killara winces, pulling back with a smile. "Let's go back to the booth!"

So we go back to the booth, a place where we can link hands across the table again, and I can glance up at the photos of Chris, Jordie, Love, and Mateo as I speak the words I've buried inside me for so long, fearing they're not true. Words that a ghost in a bathroom revealed are truer than anything else.

"I'm non-binary," I repeat. "I'm non-binary, and that will never change. I'm feminine, and I like my stereotypical obsession with pink. I'm autistic, and I can't wear a binder because of my sensory issues. I'm not open and loud about my identity, but I want to be."

Killara's smile drips with adoration, and I drink it up. "Yeah, love, I know." She rubs her thumb over the back of my hand, so soothing, so wonderful. "What's brought this about?"

"I…" It's hard not to tell her what really happened, but I know I can't. Aside from the fact that it's not believable at all, it's also something that just belongs to me. "I had that meltdown, and after I calmed down, I just… saw those people in the pictures. They lived in a time so difficult for queer people, and they were still so proud, even when they died for the very same thing they were proud of."

Killara tilts her head, trying to understand.

"AIDS," I mutter, then point up at the pictures as I go through them. "That's Mateo. Ze died of AIDS. That's Kit and Love, they both died by suicide after Kit's dad kicked him out." Air floods my lungs, and I hold onto it, in case I stop breathing altogether. "And that's Chris. They were amazing. But they were murdered in 1986, in this very building."

My girlfriend's jaw drops. "What the *fuck*."

"Yeah," I say. But then I turn my head, and at the bar, an older Armenian lady mixes drinks for our friends. "That's Jordie. Chris' sister."

"Holy shit. You really did your research."

Behind the bar, there's a plaque over the top of Jordie's head. It's silver, dust-free, and engraved into it is the best message I've ever read.

THE LOVE CLUB: IN MEMORY OF MATEO, LOVE, AND CHRIS.

EARTH WAS NOT DESERVING OF YOUR LAUGHTER.

I tear up. My body isn't the perfect non-binary body. I can't wear a binder. The shirt I'm wearing is pink. I'm autistic, and I'm trans, and it isn't the best combination at all.

But I'm fucking proud. I love who I am, no matter how little I conform or whatever, and that's what's important. That I'm proud. That I'm the kind of person those before me would be proud of.

In my pocket, I can feel the insistent shape of a circle. My spare hand digs through fabric to find it, coming back with the pin Killara bought me. It takes a bit of effort, but I manage to align it with the location of my heart, poking the sharpness through the outer layer of my clothes.

Then I say, "Something like that."

Killara is crying just a bit too. Now we match. She's wearing her 'SHE/HER' pronoun pin, and I'm wearing my 'THEY/THEM' one. We're in love.

I lean in to kiss her, my shoulders light for the first time in forever.

When our lips disconnect, we stay near each other. "I love you," I whisper.

"I love you too," she responds. "Happy birthday."

And then we sit together, smiles on our faces, as our friends get progressively drunker. Jordie and I look at each other from across the club, and I don't know how, but I'm certain she recognises me, because there's a twinkle in the brown of her eye.

Pixie dust sits with me in the booth, glistening on my skin. I no longer feel like death.

Holden Caulfield may be the Love certified expert on being different, on being unique, but nobody else can say they were taught how to live by the ghost on Oxford Street, and that makes me feel like the most special person of all.

# Hyacinths & Other Purple Plants

## Alex Lakej

Content Warnings: Confinement

Author's Note:

When I first wrote "Hyacinths & Other Purple Plants", it was the summer after my junior year of college. I had a completely different plan for my future than I do now. A different career path, a different academic journey. Now in 2023, I sit here having graduated college after a whirlwind of changed plans, reading about two characters I created on the precipice of their own graduation, their own journey into a new world.

During my time in the education system, despite my good grades, I always struggled to keep up with my peers socially. Every day at school drained me, and as a late-diagnosed autistic, I failed to understand the importance of safe spaces, spaces where I could fully unmask and people I could fully unmask with. I wrote this story because I wanted to give these characters the safe place/person I never had. I wanted other autistic people, whether in school or not, to see that we deserve to exist and be accommodated in all aspects of our lives. That we have the right to carve out our own spaces to decompress.

This idea came to me at a time where I was processing my own diagnosis. I was still in the stage of accepting the fact that I needed to accommodate myself. Calliope and Rory finding the greenhouse inspired me to create my own safe space. They also made me realise how healing it is to write characters that are so casually and unapologetically autistic and trans. I learned more from them than I ever thought I could writing a short story. I am proud to have them be

231

the focus of my first published work. And now, Reader, I give them to you.

Thank you for taking a chance on this anthology and may we all one day find our greenhouse. <3

# Hyacinths & Other Purple Plants

Alex Lakej

### Calliope

RORY ANDREWS SET fire to the chemistry lab. Calliope stares in shock at the flames, watching as they warm her brown skin. She knows Rory will still somehow get an A on their assignment. As she's pulled onto the green of the football field, she knows that Rory's A will sit alongside her own, like their grades always do. And while Calliope works hard for her grades, actually *cares* about her grades, Rory barely does anything. It's infuriating.

This isn't about valedictorian anymore. It's about the fact that Rory can do whatever they want and still come out on top. Their name even comes before Calliope's on the attendance sheet when all her life she's been first.

*Andrews, Rory. (they/them)*

*Atkinson, Calliope. (she/they)*

She wouldn't have cared about coming in second if it wasn't for Rory's whole schtick. They're always late. They're always messing around in class. They never hand in anything on time, yet still manage to provide a sob story believable enough that the teachers give them full credit anyway. Rory always gets their way without even trying.

It's obnoxious and annoying and *aggravating* and–

"Andrews! Stay with your class!"

Calliope looks over to see Rory walking along the forest that surrounds their school. They almost blend in with the trees with their shaggy green hair being tossed around by the wind and their striped brown button-up fluttering around them like wings. The only things

233

that stand out are their pale arms as they reach up to inspect some leaves. It's the quietest Calliope has ever seen them.

One of the teachers calls out their name a second time. Rory lets their arm fall back to their side. The irritating smile they usually wear is back on their face before Calliope can even blink. As they saunter back over to the class and spot Calliope watching them, she can't look away fast enough. *Great.* She tries to ignore them, crossing her arms and staring pointedly at her shoes, chanting *please don't stand next to me* over and over in her head.

But the chanting isn't enough.

Because Rory still comes up to them.

At first, everything is quiet. Calliope thinks Rory's exhausted their words for once, but really, in what reality would that happen? So, she braces herself. She waits one second, then two, then three, then–

"You know that fire wasn't *technically* my fault," Rory says.

Calliope whips her head up fast, her box braids flying behind her. She couldn't come up with a response to that if she tried. She was there. She saw Rory do it, even if it was an accident. Rory, upon noticing the bewilderment on Calliope's face, shrugs. They just... *shrug.* "What? The instructions should've been clearer."

"You didn't even *read* the instructions," Calliope says.

Rory shrugs again, like it's not a big deal. "Okay, then they should've been more interesting," they say. "And much shorter."

Calliope is too stunned to speak. Instead of thinking up a reply, she takes a deep breath and puts as much distance between her and Rory as she can.

The next day isn't much better. Calliope kept waking up throughout the night, leaving her exhausted the next morning. She *could* sleep in for a few extra minutes if she skips some steps in her routine, but that isn't a possibility for her. So she gets up, all dizzy and disoriented, and goes through the motions.

When she gets to school, Calliope wishes, not for the first time, that it was socially acceptable to wear sunglasses inside, that people wouldn't look at her and think she was full of herself for having them on. She sure could have used them now. Along with their constant buzzing, the fluorescent lights are a little too bright today. Usually, Calliope can put up with it, but with their head already pounding from the incessant hallway noise, the lights make everything worse. English twelve, Calliope's first class of the day, doesn't help anything either. English is normally her favourite. She likes discussing the books they've read, analysing how the story was constructed and talking about allusions made to different mythologies, specifically Greek. But today is different. Today, the scribbled writing on the chalkboard makes her want to turn around and go back home.

*Line up in front of my desk for new seating placements.*

A seat change day.

Calliope hates seat change days. They completely disrupt her orientation in the classroom. She'll have to get used to seeing the board from the different angle, to having new people around her, to the physical chair itself. All she can do is hope to get placed in the back of the room, or to at least have a seat against a wall.

Mrs Ricci, their teacher, smiles when she spots Calliope. Calliope likes Mrs Ricci, really, she does, but it's hard to smile back when she knows what's coming.

"Ah, Calliope, yes. Let's see where I put you." Mrs Ricci examines the new seating chart in front of her, pushes her glasses up, then trails a finger down the rows of names. "Okay, you are next to the window, third seat from the back.

Calliope nods in thanks and forces a smile again before going where they're told.

A window seat.

Okay. Not as bad as it could be, but still not ideal.

A window seat means they'll have to deal with the sun as well as the overhead lights. A seat that's third from the back means they'll have someone sitting behind them, someone they can't see, which means they'll be tense and still the whole period. Sure, they could ask to be moved to the back row, but that means going up and explaining everything to Mrs Ricci. It means risking Mrs Ricci not understanding and telling Calliope that it's not a big deal, that she's graduating at the end of the quarter, and she can handle it.

So Calliope sits down and doesn't complain. She never complains. She simply folds her hands in front of her and tells herself that everything is going to be fine. They're so in their head that they don't notice when the bell rings to signal the start of class. They don't notice when Mrs Ricci starts speaking. They especially don't notice that the seat next to theirs is still empty. Until: "I'm here!" Rory runs into the classroom. Their backpack and button-up are falling off one of their shoulders showing off even more of their dark grey binder and thick waist.

"I'm here," they say again through heavy breaths.

"Rory Andrews. How nice of you to join us," Mrs Ricci says. "Your new seat is next to Calliope. Hopefully her good attitude will rub off on you."

Calliope blinks, not sure they understood her correctly, but when they look at Rory and see the smug smile on their face, they know they heard everything perfectly. It takes everything in them to hold back a groan. Isn't it bad enough that they're lab partners? Now Calliope has to tolerate them in this class too?

Rory lets their bag fall loudly to the floor, making Calliope jump. They whisper an apology, but the grin on their face tells Calliope that they're not sorry at all. She shakes her head and faces the front of the class again, determined to pretend like Rory isn't there for the rest of the semester.

But Rory has decided to make that unequivocally hard for her.

"Psst."

The noise is like a fly in their ear.

"Psst."

Calliope doesn't budge.

"Calliope."

They squeeze their eyes shut before begrudgingly glancing over at Rory. "Has no one ever taught you how to whisper?"

The corner of Rory's mouth twitches up a bit. They hold up their mechanical pencil and click the eraser a few times. "I'm out of lead," they say.

"I don't see how that's my problem," Calliope whispers back.

"C'mon, just let me borrow a pencil."

"Borrow?" Calliope almost laughs. "As if you're gonna give it back."

"I will! I promise!"

"No."

"Please?"

"I said no, just drop it," Calliope says, a bit louder than they meant to.

"But–"

"Rory. Calliope," Mrs Ricci calls from the front of the class. Calliope didn't realise she'd stopped talking. "Would either of you like to repeat back what I just said?"

Rory doesn't say a word. They lean back in their chair as if nothing is happening. Mrs Ricci already knows Rory wasn't paying attention, so what's the point in asking a question like that? She turns to Calliope after a moment, waiting.

Calliope bites her lip before shaking her head ever so slightly.

Mrs Ricci sighs, like she's disappointed. An ick crawls up Calliope's chest. They can't remember the last time someone was disappointed in them. They try so hard to avoid that in their day-to-day life that they feel a lump start to form in their throat.

Calliope can't handle the eye contact anymore. She casts her eyes down at her desk, letting her braids shield the sides of her face.

Mrs Ricci clears her throat. "Pay attention everyone," she says, addressing the class. "I will not be repeating myself a third time."

Calliope tries to listen, but it's nearly impossible with the heat spreading across their face, and the anxiety churning in their gut.


The rest of the day is a specific kind of torture. By the end of it, Calliope is ready to collapse. The entrance they usually leave out of is blocked, so they have to take the long way around. It only adds to the constriction in their chest.

They're not sure if they can handle the walk home when they already want to sink to the ground and sob. With all the noise from passing cars and the heat that's settled on the concrete, it doesn't seem like a good idea.

They're about to bite the bullet and do it anyway, when they see it. Down the hill, there's a greenhouse. Calliope has heard people talk about the school's greenhouse, but they've never actually seen it themself. It's bigger than they expected. The front bit looks old, with a brick wall covered in vines to the right, and slanted glass windows to the left. The rest of it has newer-looking translucent white tiles going all around it. It curves out of the original, like it was hastily stitched on to add more room. The shadows of the plants are just barely visible from where she's standing.

*Mismatched*, Calliope muses. *I like it.*

Before they can properly think it through, they start walking toward it. The grass is wet, freshly watered. It splatters on their ankles as they make their way down the hill. The cooling sensation is a welcome reprieve from the first trickles of summer.

When Calliope makes it to the aged, white wooden door, she presses her ear against it. There's no movement coming from inside, and even if there was someone in there, wouldn't she have seen them through the glass, seen their shadow through the walls? Maybe this'll be a good place to rest. It's empty, quiet. The heat might be a bit much, but it beats walking on the side of a main road when she already feels horrible.

A few minutes won't hurt.

Calliope reaches for the handle. Is she even allowed to be in here? If no one's using it, it should be fine, right? There aren't any signs around and Calliope's never heard anyone explicitly say that they *couldn't* go inside without a teacher…

So, Calliope takes a deep breath, and opens the door.


Rory

Rory's pretty sure the greenhouse heat is stealing their brain cells and giving them to the plants. Though, if that's the case, they honestly don't mind.

Being trapped in a greenhouse sounds exactly like Rory's dream scenario. They love plants. Studying them, learning from them. Just being around them helps Rory calm down, helps them think straighter. But being held captive by them? Maybe not the best thing in the world.

Whatever. It's not like Rory has any plans.

They just have to wait until someone comes along and opens the door from the outside. It shouldn't take too long. At least, not longer than it's already been.

When the handle starts to turn, Rory hops to their feet from where they were sitting, just in time to see Calliope Atkinson walking through the door. Just in time to see the door start to swing shut behind her.

"No!" Rory shouts, holding out a hand like that would do anything.

Calliope flinches.

And the door closes.


Calliope immediately goes to try the handle. She pulls and pulls, but no matter how hard she tries, the door doesn't budge.

"That's not gonna work," Rory says. "It locks from the inside."

Calliope ignores them, like she so often does. She starts banging on the door, calling out for help. When she realises the attempt is fruitless, she checks her phone. Rory already knows what she'll find. No signal. One of the reasons they like this place so much. No one can bother them here. Though now they see that has its downsides.

They watch as Calliope thumps her head against the door. She stays like that for a while, breathing heavily. A few seconds pass before she turns around and sits on the floor, wrapping her arms around her legs. Sweat is already dripping down her forehead. Rory almost suggests she take her hoodie off, the same blue zip-up hoodie she wears to school every day, but decides against it. If Calliope's still wearing it in this heat, who's Rory to say what she should do with it?

As if they're sharing the same thought, Calliope rolls up her sleeves. Rory guesses that's better, but even they couldn't stand the feeling of their button-up clinging to their back. Now, their binder sticks to them like glue, though there's nothing they can do about it. If they got the top surgery they keep begging their parents for, Rory wouldn't need the binder at all.

Calliope bites their lip, their eyes getting glassier by the second.

Rory doesn't know what to do with that. They've never been particularly good at comforting people, but they take a step forward anyway, ignoring their racing heart. "Hey," they begin, "it's okay. Someone has to come by eventually, right?"

Apparently, that was the wrong thing to say because whatever dam Calliope had up shatters into a million pieces. She chokes back sobs as she buries her face in her knees. Rory *really* doesn't know what to do now.

So, they revert to what they're good at.

"Is being stuck here with me really that bad?" they say, kind of joking, kind of not, as they set themself next to her.

Calliope sniffles. "I just wanna go home," they say, their words wobbly. "Today's been the *worst*. Everything was too bright and too loud, and then I had to change seats and you *stole* my pencil, and I had a headache the whole day so everything was too *much*, and I came in here to sit in a quiet space for a bit so I wouldn't shut down when I walked home, but now I can't even *go* home, and it's too hot in here and I just wanna go *home*." She takes a deep, shaky breath. "Everything is out of control and I just want to go home."

Rory is silent, processing it all. They reach into their jeans pocket, pull out Calliope's pencil, and hold it out to her. She eyes it for a second before plucking it out of Rory's hand, muttering a "thank you". A shiver goes down Rory's spine from where their fingers brushed each other's. It's quiet again. Rory draws in a breath. "I get it."

"No, you don't," Calliope says, her voice quiet.

Rory wonders if she meant to say that out loud. "Actually, I do," they say.

Calliope lifts her head, finally looking them in the eye. Rory's heartbeat picks up the slightest bit.

"Really," she says. "You know what it's like to hear the lights buzzing when no one else can, so you just have to sit there and hope that you can handle it? Or what it's like to hear someone's voice through a wall and feel like you can't breathe or like your whole body is about to collapse in on itself?"

"I mean, I'm autistic, so that's pretty run of the mill for me," Rory says. Something dawns on Calliope's face, but Rory can't quite read the emotion. "What? Are you gonna tell me I 'don't look autistic' or something?"

"What? No, why would I do that?" Calliope shakes their head. "No, I think… I think maybe I am too."

Rory nods, giving them the space to talk.

"I mean, I've been researching and… yeah."

Rory nods again. "Cool."

Calliope chuckles the slightest bit.

A spark thrums through Rory's chest, their mouth pulling into a proud grin. This time, they don't even bother trying to smother the feeling. "Wow, did I just make Calliope Atkinson laugh?"

Calliope rolls their eyes. "Shut up," they say, but the smile doesn't leave their face, even if it's a small one. "It's just, you're the first person I've told so…"

The two of them go quiet again, like they don't know how to interact with one another. Though, Rory supposes that they don't. For the most part, their conversations are short and to the point. If they go on for any longer than a minute or two, they usually start to argue. This, whatever they're doing now, doesn't fit into their little game. And while Rory loves their little game, they think they like this better.

"So," Calliope starts. "Why are you here? Is it for the same reason as me or…"

"Kinda?" Rory answers. "I mean, not the exact same reason but… I like the plants. They help me relax, so I come here after school to just hang out and make sure they're doing okay." Rory knows it sounds weird, but Calliope nods like it's the most normal thing in the world. Maybe it is normal. It's Rory's normal, at least.

"And you just… locked yourself in?" Calliope asks.

"Well, that part was an accident."

"But you've been in here before."

Rory nods.

"And you didn't know that the door locks from the inside?"

"Look, we all make mistakes," Rory proclaims dramatically.

Calliope laughs again, a little louder this time, and Rory has to wonder what they've done to deserve two laughs from Calliope Atkinson in a single day.

They think for a moment, a question running through their mind. Asking it will pop the fragile bubble they've found themselves in. Rory *knows* it will, but they have to ask, they have to know.

"You don't actually hate me, do you?"

The smile on Calliope's face falls slowly. Rory instantly regrets asking the question. They almost dismiss the whole thing, almost tell Calliope nevermind and that it doesn't matter. But they don't. They sit and wait as Calliope drops her gaze to the floor.

"I don't hate you," she says finally. "I just—"

"Wanna win valedictorian," Rory finishes for her.

"No! I mean, yes but…" She pauses for a moment. "I work so hard for the grades I get and you… you seem like you don't care about any of it, you know? It kinda feels like a slap in the face."

Rory didn't know what they were expecting, but it definitely wasn't that. "It's not that I don't *care*," they explain. "It's just that if I don't try, if I BS everything, then it's okay if I fail because I didn't actually put any effort in."

Calliope stays silent.

"But if I try and *then* fail, it's all on me."

Rory stares at the side of Calliope's head for what feels like hours. The wind from outside beats against the plastic walls. Birds chirp and bushes rustle, but the inside of the greenhouse is completely quiet.

Until Calliope takes a breath.

"So, you're into plants, huh?"

What?

Rory blinks a couple of times, confused. "Uh, yeah."

Calliope nods and cranes her neck to look around the room. "What does that plant do?" she asks, pointing to a Venus flytrap in the corner closest to them.

"What does it do?"

"Yeah," she says. "What does it do?"

They stare at each other. Rory's eyes keep focusing on different parts of Calliope's face, unable to stay still. Everything about this moment seems so unreal, yet here they are, with a person they thought hated them a couple of seconds ago. A person that twists their guts in knots and makes their face feel warm. A person they thought they'd never get to speak to like this. Like… they were actually friends.

Rory can't help but smile. They look at the plant, then back at Calliope. "You really wanna know?" they ask.

"I really wanna know," she says.

"It could take a while."

Calliope reaches up and jimmies the door handle. It's still locked, as expected. She faces Rory and shrugs. "We've got time."


After Rory thoroughly explains the different functions of a Venus flytrap, Calliope asks about the other plants in the greenhouse. She asks about what they do, how to properly care for them, what their scientific names are. And she actually listens when Rory answers. Rory's so used to being tuned out when they talk about plants, when they talk about anything they're passionate about really, that having Calliope there, actively listening and asking questions is surreal.

They talk about plants for another half hour before they hear footsteps crunching on the grass outside. Calliope's the first to get up, shooting to their feet, and banging on the door as loud as they can and, as much as Rory wants to get out of here, they're also a little sad about it.

The two of them stand back as the door opens, revealing Mx Morrow, the teacher that's normally tasked with taking care of the greenhouse. Calliope thanks them and speeds out the door, hauling their backpack over their shoulder.

Mx Morrow watches them go before facing Rory. "Got locked in again?"

Rory steps out of the greenhouse, hanging their head. "Yeah."

Mx Morrow hums. "You had company this time."

Rory lets their gaze wander toward the hill. Calliope is already halfway up it, making their way to the paved road. She must've felt the eyes on her back because she stops and looks over her shoulder. She gives Rory a small wave.

Rory waves back. "Yeah," they say as Calliope continues walking. "Yeah, I did."


Calliope

Calliope is used to Rory taking up space in their brain. Anytime they're in a room together, Calliope can't help but look over at them, to see what they're up to, to prepare for when they inevitably come over to talk to her. Now though, it's different. Now Calliope looks for proof of the greenhouse on their face.

Neither of them have brought it up yet. In fact, they haven't talked much at all. For the past week, Rory has been quieter in English, more attentive in lab. Calliope doesn't understand the sudden change. She thinks if she goes back to the greenhouse, she can figure it out.

So every day after school, they stand at the top of the hill, watching Rory's shadow as it moves through the plants. They debate going in. What are the pros and cons? Does is really matter that much that Rory's changed? Does Rory even want them there? They did mention that they went there to relax after school. No matter how much Calliope sort of, kind of, dislikes Rory, she doesn't want to intrude on their space.

Every day, the same thought process runs through their head and, every day, they leave. They go home and wonder what would've happened if they didn't.

It becomes a routine of sorts. On Friday, the routine continues. Calliope stands on top of the hill and watches, debating with themself inside their head. Only, something's different, something's off. There's no shadow moving around inside.

Without another thought, Calliope walks down the hill. When she gets to the greenhouse, the door is closed. She thinks Rory got themself locked in again, but when she opens the door, there's no one inside.

"Hello?" they call out for good measure. No one jumps up. No one responds. It's just... empty. Did Rory leave for the day? They were in English and chem. Maybe they felt sick and left after that? Rory didn't *look* sick during class, but maybe that's the reason they've been so quiet lately. Maybe–

"Calliope?"

Calliope jumps, shrieking and losing their hold on the door. It swings shut, only allowing them a brief glimpse of green hair. A second passes and the door opens again, Rory standing outside with an armful of purple flowers and a goofy grin on their face.

"You don't wanna get stuck in here again," they tease.

Calliope doesn't laugh, still recovering from the scare. They can't help but notice how different Rory looks from the last time they were in here. Last time, their shoulders were bare, their loose jeans rolled up as far as they could go. Their makeup, usually dark and precise, was smudged by sweat and humidity. Now, they look like they always do. They look like the same old Rory. Calliope feels like she's talking to a completely different person.

"So..." Rory says. "What're you doing here?"

"Um," Calliope doesn't know what to say. She can't tell them the truth. That they've been debating coming back all week. That the only reason she decided to come here today is because she didn't see their shadow moving back and forth. "Sorry," she says, and starts to move past Rory to get back outside. "Sorry, I shouldn't be here. I'll just–"

"Wait." Rory holds out a hand, almost dropping their flowers. "You don't have to go."

There's something in their eyes that Calliope can't fully place.

"Really, it's fine. This is your space," she says.

Rory snorts. "Pretty sure this is school property."

"You know what I mean," Calliope says. "You were here first."

"And you were here second." Rory hikes up the plant pots in their arms. "A little help?"

Calliope looks behind her, then to the flowers Rory's carrying, then to Rory themself. They're still watching Calliope, eyebrows raised.

She could've walked away, left and gone home. Calliope already knows that Rory's brain works similar to theirs. They don't have to follow the regular norms of the situation. Rory wouldn't hate them if they didn't.

Not that Calliope cares about that. Nope. Definitely not.

Against their better judgement, Calliope takes two of the flowerpots and follows Rory back inside the greenhouse, making sure the door stays propped open behind them.


"These are new," Calliope says, gesturing to the plants they just set down. "They weren't here last time."

"Yeah, we just got them in today. Mx Morrow's letting me set them up." Rory gets up from the crouch they were in and dusts off their hands. "They're–"

"Hyacinths," Calliope finishes.

Rory blinks a couple of times, a slight grin growing on their face. "Yeah, that's right. How did you know?"

Calliope pauses for a moment. "Flowers are just easier to recognise," they say, not totally a lie.

Rory narrows their eyes at her. "Right. Now, what's the *actual* reason?"

Calliope hesitates. "They're part of one of my favourite Greek myths, that's all," she says.

"Really?"

"Yeah."

Rory nods. Silence stretches out between them, but Calliope doesn't mind. It's kind of nice. Rory breaks it a moment later. "Will you tell me the story? About the hyacinth, I mean."

"I don't know…" Calliope says. This is why she didn't want to say anything; she doesn't want to ramble. She knows that, once she gets going, it'll be hard to stop.

Rory nudges them lightly. "C'mon," they say. "I really wanna know."

Calliope vaguely remembers saying the same thing last week. She looks at Rory, searching their face for anything disingenuous, but there's nothing there.

So she tells them.

She tells them about the beautiful prince named Hyacinthus that drew the eye of both Zephyrus and Apollo. She tells them about both gods showing off for the prince and letting him choose who he liked best. About how Apollo won and how they fell in love, only for all that to be taken away in an instant when Zephyrus' winds blew a discus into the side of Hyacinthus' head, killing him. How Apollo used the dying prince's blood to create a flower: the hyacinth.

Everything goes quiet after that. Rory stares at the flower in front of them, gently fidgeting with its silky petals. They suck in a breath. "That was really sad."

"It's a Greek myth," Calliope says, her voice low and soft. "They're all sad."

"I'm sure there's at least one happy one," Rory retorts in the same tone.

"Well, there are *some* happy ones, but that's not really the norm. Plus, even if a story is technically happy, there's still sad stuff that happens within it."

"Happy is happy," Rory says, like it's the simplest thing in the world. "The good shouldn't be discarded just because bad things happened, you know? Apollo was in love before Hyacinthus died. Shouldn't that count for something?"

"I guess so." But Calliope's never been able to see it that way. To her, these myths have always been tragedies, even the happy ones. Sure, Perseus gets to save his mother, but Medusa dies despite living in isolation so she wouldn't hurt anyone. All the men she turned to stone sought her out, trying to prove themselves, trying to slay the 'hideous beast'.

Rory goes silent again, thinking while they continue examining the hyacinths. "Will you tell me one of the happy stories?" they ask, "On Monday?"

Calliope bites their lip. Do they really want to commit to this? What if it's all a distraction so that they don't win valedictorian? A week ago, Calliope would've thought that was the case, that Rory would rather put the effort into getting her to slip up rather than working harder for themself.

But now Calliope's not so sure.

"I mean, you don't have to if you don't want to," Rory says. "Like, you probably have better things to do after school, so definitely don't feel like you have to say yes. Like–" Rory goes on rambling like that for a few more seconds. Calliope's never seen them like this before. It's as if they're nervous or something. Nervous about what? About hanging out with her? Something pulls in her chest.

Is that– Does she find this *cute*? Is that what this feeling is?

No. Absolutely not. This is not something Calliope wants to be thinking about. They shove it down and try their best to ignore it, focusing back on what Rory's saying.

"So, yeah, like, it's totally okay if you don't show up and–"

"Monday," Calliope says, cutting them off. "I'll be here."

Rory's ears turn a faint shade of red. If they were any redder, the colour would clash with their hair. It's kind of– *Don't say it. Don't even think it.*

"Cool," Rory says, "Monday."


Rory

Calliope shows up on Monday, as promised. She tells Rory about Atalanta, a strong woman who would only get married if the guy could beat her in a race. After many men try and fail, someone finally beats her with Aphrodite's help. Atalanta keeps her word and gets married. They both get turned into lions at the end, but still. That counts as a happy ending in Rory's book.

Calliope shows up again on Tuesday, telling the story of Perseus. She goes on a long rant about how Medusa was wronged and deserved better. The two of them come up with endless redemption arcs for her.

It happens again on Wednesday, then on Thursday, then on Friday. Their after school meet ups become an unspoken agreement. The greenhouse, which used to be Rory's alone, is suddenly a space for both of them. Rory exchanges plant facts for stories. Calliope exchanges stories for plant facts.

It doesn't end in the greenhouse either. Calliope smiles at Rory in class, waves at them when they pass in the hallway. They're actually friends, of a sort. And even though Calliope's still quiet during the school day, in the greenhouse, they're way more talkative than Rory could have ever imagined.

Rory knows they've got it bad. They try to convince themself otherwise, but it's no use. When it first started, they thought it was a friend crush, nothing more. The both of them moved on to competing for valedictorian and Rory knew, they *knew*, it would be stupid to crush on her, to fall for her. Repressing it had worked for a while. They kept telling themself that they'd get over it eventually, that if they tried, they could let it go.

And then Calliope got locked in the greenhouse.

And then Calliope smiled.

And then Calliope laughed.

And the dams Rory put up were no match for that.


When the myths run out and there are no more plants in the greenhouse to study, Calliope and Rory talk about themselves. They find out that they're going to the same college. They find out that they're both commuting since neither of them can stand the thought of not having a space of their own.

"Like, I don't wanna have to pick between a 'boy's dorm' and a 'girl's dorm', but also, like, being around someone twenty-four/seven? I wouldn't be able to relax," Rory says.

Calliope nods along. They understand. They always understand.

Grades are the furthest thing from Rory's mind. They can't believe it was ever such a priority for them. Sure, they might have slipped a little, but who cares? School is about test taking and rules and Rory knows they're smart in the way that matters, in the way that counts, to them at least. Everything's going so well that Rory doesn't notice the signs; doesn't notice Calliope getting quieter and quieter. At first, Rory thinks she's just had a bad day. They both have bad days from time to time. Days where the noise is too much or where the wind feels like someone poking them over and over and over. Days where the tightness in their chest doesn't go away no matter how hard they try.

Rory assumes it's one of those days. When it keeps happening, Rory assumes it's one of those weeks. Rory knows what those weeks feel like. They wait for Calliope to acknowledge it, not wanting to push. Sometimes, Rory can't stand anything more than silence, but other times, a distraction is welcome. They don't know what Calliope's like, so they wait for them to say something.

But they don't.

So Rory keeps talking.

Until they get in their head and tell themself, *Tomorrow. Tomorrow I'll ask Calliope about it*. Tomorrow comes and Rory's having one of Those Days. The lights are too loud. Their binder is sticking too tightly to their skin. They get the worst grade they've gotten in ages and, as much as Rory thinks the education system is a scam, it still stings a little.

Their only reprieve is seeing Calliope in English, then again in chem. For the rest of the day, the thought of hanging out with her after school is what keeps them going.

Rory all but runs down the hill and into the greenhouse. They prop the door open and say hello to all the plants, checking them over for spotting or wilting leaves, before settling into the corner they always sit in with Calliope.

A couple of minutes go by, and Calliope still hasn't shown up. Rory tells themself not to worry. She's just caught up with a teacher or a friend. Yeah. That has to be it.

After a couple more minutes, Rory pulls out their phone and realises that they never exchanged numbers. Why have they never exchanged numbers? There was never any room in their conversations to ask, but now Rory wishes they *made* room. For a brief moment, Rory thinks about searching for a signal to try and find Calliope's Instagram, but decides against it. That would be weird, right?

Yes. It would be weird. Best not to take the chance.

A few minutes turns into twenty minutes which turns into forty minutes which turns into an hour. Calliope isn't coming. Rory only leaves when Mx Morrow shows up. They don't stop to talk like they usually do. Mx Morrow gives them a concerned look, but Rory doesn't pay it any mind. *Maybe she's sick and went home early.*

*Yeah.* Rory tells themself. *Yeah, that's it.*


But Calliope doesn't show up to the greenhouse the next day—or the next, or the next—despite being in school. Rory tries to talk to her in class, but she pretends like she can't hear them, and Rory doesn't want to risk getting her in trouble again.

When the bell rings at the end of period, Calliope speeds out of the room before Rory can even begin to process what's going on. She doesn't look at them in lab, only speaking in short, to the point sentences.

"Are we gonna talk about this?" Rory asks halfway through their allotted experiment time.

"Talk about what?" Calliope keeps their eyes trained on the slick, black surface of their table.

"You know what."

Calliope looks up. They lock eyes for the first time in a while. Rory feels hopeful, like maybe she'll tell them it was all a big joke. But she doesn't. And it isn't.

"Nope. Sorry," she says, and continues on with their experiment.


Exam schedules come out later that night. Right. Of course, Calliope needs to study. They can't have Rory distracting them after school every day if they want to keep their top spot. Rory gets it. They're fine with it. Really, they are.

So, that's it then.

Everything goes back to the way it was.


Calliope

The ache in Calliope's chest started the day they stopped going to the greenhouse. It hasn't stopped since, lingering and spiking with every reminder of what they lost, what they gave up. They felt bad, but what else were they supposed to do?

She watched as Rory's grades dropped little by little, glancing over in class to see red Bs and Cs circled on their papers. Calliope couldn't help but feel like it was her fault. She didn't know if Rory was tanking on purpose so that she'd win valedictorian or if she was just distracting them, but none of that mattered. She didn't want to win because Rory threw the competition. She didn't want to win because she distracted the opponent.

More importantly—*most* importantly—she didn't want Rory to resent her.

Initially, she thought about talking it out, but decided against it. Because what if Rory lied? What if Rory said they weren't throwing the competition when they really were? What if they said they didn't care about their grades, when they really did? Even subconsciously?

There were too many possibilities. Too many variables.

She couldn't take the risk. She *wouldn't.*

The day she decided to do what she did was the day she saw Rory getting lectured by Mrs Ricci. Calliope's seen Rory get lectured before, but never like this, never over failing grades.

So, they bite the bullet. They shut Rory out, no matter how much it hurts.


Rory

Rory stands in the greenhouse one last time. They walk around, dragging their fingers across leaves, naming plants as they go. They're sure they can find a way to sneak in after today, but it won't be the same. It wouldn't be them going there after a rough day of school, trying to do their homework but getting distracted by all the foliage instead. It wouldn't be them kneeling in front of a flower and sketching it out, leaving just enough room for a description underneath. They breathe in the scent of flora, holding it deep within their lungs. How will they ever find another sanctuary like this?

Rory looked it up the other day. Their college has something of a greenhouse, but it's not as homey as this one. They wonder if Calliope feels the same, if Calliope even thought to check in the first place.

Rory makes their way over to the hyacinths. Even now, their chest still pangs at the memories of deities and demigods and mythical creatures. Of fleeces made of gold and flowers made from lovers. After they make their rounds of the greenhouse, they sit cross-legged in front of the purple flowers, letting themself think for once.

Their grades went up a bit after Calliope stopped talking to them, so maybe if was a good thing. For the best. That's what they keep telling themself. That it's okay. That they can remember the good, even after the bad things happened. Still, it was hard for them to care about school after that. Mustering up the motivation to actually try, actually give Calliope a run for their money, was difficult. In the end, they stopped caring altogether.

Calliope's grades stayed consistent from what they've heard. That's just who Calliope is: consistent. The loudspeaker this morning listed off the top twenty students in the grade; Rory was glad to hear her name at the top. She deserved it; worked hard for it. Rory always expected to be right behind her. Salutatorian. But they weren't. They weren't even in the top three.

Rory came seventh in overall class rank, which isn't bad in the grand scheme of things. Not that it matters. Not that they care. They're sure some of the teachers were happy that they dropped so fast after messing around all year.

Maybe they deserved it.

Maybe they deserved to fall.

The door to the greenhouse squeaks, breaking them from their thoughts. Rory jumps to their feet, thinking the wind is about to lock them in there yet again. *Maybe it's Zephyrus getting back at me for being on*

*Apollo's side*. The joke is painful, but Rory still manages a grin. When they finally get a proper view of the door, they see it's not Zephyrus.

It's Calliope. They look almost exactly the same as the first time they were here. Same blue zip-up hoodie, same black shirt, same ripped jeans. The only difference is their hair, in twists instead of box braids. Rory was so sure that they wouldn't see her again until their graduation ceremony. Now, Rory doesn't know what to do.

For a moment, they debate hiding and trying to sneak out, but Calliope spots them before they can make up their mind.

They walk toward each other awkwardly.

"Congrats on making valedictorian," Rory says once they're close enough.

They're quiet for a moment. Calliope stares at Rory's shoes. She inhales sharply and looks up, their brown eyes meeting Rory's hazel ones. "I don't know how to do this," she says.

"Do what?" Rory asks.

"Explain what I did without it sounding like an excuse."

Rory nods. They take a deep breath. "Just explain. I'll listen."

And so, after searching Rory's face for something incomprehensible, she does. "I'm so sorry," she says. "I'm sorry for ignoring you and pushing you away. I should've just *talked* to you when I noticed your grades slipping, but I didn't want you to say it was okay and hate me for it later, so… so I thought if I just stopped coming here after school, you'd do better and we could go back to the way things were so you wouldn't resent me for winning."

The silence ticks on until Rory can't hold back the laugh anymore. "Grades?" they say through their laughter. "This whole thing was about *grades*?"

"Kinda," Calliope says sheepishly.

Rory starts laughing again,

"Did I say something funny?"

"No," Rory says, dragging a hand over their face to lessen their grin. "I'm just… I'm just glad that's all it was."

"So…" Calliope crosses her arms. "You're not mad at me?"

"No, I'm not mad at you," Rory says. "I mean, I was for a while, in the beginning, but then I just kinda settled. I thought you went back to hating me, you know?"

"I never really hated you. You know that," Calliope says. "Maybe I didn't *like* you, found you loud and irritating and–"

Rory cuts her off. "Okay, I get the picture."

Calliope smiles the slightest bit. "But I definitely don't feel like that now."

"How *do* you feel now?"

Calliope gets this look on their face, kind of how they look when they're taking a test or giving a presentation, determined and a little anxious. Rory knows that face well. She opens her mouth, then closes it again, huffing through her nose. "Are you really gonna make me say it?"

Rory grins. "I kinda need things spelled out for me," they say, only half joking.

Calliope sighs, frustrated. It's kind of cute, seeing her like this. They think they know what she's about to say. They hope. She takes in another breath, straightening her back. The face is back. The determination. The anxiety.

"I…" she begins and immediately folds back in on herself. "I like you, okay? You know, like *that.*"

Rory can feel their heart pounding in their ears. "Like what?" they ask, in mock confusion.

Calliope rolls her eyes. "I hate you," she says, but the tone is sweet and soft, no malice to be found.

Rory snorts. "I like you too," they say. "Like *that*."

Calliope tilts her head. "Really? For how long?"

"Pretty much the whole time I've known you," they answer, trying to sound casual, but they can already feel the tips of their ears turning red.

"The whole time?" Calliope asks.

"The whole time," Rory says.

Laughter bubbles up from within them until they can't hold it anymore. Calliope follows suit, a hand covering her mouth. They calm down after a minute or two, standing closer than before. Rory glances up from their almost-touching shoes to find that Calliope is already looking at them.

Rory isn't sure what they're supposed to do now. All those movies and books and they still don't know how to proceed in this situation. "So, I'm guessing prom is out of the question?" they ask, because that seems like the right next step.

"Yeah, flashing lights, loud music, and crowds aren't really my thing," Calliope responds.

"I figured," Rory says. "Maybe we can do something after graduation then? Like a date?"

Calliope smiles, teeth and all. She reaches out a hand. Rory meets her in the middle, lacing their fingers together. "Yeah," she says. "That sounds nice."

The thumping in Rory's chest grows louder and louder, even as they let go of each other's hands to exchange phone numbers. They're just so glad they get to be here, with Calliope again. Even if it is for the last time.

"I think we have to get out of here soon," Rory says.

"Do we?" Calliope hums, glancing over their shoulder at the door. When they start walking toward it, Rory thinks they're about to leave. Something drops in their chest. They want to get on the floor and hold onto a table leg for dear life. It's too soon to leave, too soon to go.

But when Calliope gets to the door, she doesn't leave. She merely gives it a little kick, so that it swings shut and locks them inside.

"Whoops," she says. "Looks like we're stuck here."

Rory watches them, bewildered, before cackling. "I can't believe you just did that."

Calliope grins. "Did what?" they ask innocently as they sit down, back against the plastic walls. "That sure was a strong gust of wind."

Rory laughs again and sits down next to her. "Yeah," they say. "The wind."

The two shuffle closer together. They lean against each other, breathing in the smell of flowers and earth.

"Calliope," Rory says.

"Hmm?"

"No, your name. Calliope. She's a goddess, isn't she?"

Calliope nods.

"Will you tell me about her?" Rory asks.

In that moment, Rory swears Calliope glows. She takes a deep breath, tracing lines on Rory's palm. "Calliope is one of the nine muses," she starts.

And, as they wait in their hidden place, the story is told; the good and the bad.

# Who Were You, What Are You

Andrew Joseph White

Content Warnings: Partner Violence, Transphobia, Ableism, Slurs

Author's Note:

If I remember correctly, I wrote this short story during the last year of my master's degree, for a class on suspense I took to meet my funding requirements; this was also the year I began attempting to unmask my autism in earnest. Even with endless support from my classmates and professors, it was nerve-racking. I stopped forcing eye contact, fidgeted with toys at my desk, and allowed myself to flap my hands and rock. It was a year of coming to terms with parts of myself I'd locked up to appear normal.

In turn, "Who Were You, What Are You" was the first story in my academic career to use the word "autistic." I'd skirted around it previously—lots of my stories were set in times and places where the word simply didn't exist, allowing me to avoid calling my characters what they clearly were. But my debut novel, *Hell Followed With Us*, would be coming out in a few short months. The book says "autistic" on page, out loud. And I was nervous.

So I decided to rip off the bandage, and this short story was born.

Cameron is a messy kid, but so much of him is based on me and my fears, theorising who I could've been if I knew about my transness and autism earlier in life. After all, what is all of my YA work, if not that? I can't wait for you to meet him, and thank you for reading.

# Who Were You, What Are You

Andrew Joseph White

MY FRIEND DUNE texts me while I'm sitting at the only traffic light for forty miles:

TEENAGERS DONT GO TO COUPLES THERAPY.

My pinkie—unused to precision work but forced into it due to the splints swaddling my pointer and middle fingers—fumbles helplessly against the touch screen. Maybe referring to dog-sitting as 'couple's therapy' was a mistake. I'd meant it as a joke.

THEY JUST FUCKING BREAK UP.

We're the only car at the intersection. The road is lined with empty buildings under a blanket of woolly grey clouds. In the shotgun seat, my boyfriend, Jake, plays a game on his phone—PUBG, I think. He has one earbud in, allowing him to split his attention between the screen (where he grabs a weapon and downs another player with the chattering of stock bullet noises) and the road, as if I've suddenly lost the ability to drive. He's been like this the whole trip. I graduated from my learner's a few months ago but he's still saying "brake, brake" whenever I get within ten yards of another car, or pointing out upcoming exits as if I can't read Google Maps.

I chew on my thumbnail as I skim Dune's texts. Jake is only doing it because he's worried about me. Not because he thinks I can't actually do it.

Jake is nothing like my ex.

I have to remind myself of that a few times a day.

"Emmy—I mean, Cam," Jake suddenly says. He has to pitch his voice above the music; he tried to make an autism joke when my playlist repeated for the third time half an hour back, but I hadn't found it amusing. For a neurotypical, his autism jokes are honestly kind of funny, but it's hard to find anything funny when he keeps fucking up my name. I know he's not doing it on purpose, but... "*Cam.* Light's green."

"I saw," I lie, switching back to Google Maps and hitting the gas. "I can drive."

Dune's next text jams itself at the top of my screen:

I KNOW YOU DON'T HAVE ANY BARS DOWN THERE BUT JESUS CHRIST CAMERON THIS IS HOW GUYS LIKE YOU GET MURDERED.

The words sting. I take one hand off the wheel to slap my arm as if swatting away wasps.

"You good?" Jake says.

"Yeah. I just–" I jerk my head to the side to get the feeling to go away. He still worries about me. After everything I did, he still worries. "–feel weird. Sorry."

The thing is, I can't blame Dune for grating an open wound they don't know about. I didn't tell them what happened two weeks ago at school, because of course I didn't. I know better. If I tell them, they'll steal their dad's car and tear from New York to Virginia to do the following:

1. Make sure I change all my bandages on time and gently bully me into taking my painkillers because I hate pills,

2. Tell Jake to fuck off, which would probably involve a fist fight, and

3. Murder Adam Rhys, the boy who called me a "retarded, cheating faggot slut" and pushed me down the concrete steps of the school's

back stairwell, breaking my nose, two of my fingers, and at least three other bones in my face.

Because two weeks ago, Adam—my ex-boyfriend, the track star I'd been dating for just over a year—found out I'd been cheating on him with his best friend for months.

And also I'm a boy.

And *also* also, that best friend was Jake.

Yeah. I'm a piece of shit. I know.

As I pull away from the intersection, we pass two empty parking lots before the road takes us right back out of town, swallowed by looming trees. They're old and creaky with dark leaves and black bark. The county can't get the funding to trim them, especially since my mamaw was just telling me about a slew of water testing going on right now, some chemical or another, so the trees just kind of stand there, waiting to break. I keep an eye on them—a branch might finally give way and snap. I don't think AAA takes calls out here.

"Shit," Jake says. "Maps just stopped."

"What? Fuck." I try disabling the useless wi-fi and rebooting the 4G, but nothing happens. I hate this part of Virginia. It's all dead air and roadkill. "It's fine. I can get us there."

Something like blood wells in my mouth—I'm alone with a boy for the first time since one put me in the hospital. I swallow it down and I hate that I savour the recoil of my throat muscles, the fact that they still move.

I think Adam would have killed me if he got the chance, because he'd brought his father's hunting knife to school, stood over my crumpled body and said he'd put it right through me. But the gym teacher threw him across the stairwell and I heard something crunch maybe, probably, and it was the most beautiful sound I'd ever heard. I

266

wanted to devour it whole. I wish I'd done it myself. I imagine doing it over and over until Adam's head comes apart like mine did.

I think Jake's only still with me because he has to be. Because he'd be a terrible person if he left me now. Because he didn't know I was dating Adam at all and only found out when I was escorted, bloody and shattered, out of the school.

Because he doesn't even know where to *start* breaking up with me.

That's the hardest part. If Jake had just broken up with me weeks ago, I wouldn't be so nervous. I wouldn't be so confused. I look at myself in the rearview mirror and barely recognise the mess of bruises and choppy hair that stares back.

I don't know how people work.

I just don't want to be alone right now.


Mamaw's house is a canary yellow two-bedroom sticking out from the trees like a rotten tooth begging to be pulled. We're parked in front of the garage now; I'm waiting for Jake to speak first, but maybe he's waiting for me to speak first instead. He's closed out of his game and has the earbuds slung around his neck, peering out the windshield as if trying to find something creeping in the trees.

It'd probably be more comfortable if one of us said something. I start.

"Mamaw's dog is really old. Her name is Annie and she kind of looks dead." Jake wrinkles his nose. It's a specific look he gives me sometimes, almost like confusion, which always confuses me in turn because it's not like I'm saying confusing things. "She's got cataracts half an inch thick and at least three tumours, so don't be surprised when she's a little lumpy. Plus she smells bad."

"If you're trying to distract me from how fucked up this place is," Jake says, "it's not working."

"I'm not—you know I'm not trying to distract you." I get out of the car and pop the trunk, realising too late that it may have been a joke. We haven't joked about things in a while. I'm out of practice. "Come get your bag."

Mamaw left to visit family in Ohio for the weekend and asked us to dog-sit. Well, she asked *me*, and I had to bring someone or I'd crumple into a ball of broken bones. With my parents keeping me out of class until Adam is officially expelled, today is my first day away from Mom fretting and crying, Dad calling up his lawyer friends, and neither of them willing to swallow *why* all this happened.

There's no way they don't know. That I'm a cheater, that I was forced out of the closet, that I'm not the kid they thought they raised. It makes me want to burn inside out.

(Honestly, I think Dad was more impressed that I had pulled it off at all. His great-grandfather'd had two families back in the day, and I thought I heard him joking to Mom a few days ago: *"I didn't think that was possible anymore. The time management alone–"*

*"Dear,"* Mom had hissed.)

I pull a key from the frog ornament in the garden and let us into Mamaw's house. The place smells like smoke even though Papaw died two years ago, and also dog piss. Annie—a truly unnerving chihuahua-beagle mix—sits on the kitchen floor with her big waddle-tumour, one paw in a puddle.

"Oh, Jesus," Jake says.

"I know." I dump my bag near the front door and make a beeline for the paper towels, turning on every light I can find along the way. It's not evening yet, but the clouds have made everything oppressively dark. "I got it. I said she's old."

"No, I know. It's just…" He's staring past her, out the massive glass doors at the back of the dining room that lead to the backyard and the forest beyond. "Those are creepy."

"Yep."

"You haven't had something come through? Break it or anything?"

I grab a handful of paper towels and crouch to clean up Annie's mess, nudging her until she moves. When I was little and spending the night at Mamaw's house, I refused to sleep on the pull-out couch in the living room—I was convinced I could see faces peering through the glass. Even now, I try not to look out the windows in the dark.

Maybe I should make a joke myself, a sort of olive branch. "Eh, if something does, I'm sure you could fight it off. Can you take Annie out?"

Jake deftly gets her out the door after a bit of cajoling and promising to give her treats once they're back inside. Jake is better with dogs than I am. He's also on the track team, with shotput shoulders and 400 metre-hurdle legs, and my mouth floods with a bitter swarm of jealously: that he gets to have those when I don't, that someone else will get to have them once he breaks up with me.

Jake and Adam were on the track team together. Adam won awards and ribbons and Jake never really won anything. Adam brought me to parties and I always found a way to sneak off with Jake, saying I was just getting something more to drink, that I was overwhelmed and needed to breathe, that I was going to head home early. It was only ever half a lie.

Jake always laughed at Adam's jokes, even the ones that made me sick. I wonder if he felt like he had to, the same way I did.

I wonder if he actually found them funny.

I get up off the floor and throw the paper towels in the trash.

Maybe Dune was right. Maybe this was a mistake.

Annie falls asleep on the back of the couch, which has a permanent indent from her body, and Jake and I pull apart Mamaw's pantry in search of dinner. We find a stuffed crust pizza underneath freezer-burned tubs of praline ice cream.

We sit at the breakfast bar while it cooks.

"So," Jake says. He's not good at starting conversations. No guys are. He's put his phone down too, which means it's serious.

I turn my book over to show I'm listening. "So," I repeat.

"Where do we want to start?"

Right. When I called this couple's therapy, I was making a joke, but it was only funny because it was true. I suddenly feel nauseated. I hold out my hand and Jake reaches over to my bag to give me one of the several cheap rubber animals he'd bought me from the Walmart toy section, the kind that's filled with sand and stretches to weird proportions. This one is a snake. I take it and squeeze it hard between my palms.

Jake wasn't the first person I told I'm autistic, but he was the first person who wasn't my parents or Dune. I'd been thinking about it for at least a year before I worked up the guts to ask Mom and Dad about getting tested. Everything lined up, and Dune—who got diagnosed last year after a nasty meltdown—said they believed me, that I didn't have to go through the months-long and humiliating process if I didn't want to, but I just wanted that little signature. That... that *proof.* The *power* of being proved correct in a way someone might actually listen to.

Well, my parents simply informed me that they weren't coughing up several thousand dollars for a shrink to tell them what they already knew: that I'm just bad with people and need to try harder, as if I wasn't already trying so hard I hated myself. So, of course, I told Jake when I showed up at his house crying, tired of pretending to be someone I wasn't.

I told him first. Not Adam. *Him.*

"There's a lot of places to start," I say, turning the snake over in my hands. *Are you okay? Did you know? Why did you laugh when Adam called things retarded, even though I told you how much I hated it? When you laughed at his homophobic jokes, were you agreeing with him, or just scared he'd single you out if you didn't?*

*Why didn't you help when you saw Adam drag me into the stairwell? Why haven't you broken up with me?*

I say, "You pick."

"Alright," Jake says. "Are you okay?"

Not sure what I was expecting. "I'm fine."

"Are you sure?"

"I'd know if I wasn't fine." We both know I'm not the kind of person to do anything about it if I wasn't, though. Jake sighs.

"When did you start dating Adam?"

No use lying. "He asked me to homecoming junior year. So… Little over a year ago."

He mulls over that for a moment, like he's trying to remember me at homecoming. I wasn't much to look at, huddling in a corner in the only dress I owned—the one I'd bought for Papaw's funeral. I wouldn't have gone if Adam hadn't asked me, if I hadn't been so desperate for someone to make me feel normal. "So I'm the homewrecker, then."

"No." My fingers dig into the rubber snake, the sand inside it grinding loudly. Cheap paint flakes off its body. "I didn't like him half as much as I like you."

Jake looks puzzled by this. Or maybe hurt. "So why not just, I dunno, break up with him?"

The truth chokes me before I can say it. It tastes like bile. I stayed with him because I was afraid: of him, of what I'd be without him. One time, Adam took me to his house and showed me the hunting knife he'd try to kill me with, joking about what he'd do with it in a way that I couldn't tell if he was *actually* joking or using his smile as a cover for meaning it. The first and only time I shook out my hands in front of his friends, he grabbed my wrist and said something about the short bus. With him, I was small and hidden, but without him, I was nothing at all.

Until Jake.

So instead of saying any of that, I hold up my splinted hand.

It gets the point across. Jake buries his face in his elbow and we don't talk again until the pizza is ready, when we discuss browsing Mamaw's early 2000s DVD collection for something that doesn't suck. Papaw owned half a dozen copies of Top Gun. We eventually decide on School of Rock because it's the only one I'm sure doesn't have any shitty jokes.

But while washing dishes:

"So," Jake says. He's scrubbing the plates, then I dry them—Mamaw doesn't have a dishwasher and I have a very low tolerance for hot water. Jake does a lot of things to accommodate me. It makes me feel bad. "You're a guy now."

I pause for a second. It doesn't work like that. At least not for me. "I always was. I just figured it out is all."

"Oh." The word comes out of his mouth weirdly small. "Okay."

Annie waddles into the kitchen and begs to be let out. I kick open the door so she can sit on the porch and stare into the woods. Nothing's out there. I don't think. Something prickles at the back of my neck.

"Annie," I call, opening the door again. "If you're not going to piss, come back in."

We watch the movie. It's okay. Jake and I don't sleep in the same bed that night, but it doesn't feel right to be in different rooms, so we sleep across from the each other on two different couches. We keep the QVC channel on, muted, because Annie needs the light—and I don't like knowing the trees can see me with those big, big windows.

I'm woken up by a horrendous scratching and ghoulish wailing, catapulting me off the couch and directly into Mamaw's coffee table. The candy dish full of Werther's rattles. Jake sits up with a start, his eyes blown wide.

"What was that?" he wheezes.

I stare at him, shaking my head. *I don't know.*

Another scratch. Another throaty howl.

Oh.

"Fuck," I manage, unsteadily getting my balance. A blonde lady on QVC is selling orthopaedic shoes. For a moment, I'm disappointed that it's not the gay goat farmers hawking face wipes—at least that would be comforting. "It's just the dog. Sorry."

"The dog?" Jake blinks owlishly. "That's the dog?"

"Told you. Pretty sure she's a zombie."

Jake groans and pulls the quilt over his head, turning to face the cushions. I fumble into the kitchen, where Annie is indeed sitting by the big glass door, her tail whapping against the floor.

"Christ, dog. Scared the shit out of us." I open the door for her anyway.

I go out too because there are foxes and raccoons sometimes, and in a fight against one of those, Annie would lose three times over. Moths and crane flies bumble around the porch light. I'm in a hoodie and boxers. I know I dressed like this when everyone thought I was a girl but I wonder if it reads differently to Jake now—with all my chopped-off hair and the eyebrows I've started filling in thick to give my face a heavier, desperately-boyish look. I chew on my thumbnail as Annie wanders off the porch and into the grass.

Then.

"He really did a number on your face this time, huh?"

There's a man beside me.

Mid-twenties, maybe. Staring out into the forest. Sitting in one of the mouldy lawn chairs Mamaw tossed out here and forgot about, a foot propped up on his knee. He's dressed the way everyone dresses out here, with sanded jeans and a flannel coat unzipped to show a muddy white tee. Heavy boots, a working man's boots. A pack of Camels tucked in his pocket and two day's stubble.

He looks like–

Me.

Me, if I had been born with a dick and testosterone.

Exactly like me.

I reach for the door, slowly stepping back, and the man tilts his head as if the trees beyond us have done something mildly interesting. His hair goes from auburn to gold in the light, the same way mine does. It looks better on him.

"I wouldn't if I were you," he says. His voice isn't as deep as I was expecting. For some reason, that's what I focus on. That is what my brain rolls over like a shiny rock. *Even when you get out of your town and away from your fucking family and finally start hormones, your voice will never be as deep as you want it.* "I understand, really, considering what you've been through. But I still wouldn't."

My tongue is jammed in my mouth, my head a storm of static. I try to speak once, twice, but all that comes out is a low, rasping wheeze. Finally, one painful word at a time, I fight for them:

"My boyfriend is in there. If you do anything, he'll hear."

"Quit bitching. I'm here to help." The man reaches into his pocket, pulls out the Camels, and offers them to me over his shoulder. A single one sticks out of the pack like they do in old movies. He has a scar on his finger. The same kind of scar I'll probably have once my hand heals.

"Cigarette?"

"No."

"Suit yourself." He puts one between his lips and lights it with a Zippo. "You know, if you were a cis boy, you'd be stuck on these already. You pick up the habit junior year when a cute guy offers you one and you're too gay to turn it down. And before you bring it up, yeah, they are sensory hell at first. But you're good at hiding that." A long drag, a long breath out. "You get addicted to things easily, huh? Cigarettes, routines, boys. That and you'll do anything not to draw attention to yourself. Trying to quit smoking, breaking up with someone even when you start fucking his best friend behind his back... it's just too much of the spotlight. You'd rather die."

My head hurts. "It's not like that."

"Sure it's not. Adam made you normal and Jake made you happy. Especially when Adam started getting–" The man gestures to my wrecked face and laughs, which makes smoke pour out from his mouth. The end of the cigarette burns cherry-red. It's the same brand

Papaw used to smoke. "Shame they found out about each other. And the whole *being a boy* thing too."

"If you don't get away from me right now, I'll scream."

The man tilts his head. "How very *girl* of you."

I hate how he says it. I hate that it's true.

"Wouldn't it be better if you never had to say that again?"

"What?"

Annie comes up from the grass, toddles across the porch, and nudges up against the man's leg. He reaches down to pat her back, and she drops the severed bird leg she found in the bushes at his feet.

"Wouldn't it be better," he says, "if you had been the one to make Adam regret it? Not some poor bastard who's probably going to get fired for putting his hands on a student—*you*. And wouldn't it be so, so much better if you could stop being scared of Jake?"

Something terrible wells in the back of my throat. "I'm not scared of Jake."

*Why did you go along with everything Adam said? Why didn't you stop him?*

*Please don't leave me alone.*

"You hurt his feelings, Cam," the man says. "He can't ignore how much of a shit his best friend is anymore and, plus, you retroactively made him gay, didn't you? If you ask me–" He glances towards the glass door, and I look too, just to see what he sees, and it's nothing. "You should be watching your back. This is how guys like you get murdered."

My mouth is dry and my limbs are heavy and my head feels like it's stuffed with cotton and down. "I won't tell Jake you were here. Just let me go back inside."

"I can make it easier if you want."

The man waves his hand. "I'm not stopping you. Cute dog, by the way."

I open the door a crack, pushing Annie through the gap with my ankle, and then throw myself in and lock it behind me, and sit on the floor and stare and stare and stare out into the woods until I remember how to breathe again, until I crane my neck to see the mouldy chair empty again.

When Jake finally crawls off the couch and wanders bleary-eyed into the kitchen, I'm halfway through my second bowl of cereal.

"Morning," I say. "Hope you like stale Fruity Pebbles because it's all we got."

My voice comes out weirdly normal. Calm. I guess all those years of cramming down my feelings to act 'like everyone else' are finally coming in handy.

I have come to the decision that the man wasn't real. He couldn't have been. He knew too much, he looked too much like me, and that sort of thing doesn't happen, so I have chalked it up to a combination of stress and either sleepwalking or a weird dream. Brains are garbage piles of meat that are prone to glitching. That's why I'm not saying anything. That's why I'm not telling Jake.

Besides, he was wrong. Jake wouldn't hurt me. Not like Adam did.

*Why didn't you stop him?*

"The sugar content in this is a war crime." Jake picks up the cereal box and turns it over, squinting at the nutrition label. "I have a meet in Shenandoah next week." *In place of Adam*, he doesn't say. With everything going on, Adam's been disqualified from the team— permanently, if he can't find a way to weasel out of this.

277

Jake makes himself a bowl anyway. He's not picking up his phone for PUBG. Something's coming. I'm already on edge. "You okay?"

"Yeah, why?"

"You just look a little–" He gestures at his face. I wrinkle my nose. "No, I know, not like that. You know what I mean. Like you've seen a ghost."

"I don't believe in ghosts."

"Fuck it. Can we talk about the *guy* thing?"

The man's words come back like a spider crawling up my spine. I've suddenly lost my appetite. "If you're going to ask if this makes you gay, I'm going to say it's up to you."

Being a gay trans guy is a mess of nasty feelings I don't know how to explain to someone like Jake, who probably didn't even know trans people could be gay before I came out. (Better than my parents though, who probably think trans people are gays who are just More Committed To The Bit.) Like, looking at a cis boy and never knowing if you want to have him or be him. Knowing that most of them will never see you as an equal, the ever-present nagging doubt that they think of you as a girl they're humouring in exchange for blowjobs.

*Wouldn't it be better–*

Jake says, through a mouthful of cereal, "Do you want a dick?"

"Christ."

"It's an honest question."

"No. Maybe? Probably not? They're weird." Jake looks strangely hurt. "Come on. You know they're weird. I'm not insulting yours or anything, I'm just saying—you can't tell me they don't look like sea cucumbers. I'm not gonna pay several thousand dollars for a doctor to make a sea cucumber out of my leg skin."

*"Leg skin?"*

I can see the gears in Jake's head turning, trying to figure out how to excise the flesh to build something else—a graft to build something 'unnatural'. My stomach turns at the idea. The word 'unnatural' always worms its way into conversations like this, right next to the word 'mutilation', put there by mothers distraught about the loss of their beautiful daughters, accusing them of destroying healthy tissue with binding and mastectomies, forsaking their God-given beauty with ugly hormones.

Women lose daughters. Men lose breeding stock.

All that slams into my brain at once, a mess of knotted thoughts that slot into place like a needle slipping into a vein. My thoughts never come naturally as words, but as something else I have to untangle and translate. I slide off the chair and root through my bag, looking for the silicone bracelet I tucked away in one of the back pockets. Without a word, I wash it in the sink and begin to chew on it. My cereal has gone soggy. The texture is unpalatable now. I realise, belatedly, that this is why Dune only dates other trans people, and that maybe I should have listened to them.

Jake doesn't think of me that way. Adam might have but Jake doesn't. He can't. He can't be the reason fear is rising in the back of my throat, reminding me of flashing metal and the crackling pain in my fingers and the suffocating numbness in my face.

That is what boys to do people like me. That Jake hasn't acted on it is a gift he can take away whenever he wants. And the fact that I don't know for sure, that I can't, that my brain is built in a way that makes my boyfriend into an alien—

*You should be watching your back. This is how guys like you get murdered.*

*Why didn't you stop him?*

*Wouldn't it be better if you never had to scream again?*

I don't want to be alone again.


There's nothing to do out here. Mamaw's basic cable package is garbage, or maybe I just don't like TV. Her old computer by the pellet stove has Microsoft Word, a Disney-themed art program, and still runs on Windows 98. I need a break from class readings and picking through the half-dozen junk drawers. I'm about to dump out the decorative jar of assorted beans on the fridge to start sorting them by type when Jake catches my attention.

"Going to go for a run," he says, filling up his water bottle at the sink. Right—he has that meet to practice for. "Wanna come?"

"The well water here is bad." I pull three plastic bottles from the stack beside the fridge. "Use these."

Jake sighs as he pours the well water out. "Fine. Still. You want to come with me?"

"I don't run."

Something glimmers in his eye. We go back and forth like this every time. It's comforting. "You can walk. I just need someone to carry my bottle." He rips open a small flavour packet with his teeth. "Please?"

I glance out the big glass door. I told myself that the man wasn't real, but here I am, looking for him, trying to judge how safe it is to walk outside. The mossy lawn chair is still in the same spot. There's nobody but us.

I just want us to be normal.

"Okay," I say. "Let me get Annie in her harness."

We go, me carrying Jake's bottle under one arm. I walk at Annie's speed, and Jake trots beside us, doing that half-jog thing where you move your legs like you're running but you're going an inch at a time.

We go down Mamaw's twisting quarter-mile driveway and hit the main road. Out from under the tree canopy, with the sun shining, it's actually kind of beautiful here. The trees are still dark and overgrown, but if you squint between them, you can see the start of farmland. I point out some cows, and even a goat. Jake leaps through the ditch to make goat noises. One picks up its head, ears twitching. Annie barks at a squirrel.

"I think there's a horse farm if we go far enough," I say.

Jake's eyes light up. "Wait, really? Dude, I love horses. We *have* to go."

So we do. There's a cranky old gelding who hangs out by the fence sometimes. He's there when we arrive, Annie wheezing and waddling, and Jake climbs halfway up the fence to feed him weeds. I can feel myself smiling.

This is what this trip was supposed to be. Not what Adam did to it.

Something strange wells up in the back of my throat, though. I try to swallow it down but it gets stuck, a little pebble at the back of my tongue.

I haven't been able to stop thinking about it since it happened.

And I should get to ask a question for once.

We start back towards the house, Jake still marvelling at how soft a horse's nose is—*like velvet*, he'd said in awe. He asks for his water bottle. I hand it to him. He spills some over his chin and hands it back.

I say, "You saw Adam grab me that day, didn't you."

Jake says, "What?"

"In the hallway, before Statistics. You saw us."

Jake stops in the middle of the road. There are no cars coming—a car has not come down this street since we arrived yesterday. A sheen of sweat has gathered on his upper lip.

"Cam," he says.

"It hurt."

It comes out before I can stop myself. My face doesn't always reflect what I'm feeling, so just in case, I need him to know. I need there to be no way for him to doubt what I felt.

"I–"

"And you didn't do anything."

"Are you–" He stammers. "Are you saying I was in on it?"

"No!" I wrangle my tone. Shit, why did I say anything? I should have kept my mouth shut, or at least written this down before I tried to speak. "I'm sorry. That's not what I meant. I'm just saying, I thought you would have done something."

Jake says, "I knew you and Adam were close. I just didn't think…"

"You didn't know we were close then. You had no fucking idea."

He looks away from me with a huff. Annie whines. My hand is starting to shake. I pull at the silicone bracelet until it bites against the sensitive skin of my wrist.

"Adam's my friend," he finally says.

"'Is'?"

He doesn't say anything.

"'Is'?" I repeat.

"Cameron."

"Look. I'm sorry. I'm sorry for everything I did. Really, I really am." Despite the fact that my face refuses to reflect that perfect grief-stricken expression we see in every book and movie and TV show, tears still burn my eyes. "It was selfish and awful. But Adam pulled a knife on me over it. That's not okay. Right? You think he's a bad person too, right? Not just me?"

Silence.

For a long time.

"Let's head back," Jake says, changing the subject. That's what I do; that's how it seems to other people who can't follow me the way Jake can. It almost feels pointed, like he's making fun of me. "Annie looks tired."

"Yeah." I don't want to talk about this anymore. "Let's go."

I text Dune when the phone signal comes through, just for a little bit:

I'm kind of busy this weekend, but when I get home Monday, can we talk? I have a lot of things I need to tell you.


I sleep in the guest bedroom instead of on the couch that night. The silence is bad but being away from Jake is worse.

Or better.

I don't know.


That night, when Annie begs to be let out, I usher her through the door and follow her into the dark. At the edge of the property, a deer plods along beside the wire fence, nose down to the ground as it searches for some of the corn left behind. Mamaw leaves some out every now and then. Papaw used to bait them to the edge of the lawn during hunting season, but now that he's gone, Mamaw does it just to see the animals up close.

I drag the mouldy chair into the grass, the silicone bracelet still between my teeth. It's easier for me to focus like this. The material is tough, making my jaw ache, but at least it's better than Camels.

I can see myself starting on them, though. Awestruck by a boy who looks at me the right way, unable to say no, suppressing a coughing fit when the smoke hits my lungs. I would be too embarrassed to flap my hands or bob my head to help stomach it; I'd just stand there and suffer and maybe smile when he asked how I was taking the drag.

When I decided I would come back out here, I started practising what I was going to say to the man when I saw him. I am not going to make the same mistake I did with Jake.

But when I hear the gentle *click* of a Zippo, I forget all of it.

"You're here," the man notes. There's no hint of surprise—I don't know if that means he really isn't surprised, or he just isn't putting in the energy to make his voice sound that way.

I turn to look at him. He's taking the first pull of his cigarette, the red tip flaring bright. Now that we're closer, I can see the hairline scar over his cheek. Interesting, then, that even in a world where I was born a cis boy, I still get pushed down the stairs.

It's funny that this version of me isn't the kind of person I want to transition into, not really. I mean, I guess aesthetic-wise, this is kind of what I'm going for. Scruffy, stocky, with solid, well-worn clothes. Maybe the voice isn't as deep as I would want, but that's the kind of thing I get from my dad anyway. But—cis? I don't want to be cis. I never want to be mistaken for cis. I want to be a man, *recognisable* as a man, while still owning my transness. And if that means hands where the bones fused small and delicate, or feminine facial fat that never really redistributes, or top surgery scars or a trans flag tattoo, then so be it.

But not this. Whatever this is.

I say, "When you said you could *make it easier*, what did you mean?"

The man laughs but it still somehow manages to be flat. "If you really wanted it, you wouldn't ask."

"No. Don't give me that. Because–" I swallow hard. "Because if you're going to make me not trans, or not autistic–"

"Jesus. You think I could do that? You think I can just reach into your head and rewrite you from scratch? I can do a lot, but I can't do that." He shakes his head. "All I'd do is move you a little to the left."

I pause to look at the grass and the patch of dirt a few inches from my left foot.

"Metaphorically," the man says. "Like, in the scheme of things."

I bite down on my bracelet hard. A tear I'd given it a few weeks back during an AP Bio test deepens. Or maybe I put it there by the horse farm. "Oh."

Annie comes up to us then, her swollen neck wobbling, bugging eyes darting between us as if one of us might have a midnight snack. I really don't like this dog but she's the one thing keeping me grounded. Even the distant glow of QVC through the glass doors is too dim.

"It wouldn't be hard. It won't even hurt." The man takes the cigarette from his mouth. He still won't look at me. Not in the eye, I hate being looked at in the eye, but in my direction at all.

"The thing is, I can't build something out of nothing. I'm gonna need something from you, Cam."

I can't ask Jake to talk me through a neurotypical view of the situation. I can't text Dune to double-check my words. It's just me.

Alone.

"What is it?"

The man looks towards the house. "You can only have power if you take it from somebody else."


When Jake sleeps, he reminds me of a Golden Retriever—I mean, he always does, with his hair falling over his eyes and the spark in his smile when he sees me in the stands during his track meets, raising a hand to me as he collapses, exhausted, to the grass—but even more now, with the quilt tucked up to his chin and brows furrowed as if dreaming.

"Call now," mouths the QVC lady, translated by the closed captioning, "and we'll throw in a second pair absolutely free!"

Annie paces the living room once, twice, then settles into her bed under the coffee table.

Someone drives down the dark road, high beams cutting through the trees for a moment before disappearing again. The first car I've seen the whole trip.

We leave tomorrow, before the sun comes up, so I can get Jake back to school on time.

I think Adam would have killed me if he got the chance, because he'd brought his father's hunting knife to school, stood over my crumpled body and said he'd put it right through me.

*I heard something crunch, maybe, probably, and it was the most beautiful sound I'd ever heard.*

*Wouldn't it be better if you never had to scream again?*

*This is how guys like you get murdered.*

I don't want to be alone.

"Jake," I whisper, putting a hand on his shoulder. "Jake?"

He makes a small, quiet noise. His eyes flutter open, lashes batting in confusion as he squints against the weight of sleep. "Cam? Is something wrong?"

But taking power by force is what boys like Adam do and, and here, here's the thing. Being a trans man is making a promise to nurture masculinity into a new, kinder beast. That's the beauty of being a boy like this. And a gift that autism gives too; when nothing comes naturally, when you have to build it all yourself, you get to decide what to keep and what to set aside.

I cannot survive if I want to rip apart every boy that gets too close.

Adam does not get to do this to me. He does not get to *take* that from me.

And if Jake has any power over me right now—this is how I get it back.

I swallow hard.

Dune would be so proud of me.

I say, "I think I'm breaking up with you."

# Wandering Stars

## Isa Elias Boog

Content Warnings: Climate Disaster, Human-Made Apocalypse

Author's Note:

Several years ago, I created a player character for a table-top role playing game (TTRPG) I was playing with my partner and my oldest brother. I wanted to create a character that was unapologetically autistic and genderqueer without caring if they would be 'too much'. A character with a xenogender who used neopronouns, whose queerness was directly tied to xyr autism. All the traits I was too afraid to express in myself, I put into Aster. For this story, I returned to xyr before the events of that TTRPG, when xe was a teen still trying to figure out life. If you have ever worried about being too much—too autistic, too trans, too strange—this story is for you.

# Wandering Stars

Isa Elias Boog

BEFORE PEOPLE KNEW about planets, they thought they were a type of star that moved around erratically rather than following a predictable trajectory. The word 'planet' actually comes from the Greek 'πλανήτης' (planetes) meaning 'wanderers', from 'πλάνητες ἀστέρες' (planetes asteres) meaning 'wandering stars'.

I named myself Aster, star, because the night sky has always felt like home; one steady, predictable thing in a life full of constant change. Though unfortunately, right now I can't see any planets (except for the one I'm on) and barely any stars. Even outside the sea wall, away from the Randstad's streets and buildings, the light pollution makes for a very limited view of the night sky. In between the many satellites I've spotted the big dipper, and Orion, and the North Star— but I wonder what the sky looked like long ago, back when we still thought the planets were wandering stars.

I'm about to get up from the cold sand I've been sitting on for a few blissfully quiet minutes, and call my dog, Jamie, back to me, when I notice something out of place. On the shoreline, not a hundred metres away from me, lies a… blob. Moonlight catches on the curved edges of a vaguely circular shape. Like a rock, but softer. Jamie hasn't noticed it yet, having run off the other way to sniff around some driftwood. Which is fortunate, because I think I see the shape move.

I start walking before my conscious mind has had the chance to catch up to my body. As I close the distance between me and the shape, I see that it's definitely some kind of aquatic animal. It has a dog-like face with a long snout but no visible ears, a soft oval body, two front flippers, and a tail ending in two similar flippers. I expect it to move away, disappear into the ocean at my approach, but the animal stays exactly where it is. The only movement is its slow and steady breathing. When I've come within a few metres of the creature, I sit down in the sand to leave it a respectable distance and show it I mean no harm. I stare at the creature and it stares at me. What now?


Zoology has been my special interest for years. There's no future in it, I've known that for about as long as I've known I wanted to spend my life studying it. No one cares about non-human animals when we're fighting for our own species' survival. Or at least, no one in power does. I'll be graduating secondary school in a year and I need to look for actually viable career prospects, but all I want to do is work with animals.

Ever since I remember, I have been studying the few animals that were around in my underground apartment block: a handful of neighbourhood pets, including our family dog; the occasional bird or mouse I encountered on my walks on the surface; the metro rats my parents were constantly trying to convince me to stay away from. Once I could read, which was fairly young, I read every book about animals I could get my hands on. This is why my answer to the question 'what now?' is to open one of the many books I have saved to my phone.


I don't have a ton of books on local fauna, mainly because there isn't much left of it. The rogue nanobots that have been sapping the energy from this planet for decades now disrupted many of the world's ecosystems, already fragile from the climate disasters we were too late to prevent. There is one book though, in which I suspect I might find something on the creature on the beach before me. The gentle light of the holoscreen projected from my wrist illuminates my face as I open Extinct & Endangered: A History of Native Species of the Netherlands.

As I scan the chapter headings to find what I'm looking for, I hear Jamie approaching behind me. I motion for him to stay with me, and, though he looks at the strange animal curiously, he crawls underneath my outstretched arm and lies down beside me. I've found the section on North Sea animals and there it is: the grey seal. One of two seal species that once made the Dutch coast their home, it was thought to have gone extinct as a result of nanos contaminating the global oceanic food chain. Though, obviously, they aren't actually extinct.

Either the animal I'm looking at is the last of its species, or there's a seal colony somewhere around here.

In all those years reading about zoology, I've learned quite a bit about animals. I'm now realising that that knowledge does nothing to help me in a situation like this. Maybe I should just let nature run its course; go home and hope that whatever seems to be wrong with this seal will solve itself and it will go back to whatever is left of its family. On the other hand, nature has gone decidedly off course due to human mistakes and mistreatment. If it's possible to correct that even a little bit by saving this animal that's supposed to be extinct, who am I to walk away from that? There must be someone else out there who cares, who isn't too preoccupied by human survival to help other animals too. And I think I might have a way to find someone just like that.

I close the book and open my anonymous messenger app. I'm not supposed to use data outside the range of our domicile's network, but I think this counts as an emergency. If not, my parents can take it out of my allowance. I don't bother to read my unread messages and immediately type a message to my best friend.

planet.aster 22:03:

> I think I just found an extinct animal (obv not extinct) (it's alive) (but sick?)

It takes a minute before my screen lights up with a response.

sage72 22:04:

> what

> where are you? what animal? why are you outside so late?

planet.aster 22:05:

> Walking Jamie. There's a grey seal on the beach. I think it's ill or sth. It's not running away from me. Or swimming I guess.

> Didn't you say you knew some ecologists or something?

It's quiet for so long I start to get nervous. Did I say something wrong? I move my fingers in slow curling motions to ease my anxiety. Finally, my screen lights up again. The message is short.

sage72 22:09:

> where are you exactly?

For a moment, my head fills with doubt. Can I really trust Sage enough to disclose my location? There are plenty of people who wouldn't hesitate to harm the innocent creature I'm attempting to save. Those thoughts clear away just as quickly as they pop up. Sage is my best friend. If I can't trust them, I can't trust anyone. I type in which door in the sea wall I went through and the direction I walked after that. Sage's response is immediate.

sage72 22:11:

> be there in 20

Twenty minutes is a long time to wait in the cold. I huddle close to Jamie and zip my jacket up as high as possible, tucking my chin into the neckline. As the urgency of the situation becomes less pressing, feelings rush in. I pull a face as I suppress a squeal of excitement, trying not to upset the supposedly extinct animal in front of me. I'm only seventeen and I've just made a monumental scientific discovery in the field I thought I would never be able to study properly. I want to jump and flap and scream, but I channel my wild emotions into slow stims with my hands instead. After a while, I calm down and open my book again, trying to pass the time by reading more about seals and then other North Sea inhabitants of times past. I try to ignore the cold settling into my bones.


It's been getting gradually colder every year for as long as I can remember and some time before that. I've often heard my parents, both climate scientists, discussing the future of our planet: ever decreasing temperatures leading up to a new Ice Age. They've worked for many companies where they've tried to draw attention to this fact, citing how much was lost in the past because large corporations acted too late to prevent the previous climate crisis, but so far no one has listened. They'll claim to be 'working on it' while they focus more on current problems, but as my parents have both said many times, all they really care about is profit and protecting the super rich. The richest members of our society live in well-stocked, nigh impenetrable bunkers, while the people who work for them live in compounds just below the surface—and the ever-growing poorest population lives in the derelict buildings above ground.

While I make surface visits every day to walk Jamie, I can't imagine what it's like to live there. For the past sixty years or so, the nanos have been steadily destroying all surface infrastructure as they look for energy and metal to consume. While electricity is still available through underground power lines, it won't be long before the nanos get to those too. Burying deeper to escape them is only a temporary solution, as the rich in their bunkers already know. The nanos are sapping the very heat from our atmosphere and soon they will go on the hunt for our structures again.

I'm painfully stiff when I hear footsteps behind me, which startle me from my half-dozing state immediately. I know Sage uses a wheelchair and these are multiple sets of footsteps.

Despite the spike of fear in my chest, I stand and turn around slowly to avoid disturbing either of the animals near me. I lose a bit of tension when I see Sage in their chair, hovering a few centimetres above the sand. Of course I wouldn't be able to hear them approach—though I don't think they ever told me their chair could do that. Walking behind Sage are two adults both wearing coveralls and boots under their winter coats. I wave awkwardly and Sage returns the gesture.

"That's xyr," I hear them say to their companions, their voice barely carrying over the sound of the waves.

Sage and I met online through our shared interest in astronomy. It's been years since I considered studying that particular field; once I learned how much maths was involved I kind of tapped out. I much prefer reading about other people's discoveries than having to do that kind of research myself. It's remained a special interest, but I'm content with the fact that I'll never know as much about it as Sage, who is still intent on becoming an astrophysicist.

Space is not all we talk about though. We've grown close over several years of chatting, sharing memes and hanging out in video calls. Despite that, we've never met in person—I didn't even know they lived so close by. So of all the ways I've imagined us meeting, this was definitely not one. I suddenly feel massively underprepared.

They're getting close now and I walk up to meet them, and Jamie, realising we're meeting a friend, runs up and practically jumps into

Sage's lap despite being way too big for that, and Sage laughs and I laugh and now we're both petting Jamie and laughing and it's like we've met each other a thousand times already.

"Can I hug you?" Sage asks, and I skip the verbal answer and just embrace them tightly.

When I right myself, breathing deeply to temper the jittery excitement in my stomach and chest, I take in the sight of my best friend. I've seen them in photos and through video calls already, but it's still different now, in person. I've always wished I could dare to be as expressive as them, always wearing the most colourful and quirky clothes, many of which they make themself. Right now they're wearing a green hat shaped like a frog that I've previously seen many knitting progress photos of; their long, dark hair is tied into two long braids with lavender hair ties at the ends that match the colour of their soft, puffy coat. Their wheelchair—which does have wheels despite currently hovering above the ground—is decorated with loads of colourful stickers. They're wearing green leggings and white shoes with thick, rainbow soles. My blue fleece coat, jeans and black trainers look more drab than ever in contrast.

Finally, I turn to greet the two adults.

"Hello," and "Hi there," they say, nodding their heads toward me.

"Hi," I murmur.

Sage takes my hand and I'm surprised again at how comforting their touch is—from anyone else I would have recoiled.

"This is Marcus and Sarah," Sage says. "They're part of a group who want to preserve all life on Earth—not just humans."

My free hand wiggles excitedly.

"Nice to meet you, Aster," Marcus says.

"Thank you for calling this in," Sarah adds.

I nod. I feel my chest constricting as I try to form words, so I turn to Sage. Talking to strangers is hard, but Sage isn't a stranger.

"The seal is over there." The words come out quiet and stilted, but at least they come out. Marcus and Sarah thankfully don't seem to mind that I didn't speak to them directly, and nod in comprehension.

"You two—or three," Marcus smiles and gestures at Jamie, "better head back now. We don't want to cause this creature too much stress. We'll meet back up with you once we've assessed the situation."


Sage and I wait by the sea wall entrance, where the sandy beach gives way to concrete, so Sage can use their wheels again and preserve power. As we look out over the sea, I kneel down and pet Jamie. His warm presence and soft fur always manage to ground me, even with all the strange and new things going on tonight.

"So, not really how we imagined our first in-person meeting, huh?" Sage says, breaking the silence.

"Yeah," I say. After a beat, I add, "How do you know these people anyway?"

They take a moment to answer. "My family and I—we live with this group of mostly scientists who are more idealistic than any corporation would allow them to be. It's all kind of… Well, it's secret. I've been wanting to tell you more, but I'm really not allowed."

"Could I, um, gain access? At some point?"

"I hope so," they say, and smile.

We fall into another comfortable silence. Maybe other people would want to talk each other's ears off at their first in-person meeting, but I'm glad Sage is not like that. We've talked so much online already, we don't really need to now. Enjoying each other's presence is enough.

After a while—I honestly have no idea how much time has passed —Sarah comes up to us. She tells us Marcus is keeping watch over the seal and she's going to go back to help with preparations to move it to their compound where they can give it the care it needs, until it's ready to be released back into the wild. As she explains this to us, with her coat open and her hands on her hips, I notice the logo on her coveralls: a white circle with a blue 'e' inside it next to a small blue dot. Next to the logo, the letters 'ESA' are embroidered in the same white. I pretend not to have noticed anything when Sarah looks at me.

"Thanks again for calling us in, Aster," she says. "Nour is lucky to have such a conscientious friend."

"I am," Sage replies with a smile.

"You two say goodbye now—I'm taking you back home with me." She nods to Sage before leading the way off the beach.

"Nour is my given name," Sage says before I can ask. "I go by Sage online. I'm fine with either of them."

I nod. "Okay." I'm twiddling my fingers awkwardly. Now that we've finally met in person, it's weird to say goodbye. I don't know when—or even if—we'll meet again, or what's going to happen with the seal.

"Talk again soon?" Nour asks.

I nod again. "You'll let me know about…" I gesture vaguely in the direction of the seal.

"Of course!" Their smile widens. "Hug?"

We hug tightly before saying goodbye. I put Jamie back on his leash and we leave the beach. Sarah is waiting inside the sea wall by the car they drove here in. I wave them off before returning to my home, a ten minute walk away. I check the time on my phone before I get there and see it's past eleven—I've been gone for nearly two hours. My parents are not going to be happy about that. Since Sage said their organisation, or whatever it is, is secret, I'm not sure what I'm allowed to tell my parents. I decide to make up a lie about losing track of time and having to walk back farther than I thought. Thankfully, my parents buy it. They make me promise to set an alarm next time I go out and send me straight to bed. Though I obey and get ready, I know I won't be able to sleep any time soon. All through brushing my teeth and washing my face, I'm thinking about seals, secret conservationists, and ESA. I'm sure I do several parts of my routine at least twice because I'm so distracted.

Once I'm in bed, I open an incognito browser on my phone and type in my first search of the night: ESA.

Here's what I learn: ESA stands for European Space Agency. For decades they were one of the world's main space agencies alongside NASA, Roscosmos, and CNSA. They researched the universe, sent astronauts out into the solar system, and developed new technologies. At some point after the nanos went rogue, it's like they dropped off the face of the Earth. There are no records of them being disbanded, but they're also not among any of the corporations that now rule Europe. This explains why I've never heard of them, but not much else. What does a space agency have to do with conservationism? Why do they have zoologists in their employ that go out to save random seals? How did a kid like Sage, or their family, get involved with them? When my brain finally gives in to exhaustion, I feel like I have more questions than answers. I dream of seals swimming among the stars.

A couple of days later, I hear from Nour again. The seal is doing better. The people taking care of it have determined she's female and named her Betty. Nour has been asking if I can come by, but apparently I need to be vetted first—and so do my parents. I guess they don't want to encourage minors lying to their parents if they can help it. Or they don't trust me to keep the secret. Either way, the ball is in the adults' court now. I send Nour my parents' contact information and hope for the best.

I actually think ESA would be the perfect place for my parents, seeing as they're always complaining about capitalism and corporate policies destroying the planet. You never know with adults though. They'll be complaining constantly, then call any solution presented to them 'unrealistic' and do nothing.


Another day after that, my parents tell me they want to talk to me when they get home from work. They've been talking to some ESA scientists and, although they have some questions for me about how I got involved with a secret organisation, they are intrigued by the prospect of learning more and possibly working with them. I try to look contrite as they tell me this—after all, I've gotten into trouble and lied to them about it—but inside I'm squealing with joy. We're going to visit ESA this weekend, where I'll get to see Nour again and Betty too. Back in my room, I do a little dance of excitement.


I'm up much earlier than I need to be the Sunday morning we're leaving for ESA's research centre in Katwijk, about twenty-five kilometres south along the coast. We're being picked up by a car a short walking distance from our home. It's my first time inside a car; the underground neighbourhoods were laid out expanding off the existing metro system, which has been our main way to travel. Most cars on the surface were consumed by the nanos decades ago, and there hasn't been any need to build new ones, except to get a few rich people to their bunkers. And, apparently, to be used by secret organisations, who of course don't have metro stops at their doors.

We drive through the urban landscape I'm familiar with from my walks with Jamie, finally reaching a small building that functions as the entrance to ESA's underground facility. The elevator goes down much farther than I'm used to at home; this place was built to last.

Nour is waiting for me outside the elevator when the doors open, and I run to hug them. I catch a surprised look on my parents' faces before they introduce themselves; I've never had very close friends at school and I don't think they've ever seen me hug anyone who wasn't them or Jamie. Standing by Nour are Marcus and someone I don't know, who introduces themself as Farah. Farah will be giving my parents a limited tour of the facilities—I suppose they're not ready to reveal all their secrets—while Marcus will take Nour and me to see Betty.

Betty is already much more lively than when I first encountered her, swimming around in a clear blue pool. I can't take my eyes off her even while Marcus explains how she'd had too many dead nanos and too few nutrients in her system when I found her, causing her lethargy. She's been recovering quickly on a nutrient-rich diet and will be able to go back into the wild soon. I feel so much joy watching this beautiful animal, so much more energetic now that she's healthier, I feel like I might cry. Choked up, I can only nod when Marcus asks, "Would you like to see some of our other animals?"

It turns out ESA has been taking care of many more endangered animals. There's a whole bird sanctuary with various species of owls, corvids, sparrows, and many more. I get to help feed a baby bat and watch a vet dress an injured fox's wounded paw. Then there are domestic animals that ESA keeps and trains for purposes I'm not (yet) allowed to know. I finally break and start crying tears of joy when Marcus opens the door to a room with a pen full of weeks old puppies. As Nour and I sit on the ground inside the pen, puppies crawling over us, I think I'm the happiest I've ever been in my life.


It's almost time for us to meet back up with my parents when Marcus takes me aside. He looks at me with an expression I can't place and speaks in a hushed tone.

"Aster, have you ever thought about your future? Your career?"

I don't even know how to respond, because yes, obviously. I'm seventeen. School has been forcing us to think about our future careers constantly.

Marcus seems to pick up on that, because he smiles and says, "Sorry, that's a vague question. What I mean is: Nour has told me you're very interested in animals and zoology. Have you ever considered a career in that field?"

"Well, yeah," I say, "but there aren't really any jobs."

Marcus' smile widens. "I know it's tough out there, but that's not entirely true. I mean, look at me."

I frown. I feel like he's trying to tell me something without saying it. I hate when people do that.

"Listen," Marcus continues finally, "I would like you to reconsider working with animals. Someone as passionate about the field as you, and more importantly about the animals themselves, is exactly the kind of person we need here. I don't want you to make any decisions right now, but just think about it, and if you want, we'll keep in touch."

I don't tell him I really don't need to think about it, I'll jump at any chance to work with animals and, if I could move here right now, I would. Partly because I know that's the puppy-induced happiness talking, and partly because I don't want to seem overeager. So I nod, and say, "I'll think about it. Thanks."

Once the tour is finished, my parents and I are invited to have lunch with Nour and their parents. They live in one of the many identical apartments allotted to ESA's employees and their families. It's small but cosy, with pillows, rugs and artwork providing the practical set up with a personal touch. There are only four chairs at the dining table, so Nour and I sit on the couch. As we eat our lunch and the adults talk about the events of the morning, I quietly imagine living in an apartment just like this.

As we say our goodbyes, I think about the excited looks on my parents' faces and hope they are a sign of more visits to come. If they aren't convinced yet, I'm going to give everything I have to change that. I know one thing for sure: I've seen a glimpse of a life I desperately want to live, and I'm not giving that up.

In the days and weeks that follow, I learn more about ESA from both Sage and Marcus. Despite their current focus on conservation on Earth, they are still a space agency, and, though I'm still not allowed to learn about the specifics, I'm told they're preparing for some kind of big mission that includes humans and animals. I try not to get any wild ideas about space travel; I know animal trainer and astronaut are wildly different jobs, even if they're both involved in the same mission.

I meet everyone again when it's time for Betty to return into the wild. We're at the same sea wall entrance, now during the day. Marcus, Sarah, and Nour are all here. We watch from a distance as Sarah drives their truck close to the shoreline and Marcus opens Betty's cage, which is really more like a wooden box. Betty hesitates for a moment before taking off at a speed quite unexpected for the apparent awkwardness of the movement, which I've learned is called galumphing. As soon as she's in the water, she disappears under, and she's gone. I think I see her head come up for air some time later, but it's so far away I can't be sure.

We take a walk along the beach before leaving. Sage and I have been discussing our futures a lot lately. Aside from employing scientists, ESA also trains them, and Sage has always expected they'd take a course in astronomy there. Marcus has been hinting that I could continue my education there as well, and, while I haven't officially made a decision, I don't see a reason not to. It's literally the only place I'll be able to study what I actually want to study. So Sage and I have been imagining 'moving out' and sharing a room together as students at ESA. The prospect excites me, because this means it doesn't even matter what my parents decide to do. I'll have a place to go once I finish secondary school.

Sarah shakes us from our conversation to point at something. There, in the ocean, is a sandflat speckled with dark grey dots. I let out a short scream. This has to be Betty's colony! Sarah hands me a pair of binoculars that she's been carrying around her neck, while Marcus hands his own to Nour. With them pressed against my eyes, I can see the individual seals. There aren't a lot of them, only twenty or so, but...

"There are puppies!" I shout, taking a moment away from the binoculars to flap my hands excitedly. The fluffy white seal pups, their coats shiny in the sun, are some of the most adorable creatures I've ever seen. I can't tell if Betty is over there—I don't know if I would be able to recognise her at all—but I choose to believe she is. Nour and I hold hands as we look at the seals resting at the sandflat, some of them calmly swimming around in the water, others lazing about on the land. However small the life of one seal is in the span on the universe, I truly feel like we've all contributed to something monumental.

Marcus and Sarah tell us they'll continue monitoring the seal colony from now on, just like ESA is doing with many groups of wild animals across Europe and the rest of the world. There is definitely something they're not telling us about the purpose of this. Once again, I ask myself: why is a space agency so concerned with conservation?

I don't get my answer to that until months later. I'm now in my final year of secondary school and I've applied to continue my education at ESA once I've graduated. When my application to join has gone through, and I've been sworn to secrecy, I finally learn what's actually going on. The agency is working toward the biggest mission it's ever attempted: project Cadmus.

The mission is so secret, information about it isn't allowed to leave the premises of any of ESA's locations. It's all saved to local networks and encrypted in numerous ways. While Sage has heard some things about the project already, we're together when we finally get to learn the full scope of it.

We and several other prospective students and employees, all wearing plastic name tags, filter into a small classroom. Seeing 'Aster van den Berg, xe/xyr' and 'Nour Sage Nader, they/them' printed next to the ESA logo fills my stomach with squiggly excitement.

Once everyone has sat down, one of the agency's head scientists takes his place at the front of the room. They're wearing a simple shirt and tie, but the logo on their name card is different from the ones I've seen so far. Underneath the standard ESA logo is a silver oval printed as a background to the letters CADMUS, each a different colour of the light spectrum. The scientist, Dr Tyler de Groot, congratulates us on our acceptance to the program (even though most of the students among us, myself included, technically still need to pass our secondary school exams) and goes on to speak excitedly about the project he helps lead.

Cadmus is going to be a sleeper mission, a giant ship filled with those brave and/or passionate enough to volunteer to go farther than any human has gone before, all while cryogenically frozen for as long as it takes to find what they're looking for: a new home. Aside from enough humans to start a new civilisation, Cadmus will carry as many species of animals as possible, like a modern-day Noah's ark. Combined with plants and seeds and a DNA database, as well as digitally saved art collections and centuries worth of encyclopaedic knowledge, Cadmus will preserve life on Earth, long after the planet is led into destruction.

The next time Nour and I are on the beach together, it's a late night in August. The sun has just set and revealed the meagre, but beautiful, selection of stars in our night sky.

"They look different," I say.

Nour turns their head to me and raises one eyebrow. Their hair is windswept and full of tiny specks of sand. We're both lying on our backs, staring up at the sky.

"Okay, they don't really look different," I amend. "They *feel* different. The stars, I mean."

"Oh," Nour says. "Yeah. They do."

I don't have to explain any further, because I know Nour feels the same way. We're celebrating today: we've just moved into our new shared apartment. In less than a month, we'll be starting our educations in astrophysics and zoology. And in several years, we could be working on project Cadmus.

Everyone working for Cadmus has their own reasons for doing it, and their own beliefs about the future of our planet and the inevitability of its destruction. For me, I think a part of me has always known my future lies among the stars. That's why, to both of us, the twinkling lights above feel different now. Looking up at the night sky has always felt overwhelming, but I'm no longer drowning in it; I'm swimming.

In a few years, however many it takes, we'll be up there. I'll truly be a wanderer; but I won't be lost.

# Acknowledgements

There are so many people to thank here. More than could possibly fit onto one acknowledgements page. But there are a few people we could not go without thanking.

Sara Codair (they/them) is a long-time friend and author of the fantastic Evanstar Chronicles series, amongst other books. When I first decided to create this anthology, they reached out to me to give me advice from their experience writing for, and independently publishing the anthology *Distant Gardens*. It was in many ways thanks to their advice and support that Changelings was able to develop from an idea to a real book.

Amanda Shortman (she/her) has been one of this anthology's biggest supporters since its conception. Thank you for your unwavering support.

I would like to thank someone without whom, this book would not be possible. My mum, who supported this book, not only in spirit but through helping with the logistics of fundraising.

And, of course, Ocean, who conceptualised this book in the first place. This book only exists because of you.

Ryan

I'd like to dedicate this book to my mom, who is my greatest ally and biggest inspiration. Thank you for everything you do.

To Ryan, for going on this journey with me and turning my idea into something tangible.

And to you, dear reader, for giving this labour of love a chance. May you find hope within these pages.

Ocean

# Our Supporters

A.E. Bross

Aina Fairchild

Amaryllis Jeanne Quilliou

Andi Fisher

Andi Kay

Andreas L.

Andrew

Annie

Ari Miller

Athena Brown

Aubrey Shaw

Branwyn Jobes

Brian Schrader

Briar N

Brooks Moses

Cecilie Aadal Knudsen

Ceillie Simkiss

Chris Muir

Cody W

Connor Charm Cochran

Corrie S

Daphne Shaw

Dybbuk Klezmer

El H

Elizabeth J. Sargent

Elizabeth Sweeny

Elsa

Erin Lerch

ET Gilmore

Evelyn

Finbarr Farragher

I McClure

Isaac 'Will It Work' Dansicker

Jen St. Jude

Jen Wilde

John Lewis

Joseph Jerome Connell

Kabit

Kaminiwa

Kat Kellermeyer

Kayden Harper

Ken Rokos

Kit Heyam

Latitude Brown

Link Z

Linnea Peterson

Lip Wieckowski

Lisa Angiello

Logan-Ashley Kisner

Lolly S.

Lycus

Marshmallow & Pippin

Max

Michelle Mohrweis

Nathan R.G. Barnett

Ned Bunting

Nellie Cole

Olivia!

Olivia Montoya

Peregrine Farrar

Rae OHW

Ray Phillips

Robin – Books That Burn

Rose Elise Seibel

Ryan W

Sam Erin Scala

Sam Mattera

Sam Wild

Sarah Tuttle

Síle Ekaterin Liszka

Spencer Beckett

Spring

Stacey Carr

Taliesin Neith

The Blerd Newsletter

The Stauffer Family

Thomas Johnson

Vincent S.

You

Zaivy Opal Luke-Alemán